Praise for *New York Times* bestselling author B.J. Daniels

"B.J. Daniels is a sharpshooter; her books hit the target every time."
—#1 *New York Times* bestselling author Linda Lael Miller

"*Hero's Return* by B.J. Daniels is a creative masterpiece."
—*Fresh Fiction*

"B.J. Daniels has made *Cowboy's Legacy* quite a nail-biting, page-turner of a story. Guaranteed to keep you on your toes."
—*Fresh Fiction*

"With a surprising villain, a mystery full of twists and turns and engaging characters, *Renegade's Pride* is an addictive page-turner."
—*BookPage*

"The strong family ties, a love story finally coming together and, best of all, a well-written mystery make this a truly great read."
—*RT Book Reviews* on *Hard Rain*

"The heartwarming romance gets wrapped up here, but the book ends with a cliffhanger that is sure to have fans anxious for the next title in the series."
—*Library Journal* on *Lucky Shot*

"Forget slow-simmering romance…the second Montana Hamiltons is always at a rolling boil."
—*Publisher's Weekly* on *Lone Rider*

"*Wild Horses* is filled with action, intrigue, mystery and romance, in other words a classic B.J. Daniels book."
—*Fresh Fiction*

B.J. DANIELS

RANCHER'S DREAM

ISBN-13: 978-1-335-00699-8

Recycling programs for this product may not exist in your area.

Rancher's Dream

Copyright © 2018 by Barbara Heinlein

This one is for Eunice Simonson,
who brings that something special to our quilt group.
No one makes us laugh more than Eunice.
I'm so glad I've gotten to know you!

CHAPTER ONE

YOU WILL DIE in this house.

The thought seemed to rush out of the darkness as the house came into view. The premonition turned her skin clammy. Drey gripped a handful of her wedding dress, her fingers aching but unable to release the expensive fabric as she stared at her new home. A wedding gift, Ethan had said. A surprise, sprung on her at the reception.

The portent still had a death grip on her. She could see herself lying facedown in a pool of water, her auburn hair fanned out around her head, her body so pale it appeared to have been drained of all blood.

"Are you all right?" her husband asked now as he reached over to take her hand. "Dierdre?" Unlike everyone else she knew, Ethan refused to call her by her nickname, Drey.

"I'm still a little woozy from the reception," she said, desperately needing fresh air right now as she put down her window to let in the cool Montana summer night.

"I warned you about drinking too much champagne."

He'd warned her about a lot of things. But it wasn't the champagne, which she hadn't touched during the reception. He knew she didn't drink, but he'd insisted one glass of champagne at her wedding wasn't going to kill her. She'd gotten one of the waiters to bring her sparkling cider.

So it wasn't alcohol that had her stomach roiling. No, it was when Ethan had told her where they would be living. She'd assumed they would live in his New York City penthouse since that was where he spent most of his time. She'd actually been looking forward to it because she'd grown up in Gilt Edge, Montana, and had never lived in a large city before. Also it would be miles from Gilt Edge—and Hawk Cahill.

She'd never dreamed that Ethan meant for them to live here in Montana, at the place he'd named Mountain Crest. All during construction, she'd thought that the odd structure was to be used as a business retreat only. Ethan had been so proud of the high-tech house with its barred gate at the end of the paved road, she'd never let on that she knew the locals made fun of it— and its builder.

When Ethan had pulled her aside at the reception and told her that they would be living on the mountain overlooking Gilt Edge in his prized house, Dierdre hadn't been able to hide her shock. She'd never dreamed… But then, she'd never dreamed she would be married to Ethan Baxter.

"Is there a problem?" he'd asked when he'd told her the news.

She'd tried to cover her discomfort. "I just assumed we would be living in New York City, closer to your business."

"I've given up the penthouse. When I have to go to the city on business, I'll be staying in a hotel." He'd sounded a bit indignant as if she should have been more excited. "Mountain Crest will have to do."

"I didn't mean…" She had seen that there was nothing she could say that wouldn't make it worse.

Now, as she found her breath, the premonition receding only a little, she had another paralyzing thought. *You've made a terrible mistake.*

It was that thought that had made her freeze earlier, standing in the church. It had been a large wedding, the pews filled with business associates of her husband and half the town. Her bridesmaids were women she worked with at the library, women who'd been excited about her engagement and enamored by Ethan every time he came into the library looking for her.

She'd wanted her best friend, Lillie Cahill, to be her matron of honor, but she'd known Lillie would decline. *I'll be at your wedding. I'll support you to the death, but I can't do that to my brother. I would feel as if I was betraying Hawk. I hope you understand.*

Of course Drey had understood. Lillie was like a sister to her after all the years Drey had spent on the Cahill Ranch when she was dating Hawk. When the two of them had been so madly in love that everyone had expected they would be the ones marrying today.

You've made a terrible mistake. But it was too late to have second thoughts. She'd been telling herself that from the moment Ethan had sent out the announce-

ment about their engagement before he'd even offi-
cially asked her to marry him.

"I thought you loved surprises," he'd said.

She had no idea where he'd gotten that idea.

"Maybe this will make it up to you." He'd reached
into his pocket, produced the small velvet jewelry box
and opened it. Light caught the impressive diamond,
almost blinding her. She'd told herself this was every
young woman's dream. A handsome, rich businessman wanted to marry her.

"Do you like it?" he'd asked impatiently.

She'd nodded as he'd slipped it onto her finger. It
was beautiful, if a little tight on her finger. He'd promised to have it resized. And yet it had nagged at her,
him running the engagement announcement in her
hometown paper without telling her.

"What's the big deal?" he'd demanded when she'd
said something about it. "I thought you'd want your
friends to know." It hadn't been her friends he'd
wanted to know about the engagement. He'd wanted
Hawk Cahill to see it, which made her regret telling
Ethan about her first love.

As she now stared at the house growing larger and
larger as he drove nearer, she felt sicker. The rooflines
rose at odd angles as the house backed up against
the mountainside in what appeared to be six levels
of glass and rock and old timbers. The front was all
glass, behind it darkness. She got the crazy feeling
that the house was watching them approach and that
it wasn't happy.

Ethan swore under his breath and looked back down the mountain.

"What is it?" she asked, turning in her seat. A set of headlights slowly disappeared down the county road below them on the mountain.

"Nothing," he said, but he kept glancing in his rearview mirror until they came around a bend and could no longer see the road below them. "Mountain Crest," he said, his voice filling with pride as he let go of her hand to motion toward the ultramodern structure. "So what do you think?" he asked when she didn't respond. Couldn't respond.

She tried not to shudder. Two years ago, she'd heard that everyone in Gilt Edge was talking about the ultramodern mansion some rich businessman was building on the side of the mountain overlooking the valley. Few people had seen it since the property was gated down on the county road and under the watchful eye of a caretaker who stayed on the estate until recently. The rest of the property was surrounded by an eight-foot-high stone fence. Ethan was determined to have his privacy.

Over those two years, several unfortunate accidents had occurred during construction. Three laborers had been injured and the first caretaker had been found dead. All of the incidents were ruled accidents and yet rumors circulated. Locals said that Mountain Crest was cursed.

Drey had scoffed at such foolishness long before she'd met Ethan and begun dating him. It surprised her, though, that when he was in Gilt Edge overseeing the building of the house—and even after it was almost finished—he always stayed at the local hotel. When she'd asked him about it, he'd said that he wanted to wait until the house was completely finished.

She could feel Ethan waiting for her reaction. "It's breathtaking." It had certainly taken her breath away the moment the house had come into view. Followed instantly by that awful premonition. She saw at once that he'd hoped for more effusiveness. "I don't recognize the architecture." Not that as a librarian she was up on the latest architecture.

"It's my own design," her husband said a little stiffly as he drove slowly up the paved road. "It will grow on you."

Again she saw herself lying facedown in the pond, the house looming over her. She tried to hide the shiver that started at the nape of her neck and crawled with icy feet down her spine. She forced the image away. It wasn't like her to let silly rumors of a curse unnerve her. And yet when she'd glimpsed the house for the first time, she hadn't been able to shake the horrible premonition that had come out of nowhere.

"Close your window if you're cold," Ethan said, apparently having noticed her shudder. As the road had climbed up the mountain, the air had cooled.

But as she whirred up her window, she knew it wasn't the Montana air that was chilling her. The dark windows caught the glare of the headlights, casting odd shadows across the grounds—and skittering over the pond. She swallowed at the sight of the water and was glad when Ethan turned into the driveway at the front and killed the lights.

"For now, you won't have any staff."

Staff?

"I'll see to hiring a cook, housekeeper—"

"Ethan, I don't need any of those." Since he'd talked her into quitting her job, she would have plenty of time on her hands to take care of the house.

But he didn't seem to hear her as he climbed out of the car. She sat for a moment, not sure if he would want to open her door, maybe carry her over the threshold. All this had happened so fast, she still felt as if caught in a whirlwind.

To say Ethan Baxter had swept her off her feet was an understatement. One moment he walked into the library and the next they were flying to Paris for dinner or landing on a helicopter pad on a yacht in the Caribbean or getting engaged.

"I'm going to make all your dreams come true," Ethan had promised.

And here she was on her wedding night and nothing about it was as she'd once dreamed. Dierdre "Drey" Hunter Baxter. Married.

Married to the wrong man.

HAWK CAHILL HAD stayed as far away from Gilt Edge and the festivities as he could on Drey's wedding day. He'd ridden up into the mountains that surrounded the small Montana town so people would quit asking him if he'd heard about Drey marrying some New Yorker.

He'd have had to be living on the moon not to hear about the upcoming wedding.

His family had the good sense not to bring it up in the days preceding the big event. Invitations had gone out. Like that monstrosity he'd built to his ego, Ethan Baxter had made sure that his wedding would go down as the biggest event this town had ever seen.

At least that's what he was quoted as saying in the article that ran in the local paper about the engagement. Hawk had heard that Drey needed a wheelbarrow just to haul around the huge diamond on her ring finger.

He'd gritted his teeth all day, getting through it the same way he did when he had a root canal at the dentist.

But tonight, as he and his horse started out of the mountains in the dark with only the moon and starlight to guide him, he couldn't keep his mind off the fact that Drey was married. This was her wedding night—and not the one he'd envisioned for her all those years ago. He could almost laugh about the plan he'd had for *their* wedding night.

Nothing like Ethan Baxter's, that was for sure. Hawk wouldn't have taken Drey in some fancy car to some ugly mansion on the mountainside. Nope, he'd planned to erect a wall tent up by one of his favorite mountain lakes. After the wedding they would have ridden by horseback to find a lantern burning inside the white tent. The only music would be the gentle lapping of the lake at the rocky shore and the sweet sounds of their lovemaking.

With a curse, he spurred his horse, anxious to get back to the ranch and reality. His new reality. And his own fault. He'd never been able to forgive her after what had happened in college. Even now, after all these years, the pain had dulled to only an ache. He'd thought it the worst pain he'd ever experience.

But knowing that Drey would be spending this night with some other man as his wife was almost more pain than he could endure.

"You can stop her from marrying him," his little sister, Lillie, had pleaded. Drey had told him she was planning to get married. When the announcement had come out in the local newspaper, it left little doubt that it was true.

"I've never been able to stop Drey from anything," he'd told his sister, who still wouldn't let it go. "This New Yorker can give her a hell of a lot more than I can."

"Drey doesn't care about any of that," Lillie had snapped.

"You sure about that?"

His sister had been furious with him. "What happened between the two of you?" she'd demanded more times than he could remember.

"None of your business."

She'd squinted at him, determination in her gray gaze so like his own. "I'm betting you're to blame."

He'd said nothing, knowing at least part of it was true.

"You're really going to let your pigheaded stubbornness keep you from the only woman you've ever loved? Then you aren't the man I thought you were."

He hadn't bothered to argue. He wasn't the man his little sister thought he was and it hurt like hell. Especially tonight when he knew that because of his inability to forgive, he'd let the best thing he'd ever had get away.

CHAPTER TWO

STILL UPSET, DREY tried to shake off her earlier fear of the future and the house. She'd never had an over-active imagination. Little scared her, but for months now it had felt as if her life was out of her control.

"I thought you would appreciate a man who took care of you," Ethan had said when she'd mentioned that she felt powerless around him sometimes.

Admittedly it had been nice at first. She could just lie back and enjoy the whirlwind romance as if she was a heroine in a book.

So what had changed?

Nothing. Ethan was still the driven businessman who'd swept her off her feet leaving her breathless and off balance. She'd been taken by surprise by him. The extravagant lifestyle, the way he seemed to cruise through life as if master of his own destiny. Of course that had appealed to her.

And he'd wanted her—and came after her like a man who knew his mind. As he said, when he saw something he wanted, he got it. He'd wanted her and now he had her.

That thought struck her as he opened her door and offered her a hand out of the car. Her wedding dress made it hard to move—let alone get out of the sedan. She always thought she'd be married in a simple sheath wedding dress. Or maybe even jeans and boots, knowing Hawk.

But Ethan had had other ideas. When she'd showed him the dress she'd liked in the bride magazine, he'd said it wouldn't do. It was too plain for the kind of wedding he had planned for them. So here she was, her dress made of yards of billowing fabric that she'd had to fight into submission to even get into the car.

She'd wanted to change after the reception, but Ethan had pointed out that they would be home in a matter of minutes. She'd relented, even though she was anxious to get out of the dress. Or maybe just anxious, she thought as she looked again at the house looming over them.

"Watch this," Ethan said and touched his phone. "All I have to do is activate this and from now on, whenever you drive up…" Lights in the house and surrounding landscape suddenly came on, making the property look like a landing strip.

She had to admit, the house looked less scary with the lights on as he led her up the steps to the front door.

"Your thumbprint works, as well," Ethan reminded her. Back when he'd had a security expert come by the library to put her thumbprint into a small handheld device, she'd had no idea this is what it had been for. Even back then, Ethan had known they would be living in this house—and not in New York.

She felt even more intimidated by the house as

she looked at the massive carved wood door. How much of this house operated on her thumbprint? She stared at the carved face of a lion in the middle of the door for a moment as Ethan deactivated the door lock. Even the lion looked displeased to see her as if it knew she was going to fail. The thought made her want to laugh.

This wasn't like her. She was usually so self-assured and confident in her abilities. But that was before she'd gotten involved with Ethan and been thrown into his world.

Still it worried her, this feeling that she couldn't cope as if she already knew she was in over her head. What was she really afraid of, she wondered, as the door swung open.

Drey hesitated for a moment, expecting Ethan to sweep her up in his arms and carry her inside. But he was complaining about something not working properly as he frowned down at his phone before rushing in, leaving her standing on the step outside. Earlier, before he'd opened her car door, he'd been looking at his phone, as well.

She sighed. After a few moments, the night air chilling her, she stepped inside. The door closed behind her, leaving her standing on the marble floor of the foyer. Modern minimalist was what Ethan had called it. To her, it felt cold and unwelcoming, or maybe it was just the fact that she didn't feel all that well. She felt a little dizzy. She'd hardly touched a bite at the reception so she didn't think that was it. At least she hoped not.

She could hear Ethan somewhere deeper in the

house but knew better than to follow the sound. She wasn't up for a tour. But she did peer in, taking in the opulence of Mountain Crest and at the same time, its starkness. The white walls climbed to dizzying heights, while the curtainless windows and dim sconce lighting gave her the feeling of being in a mausoleum.

Polished steel railings led upstairs to the next level. Ethan had told her that there were six levels aboveground with an underground garage, wine cellar and storage area. Of course there was a helipad on one side of the house and a pond on the other. She glimpsed a glass elevator off to the left. She hated elevators and the idea of being trapped. That and drowning were her two greatest fears.

Drey shivered and quickly chastised herself. Ethan had paid a small fortune for the place with all its expensive modern furniture and high-tech devices—not to mention the cost of the actual building. This was to be her home. She knew women who would have been starstruck by the place.

What did she know about how the wealthy lived? Nothing. Her father had worked as a janitor at the high school. Her mother was a clerk at the local dime store until it closed. The two were now gone—her father from a car accident, her mother from a fast-acting cancer that had taken her years ago.

They hadn't lived long enough to see their daughter married. The thought brought tears to her eyes. *You're exhausted. No wonder you're imagining such strange things. Once you're rested, everything is going to be fine.*

BACK AT THE RANCH, Hawk was unsaddling his horse when he heard someone approach from behind him. He turned, thinking it would be Cyrus. Since college, he and his brother had run the family ranch together. His sister, Lillie, had started calling them the cranky old bachelors. She hadn't been far off on that.

To his surprise it wasn't Cyrus standing in the barn doorway. Silhouetted against the night was his little sister, who hadn't talked to him since their last argument about Drey weeks ago.

"Are you all right?" she asked, her voice small and sad.

The sound of it struck him at heart level. This was exactly what he'd hoped to avoid today. While he knew he wouldn't be able to sleep, he'd hoped to stable his horse, go inside and have a few beers and put Drey's wedding day behind him.

Lillie took a tentative step toward him as if worried about him, and yet she had to know that the last thing he wanted right now was her sympathy.

He swore under his breath. He could tell his sister all day long that he didn't care about Drey anymore, but it wouldn't do any good. It was as if she could look into his heart and see the pain he tried so hard to hide.

"I'm fine." He hadn't meant to bite off the words as if straining on a bit. He'd been telling himself the same thing all day and it was getting old.

She took another step toward him.

He saw there was no getting around it. Closing the distance between them, he let her hug him. He

hugged her, not sure who had needed the hug more—
him or her.

"I'm so sorry," she whispered against his chest.

All he could do was nod and hug her back, wondering how long it would take her before her sympathy
turned to anger at him for not riding into the wedding
chapel on his horse, grabbing Drey and riding off into
the sunset together.

Lillie pulled back to look up into his face. She
seemed to be making up her mind about something.
Patting his chest, she stepped back.

He could see her battling with her nature. She
wanted to chew him out, knock him upside the head,
stomp her feet and tell him it wasn't too late. Hell, it
was Drey's wedding night. It was more than too late.
What was Lillie going to suggest now? That maybe he
could still ride up to that big mansion on the mountain,
scale the walls of that ridiculous house and steal her
away before the marriage was consummated?

Too late for heroics. As if it hadn't been too late a
long time ago. The only way he could have stopped
this was months ago when Drey had told him she was
getting married. Except he couldn't imagine himself
begging her to reconsider—not when he had nothing
to offer her and hadn't since college. No, he hadn't
forgiven her and wasn't sure he ever could. As if he
didn't know that stubbornness ran in his family?

He watched his sister marshaling her emotions.
She swallowed and seemed to brace herself, making
him realize it was going to be worse than a tongue-

lashing or a demand for him to stop Drey before it was too late.

Instead, Lillie burst into tears.

He swore as he pulled her back into his arms. He smoothed her long dark hair, the same color as all the Cahills', and whispered, "It's going to be all right. I'm okay. It's going to be all right."

He let her cry it out before shaking out his dusty bandanna and handing it to her. She took it, blew her nose and tried to hand it back. He shook his head, smiling at her as she sniffed, blew her nose again and then stuffed the bandanna into the pocket of her jeans.

He could see that she was still sad, but that she had come to accept that there was nothing more she could do, his sister, the romantic. He'd accepted the way things were a long time ago. Or at least he had told himself he had.

Only a fool would have thought that Drey would never find someone, get married, have children. The thought made him grit his teeth. At least she would be living in New York City. He wouldn't have to see her pregnant, see her pushing a baby stroller, see her in the children she would have with another man.

"I just had to come by when I heard," Lillie said, still sniffing a little.

When she heard? He must have looked confused because she quickly added, "She's going to be living here."

He felt as if she'd punched him in the stomach. "Here?"

"In Gilt Edge."

He shook his head. "I don't know where you heard that but—"

"I was there. Ethan announced it at the reception. I heard him say they would be living at Mountain Crest."

"Mountain Crest," he mumbled under his breath. "That pretentious son of a—"

"She isn't leaving," Lillie cried, as if he was missing the point.

Oh, he'd gotten the point. His heart had dropped like a stone into a bottomless well. Now he understood why his little sister had braved his temper to come here. Why her heart was breaking for him. Drey marrying someone else was bad enough. But staying here? Living right under his nose with that other man?

There was no way he would be able to avoid seeing her—not in a town the size of Gilt Edge. Unless he became a hermit on the ranch.

He swore again, turning away from his sister. Drey had told him that she and her husband would be living in New York City. Why would she change her mind?

"Drey looked shocked when he'd announced it," Lillie said. "I don't think she's happy about it."

To make matters worse, a portion of the Baxter property bordered forest service land next to the Cahill Ranch land. He'd done his best not to ride over there. But after Drey told him she was marrying Ethan Baxter, he'd saddled up and checked out the house everyone was talking about.

He hadn't been able to imagine Drey in a house like that. They used to talk about the future and the house they would have once they were married. She loved old farmhouses with big wide front porches.

"It has to have a porch swing, of course," she'd said.

He'd smiled. "And a tree swing for the kids, I assume?"

"You know it." She'd cuddled up against him as they talked about her large country kitchen where all their friends and family would gather on holidays, and all the children they would have.

Remembering made it hurt so much worse. Now Drey was going to be living in some mansion on the side of the mountain overlooking Cahill Ranch? He thought he'd been through hell all those years ago. This was hell.

"You should get home," he said, turning to his sister. He needed to be alone. She looked so small, so young, so worried about him. "Thanks for letting me know."

She looked as if she might burst into tears again. "You can't leave. Tell me you won't leave the ranch like Tucker did," she cried, grabbing his arm.

He shook his head, smiling at her as he put his hand over hers. Their oldest brother, Tucker, had left years ago because of a woman and only recently returned. "I won't leave the ranch. I'm not going anywhere," he said as he squeezed her hand. "This isn't the end of the world."

"Isn't it?" Her gaze locked with his as she let go of him. Tears flooded her gray eyes again. "What if Drey was the one for you? The *only* one for you?"

"You know I don't believe in all that romantic stuff.

Drey wasn't my one and only." She eyed him skeptically. "Now, get on home to your husband and son," he said, turning her toward the barn door.

"I just want you to be happy," she said quietly as he walked her to the door.

"I know." He thought about telling her that he was happy. Well, as happy as he could be under the circumstances. But even that would have been a lie. He was dying inside.

She hesitated for a moment at the door. Their gazes met. He gave her a smile and a nod and she turned and left, disappearing into the darkness outside.

He stood for a long time staring into that blackness until he heard the sound of her SUV pulling away. He finished putting his tack away, then walked outside in time to see the red of his sister's taillights going up the road.

The night air was cool. A normal summer night in Montana in the mountains. He looked up at the stars for a moment. A sliver of moon hung in that big sky. He let his gaze shift to the mountain where Drey was spending her wedding night with her new husband.

"Drey," he whispered to the night. He felt his throat close with emotion. "Be happy." He said it like a wish. If he couldn't have her, then Ethan Baxter sure as hell had better be the man she needed.

With that he turned toward the house, suddenly exhausted and praying for sleep. Once inside, he started for the refrigerator to get a beer, but opted for a stiff drink of whiskey before bed. He knew one wasn't going to do it.

Grabbing the bottle, he headed up. As he passed his brother on the stairs, he lifted his glass and gave him a nod.

Cyrus was smart enough to merely nod back.

"THERE YOU ARE," Ethan said when he found her still standing in the foyer. "I was afraid I'd lost you." He moved to her and, taking her shoulders in his hands, drew her into a gentle kiss. When he pulled back, he seemed to study her face. "You are so beautiful." He said it as if he'd only just realized it was true. "I love your hair."

She'd wanted to put it up for the wedding, but he'd insisted she leave it down. He loved to run his fingers through it. Now he raked a hand over the length of it, touching her bare shoulder and making her shiver. "I never can decide what color it is," he said almost to himself. "Caramel." He nodded as if reaching the definitive answer. "Warm dark caramel."

Drey began to relax a little. This was the Ethan who'd swept her off her feet. A tender, caring man who wanted only the best for her. And they did look great together, Ethan with his blue eyes and blond hair. "The all-American couple" it had said in his company's glossy magazine-like employee newsletter.

"I'm sorry, I didn't get to carry you over the threshold, a problem with the backup generator, but I'll make it up to you. I promise," he said and kissed her neck, making her shiver again.

Everything was going to be all right, she told herself. Every woman got wedding jitters, right? Every woman felt a little nauseated at the thought of her first love on her wedding day. Every woman saw herself lying facedown, dead in a pond.

She shivered and Ethan drew her closer—as close as he could because of the dress.

He touched a screen on the wall and the door locked and the lights in the foyer dimmed. "It's all about modern technology and safety. The whole house comes alive at the touch," he said with obvious pleasure. "It works for you, as well. Here, try it."

Taking her hand, he drew her over to what she knew must be the light switch. "Just touch it with your thumb."

She pressed her thumb to the touch screen and the lights went off.

He chuckled with obvious delight. "See why I needed your thumbprint? The whole house works on just our prints." His phone made a sound. He frowned down at the screen. "Something isn't working right, though. Why don't you go on up and change into something more comfortable. Top floor. The elevator is over there. I won't be long," he said.

"Unzip me, please."

As he did, he trailed kisses down her spine. "Can you manage now?" he asked.

"Don't be long, okay?" She realized she needed reassurance. Maybe in his arms she could chase away these crazy thoughts.

"I can't wait to see you in that silk gown we bought in Paris," he said, desire sparking in his gaze. "I'll hurry. Open the wine and have a glass to relax," he said, caressing her arm. "I'll join you shortly."

She started to remind him that she didn't drink but didn't want to argue. She watched him take off down the hallway before she glanced at the elevator. Even though it was glass, she preferred the stairs. She'd never liked being closed in. At least the house, with its high ceilings and sparse decor, made her feel as if she could breathe a little easier.

The stairs rose to a landing on each floor. She found a massive living room with a sunroom and balcony off to one side of the second floor. On the next floor was a restaurant-size kitchen and a dining room table that could serve fifty it appeared. Another balcony hung off to the side with a more normal-size table and chairs.

She couldn't imagine cooking in the huge kitchen let alone the two of them eating at that enormous table. Apparently Ethan planned to entertain a lot.

On the next floor, she glimpsed a terraced sunroom and a half dozen bedrooms along with another balcony. Everywhere she looked there were windows. The next floor was just as spacious with another sunroom and what appeared to be conference rooms and a media center—and another balcony.

She was wondering where the master suite was as she climbed yet another set of stairs to find wide double doors. Pushing them open, she almost gasped. Off to her right was another balcony. To the left was the largest master suite she'd ever seen.

In a room with towering ceilings and even more

windows, there was a gas fireplace and a huge wide-screen television. At the center of it all was a giant platform bed with matching end tables and lamps. On each side of the bed appeared to be his and her bathrooms. The remaining portion of the room held two matching chairs that sat in front of the fireplace and television.

Like the rest of the house, everything was white from the marble floor to the white shag rug and the duvet on the bed and the sheets. Even the throw pillows were white. It was blinding. Her brain cried out for color. Surely Ethan would let her add at least some colorful pillows, but as she thought it, she recalled him saying that he doubted she would need to add or change anything.

She shook her head. This was so not like any life she'd ever imagined. She felt ill-prepared for it, but determined that she would adjust. Ethan was a kind and caring man. A busy businessman. But he loved her. She would help him in any way she could to run this house.

Right now it felt overwhelming, though.

She turned to look out the wall of windows. Ethan had said they would be able to see out but no one would be able to see in. She still felt exposed. She could see the lights of town. In the other direction she could almost see the Cahill ranch house.

Feeling even more nauseated, she stepped into the bathroom that was obviously hers according to the monogrammed white towels. She stood for a moment realizing the bathroom was almost larger than her old apartment. Not only that, but also everything was so modern that she wasn't sure she would even know how to turn on the faucet let alone flush the toilet.

Ethan had paid someone to move all of her personal items. In the walk-in closet, she found more clothes than she'd ever owned. Nothing looked like her style, though, she thought. Ethan had said she would need a new wardrobe so on their trips, he'd insisted they pick up a few things. A few things, indeed. She couldn't imagine wearing half of the designer gowns he'd bought her. Apparently she would, in fact, be doing a lot of entertaining.

She thought of how she used to entertain friends at her apartment. Chips and dip, shoes kicked off as they sprawled in their blue jeans and T-shirts. Strange, but she felt an ache at the sweet memory of those times. Gone now. Gone forever.

In several of the drawers, though, she was happy to see her jeans and some favorite tops, as well as her cowboy boots next to the high heels in the shoe slots. Good thing she wasn't required to dress up all the time. That was a relief. As a librarian at the local small library, she'd worn jeans and blouses with a blazer to work, since this was Montana and that had been as dressy as most people got.

Ethan, on the other hand, always wore a suit—even when in Gilt Edge, where only lawyers and undertakers dressed like that. Maybe she could encourage him to try to fit in more, she thought. Or not. He didn't seem open to change, let alone what she feared he would see as criticism.

Pushing those thoughts away, she changed into the beautiful ivory silk nightgown with a flowing matching robe that had been laid out for her. As she stood in front of the full-length mirror, she swept her hair back over her shoulders and grabbed a lock to stare down at it. Hawk had loved her hair, as well. He said it was like a sunset. She tossed the lock back, telling herself she had to quit reminiscing.

She just wished she felt better. Her stomach was bothering her and she felt woozy. She continued to stare at herself in the mirror as if seeing a stranger. She looked pale, her brown eyes huge. She pinched her cheeks to get some color back into them and then turned to her dressing room table to find some blush and a touch of lipstick. She'd never worn a lot of makeup.

As she applied a little tinted lip gloss, she caught her reflection again. The pallor of her face brought back that stupid premonition. *You will die in this house.*

She shivered and glanced at her phone to check the time, anxious now for Ethan to join her. Back in the bedroom, she opened the wine and poured Ethan a glass. He'd thoughtfully left her a bottle of the sparkling water she loved. She still felt off balance and was glad she wasn't even tempted to try the wine. Alcohol was the last thing she needed.

She took a sip of the sparkling water just to humor her husband. She knew he would ask her if she had some since he'd left it for her. She didn't want to start off her marriage lying. The least she could do was drink a little.

She tried to relax. She'd been more than tense. She finished the glass and poured herself a little more for a toast when Ethan arrived.

But after another fifteen minutes and no Ethan, she lay down on the bed to wait. Nervous exhaustion pulled at her along with that light-headed feeling that had been with her for some time now. The day had been long and stressful, especially the reception where she'd been introduced to so many of Ethan's business associates and friends. Top that off with her new husband telling her they would be staying in his house overlooking Gilt Edge instead of moving to New York City.

She felt as if she was floating. Maybe she would just close her eyes to rest until Ethan joined her.

Hours later, she woke to find the sun streaming in the windows. She lay on top of the bed in the French silk nightgown—alone in the huge bed. She reached out to find Ethan's side empty—and cold. Her head ached as she lifted it to confirm that Ethan's side was still neatly made. He hadn't slept next to her.

She sat up with a start. Her head swam and she had to hold on to the duvet for a moment. Ethan's wineglass was next to the bed, still full. Her water glass was the only one used.

With a jolt, she realized that she'd spent her wedding night alone.

CHAPTER THREE

ETHAN HADN'T JOINED her last night? A bad feeling rippled through her as she got up and quickly dressed to go looking for her husband. She told herself that he'd gotten busy with the mechanical problem in the house. Or that it had been so late he'd stayed in one of the guest rooms so as not to disturb her.

But none of that could ease her growing concern. What man didn't join his wife on their wedding night? He'd said he was going to check something and come up right away. Maybe he'd found her out cold and... She bit down on her lower lip to fight off her disappointment. She'd needed him last night. Needed reassurance. He'd thrown her so many curveballs since she'd met him... What excuse could he have for not at least spending their first night as man and wife in their bed together?

Drey shook off all the excuses because there were none that she could accept. It had been their wedding night in their new home. He should have at least come up to check on her. From what she could tell, he'd never even come into the bedroom. His bathroom had looked untouched, as did his walk-in closet and dressing area.

She took the same route she had the night before, stopping on each floor to call his name. Her theory that he might have found her dead asleep and decided not to disturb her by sleeping in one of the guest bedrooms proved wrong. There was no sign of him in any of the bedrooms—nor did any of the beds look as if they'd been slept in. Ethan wasn't the kind of man to make his own bed—let alone leave it as perfect as he'd found it. He'd always had hired help to do that for him.

When she reached the kitchen, she'd hoped to smell freshly brewed coffee so she could quit worrying about him. It would have relieved her mind, but done little to dampen her disappointment to find him hard at work at the small table in the sunroom, a cup of coffee in front of him and his cell phone at his ear. That was how she often found him the few times they'd spent the night together.

But not only wasn't Ethan in the sprawling kitchen and sunroom, there was also no coffee made. Her stomach growled. She glanced at her watch, shocked that she'd slept so late. It was almost noon. Was it possible Ethan had stayed up all night?

Maybe he'd gone into town for breakfast. The thought hurt her. Not only hadn't they spent their wedding night together, but they wouldn't be having breakfast together either? Surely he would have changed out of his wedding clothes. Was it possible he'd used the dressing room in the walk-in closet without her hearing him—or him leaving any sign?

She moved to the bank of windows and looked out on the valley. The car was where Ethan had parked it the night before. She felt relieved. He would know that his leaving without a word would upset her. This was their honeymoon, such as it was.

"I can't leave right now, but I promise in a week or two we will have the most amazing honeymoon," he'd assured her.

Given the whirlwind romance, she already felt as if they'd been on their honeymoon so she hadn't minded. In fact, she'd been looking forward to settling in and getting to explore New York City. She'd been excited to nest for a while.

Looking around the kitchen, she realized she would have to adjust her plan and settle in here. This ultra-modern house was certainly not what she'd expected. Just as she hadn't expected to wake up alone. She pushed that disappointment away, feeling guilty. *Look at this amazing place.* She was a lucky woman. She could hear her friends from the library telling her that just yesterday at the wedding.

"You've married Prince Charming," one of them had said with a laugh. "Don't you just have to pinch yourself?"

So where was her amazing prince? She wandered on down to the front entrance where they'd come in last night. As she did, she saw the pond, the surface shimmering in the morning sunlight, and felt another shudder. Even in the daylight, it reminded her of that awful premonition.

Fortunately, in the light of day, she didn't believe in premonitions, she told herself as she took in the view. She could see the small Western town of Gilt

Edge sparkling in the sun. Surrounded on four sides by four different mountain ranges, she could see why Ethan had wanted to build here. The view really was impressive. All the wide-open spaces and the towering mountain peaks still capped with snow even in early summer.

"Ethan?" she called, turning back to look up toward the other levels of the meandering house. He could be anywhere in this maze of rooms. Or he could be outside on the fifty acres he owned of this mountaintop next to even more acres of forest service land.

She turned to the windows again and looked toward the Cahill Ranch. It was almost literally a stone's throw away—if you shot the rock out of a cannon. But still so close. Which meant it was only a matter of time before she ran into Hawk.

That thought did nothing to make things better.

It took her a while to figure out the high-tech coffee maker and put on a pot, telling herself that Ethan would show up. Maybe he'd gone for a walk. That didn't seem like him, but maybe he was a different man up here on the mountain.

Stepping onto one of the balconies on this level, she looked out to a spot that had been cleared for a stable. She'd forgotten that Ethan planned to buy horses once they were settled in.

"You ride, don't you?" he'd asked.

"Yes." Hawk had taught her, taking her on horseback rides up to his favorite mountain lake for picnics and swimming in the freezing cold water, then lying with her on the huge flat rocks in the sun until their clothing dried.

"Yes, I ride," she'd said, trying to show more enthusiasm. But it had seemed so wasteful to purchase horses at the house they would only occasionally visit when in Montana. Now she realized that he'd never planned for them to live in New York City. He'd let her believe they would be moving into the penthouse knowing that he'd already sold it. Because he wanted to surprise her with the house? Or because he'd changed his mind at some point and merely failed to inform her?

So why did she feel like there was more going on than he'd told her? She shoved the thought away, hating that she was finding fault with Ethan. He'd already given her so much. She had a new wardrobe in the closet. And now she lived in this…mansion on the mountainside. She could have anything she wanted, he'd told her. Just name it.

So why couldn't she throw off that ominous feeling that something was wrong—and was about to get worse?

Angry with herself and the path her thoughts had taken, she started to turn back to the kitchen and her coffee when she spotted a red sports car coming up the paved private road.

WITH THE SCENT of her Texas chili in the air, Billie Dee Rhodes turned to see one of the co-owners of the Stagecoach Saloon come in the back door with her arms empty.

"What? No baby?" Billie Dee joked as she dried her hands and stepped away from the stove. "You know I told you not to show your face around here without that adorable son of yours." She stopped, realizing Lillie Cahill Beaumont was in no joking mood today. "Honey, what is it?"

Tears filled the young woman's eyes as she stepped into the cook's ample arms. "It's Hawk."

Billie Dee hugged her tightly. "He's not—"

Lillie shook her head.

She breathed a sigh of relief. She felt blessed that she'd become like a part of the Cahill family. It broke her heart to see any of them hurting. "What's he done now?"

"Nothing!" Lillie cried, pulling back. "That's the problem. You know Drey got married."

She nodded. Everyone in the county knew since the wedding had been a huge production. She also knew that Hawk and Dierdre "Drey" Hunter had been an item in high school as well as college before breaking up. Lillie had always thought they would get back together.

"How is Hawk taking it?" Billie Dee asked.

Lillie shook her head. "He's upset, but he has only himself to blame."

"What would you have had him do? Storm the wedding?"

"Why not? Maybe all she needs is for him to show her how much he loves her."

Older and wiser, Billie Dee suspected that was naive. Whatever had broken them up was enough that the two hadn't gotten back together after all these years. "Well, it appears there isn't anything that can be done now."

Lillie didn't seem to hear. "She's going to be living here in Gilt Edge. Well, up on that mountain."

"In Baxter Folly?"

"Is that what people call it? When I told Hawk, I could tell he was upset. We all thought she was going to be living in New York City. But at the reception Ethan Baxter announced they would be living at Mountain Crest." Lillie made a face and, drying her eyes, looked at the clock on the wall. "I have to go." She stepped into Billie Dee's open arms again and after another hug, left.

"Was that Lillie?" Ashley Jo Somerfield said as she came trotting down from the upstairs apartment and into the kitchen of the old stagecoach stop. She'd moved in there after Lillie's twin and the co-owner of the saloon, Darby Cahill, and his bride, Mariah, moved into their new house with their new baby son. "And is that Texas chili I smell cooking?" She smiled as she brushed past Billie Dee to look into the huge pot on the stove.

Laughing, Billie Dee watched the young woman pick up a spoon and carefully stir the chili. She couldn't help remembering the first time she'd seen her. Ashley Jo had come in looking for a job. Billie Dee's heart had almost stopped. She'd thought Ashley Jo was the daughter she'd given up for adoption twenty-six years ago. The young woman certainly could have been—there was that much resemblance between a young Billie Dee and Ashley Jo.

But it turned out not to be true. Their DNA hadn't matched. Not that Ashley Jo knew anything about that. Since then, though, Billie Dee had been teaching her to cook and enjoying every moment she'd spent with her.

"May I?" Ashley Jo asked, motioning to the chili.

"Of course. Get yourself a bowl," the cook said with a laugh. "What Texas girl wouldn't want chili for breakfast? You're as bad as me."

Ashley Jo grinned at her as she got a bowl down and filled it with a ladle of the chili. "Have you heard anything on the recipe contest?"

"You mean the one you forced me to enter? No, and don't get your hopes up," she said as she joined the young woman at the table after pouring them both cups of coffee. Billie Dee hadn't wanted to enter the contest but Ashley Jo had insisted.

"You're going to win, hands down," the young woman said and took a bite of chili. She closed her eyes and made a *yum* sound, making Billie Dee laugh.

She hadn't found her daughter. Or more to the point, her daughter hadn't found her yet. With the help of her fiancé, Billie Dee had her DNA up on the adoption site, so now if her daughter wanted to find her… But so far, her daughter hadn't. She tried not to think about it, but it was hard not to.

The back door swung open on a gust of summer air. She looked up and smiled as her fiancé, Henry Larson, came through the door. Billie Dee had joked that she had come to Montana to find herself a cow-boy, but at her age, she'd never guessed that one would come into her life. Fortunately, this handsome rancher had done just that.

Henry was eager for the two of them to get married. As much as she wanted that, too, her dream was that her daughter might be at their wedding. Or at least she would have met her and been able to tell her how much she loved her and that she'd never wanted to give her up.

She started to rise to pour Henry a cup of coffee, but he waved her back down, saying he could get it himself. Billie Dee watched him, seeing a change in his manner this morning that told her something had happened.

As if sensing the mood had changed, Ashley Jo grabbed her bowl and excused herself, saying she needed to do something in the bar. She took off down the hall, closing the door behind her.

"What's wrong?" Billie Dee asked as Henry turned from the stove, coffee cup in hand.

"It's your daughter."

Her heart lodged in her throat. All those years ago when she'd been forced to give her baby up for adoption she'd dreamed that one day they might be reunited.

"She contacted the adoption site. Her DNA's a match."

AFTER A RESTLESS, nightmare-filled night, Hawk woke determined to get on with his life. A door had closed, one that he told himself could never open again. He'd thought it would be a relief. He and Drey could both move on now. Wasn't that what he'd wanted? To put the past behind them? Find peace finally?

If he had regrets, he wasn't about to let himself think about them. He'd lived with the what-ifs for too much of his adult life. He and Drey...well, they'd had their chance. Now there was no going back. There was no second-guessing himself anymore. Drey was gone. Married. Honeymooning in a house near his ranch.

He swore and took a deep breath, determined not to look back anymore. The morning sun came up in a cloudless blue sky that only Montana made. The ranch, like the town of Gilt Edge, sat in a valley surrounded by mountain ranges. To him, it was the most beautiful place in the world. There was nowhere else he wanted to be—even if he was going to have to share his valley with Drey and her new husband.

He couldn't help but think of the last time he'd run into her. She'd been coming out of the post office. They'd nearly collided. There was that awkward moment, the two of them just standing there looking at each other. He'd felt the chemistry arc between them—just as it always had. Seeing her had sent his heart into overdrive—even as hard as he willed it not to.

"You look beautiful." The words were out before he could still his tongue. Her auburn hair shone in the sunlight making her brown eyes gleam.

"Thank you," she'd said, sounding embarrassed.

The breeze had stirred her long hair. Without thinking, he'd reached over and brushed a lock back from her eyes. His fingers had touched her warm skin, sending a shiver through him, and a shudder through her.

He'd quickly withdrawn his hand and let his arm drop to his side. There had been a time when they'd had so much to say to each other. But back then, they'd known each other intimately and often hadn't even needed words.

And that was a lot of water under the bridge, he thought now. So why did he still feel such an aching need for the woman? Why hadn't he broken down that wall between them? Or hell, just bounded over it and taken her?

Those kinds of thoughts did nothing for him, he realized. Drey was married. Drey was the past. He had to get that through his thick skull. Drey was gone. And he hadn't just let her go, he'd practically thrown her into another man's arms. Cursing under his breath, he headed downstairs, determined to work her out of his thoughts.

He found his brother downstairs, sitting at the breakfast bar shoveling down a bowl of cereal. Stepping behind the counter, he poured himself a cup of coffee and asked, "What's on the agenda this morning?"

Cyrus eyed him as if expecting he would be too hungover to work. "We've got all that barbed wire to string on that new section. You up to that this morning?"

Hawk didn't feel all that well after rather too much whiskey before he'd fallen into a dark, disturbing sleep. In one nightmare, Drey had come running at him in her wedding dress, screaming at the top of her lungs. The front of the dress had been covered in blood.

"I'm up to whatever you throw at me," he said, hoping it was true.

His brother laughed. "That sounds like a challenge to me."

Bring it on, Hawk thought, wanting to lose himself in a long day of backbreaking ranch work. He poured his coffee into a container to go as his brother got up to rinse out his bowl. "Then let's get on it," he said and headed for the truck.

DREY WATCHED THE car approach, thinking it must be either the caretaker or possibly someone who had come by earlier and taken Ethan into town.

She felt disappointed again that he hadn't joined her last night. Even if she had been asleep, he could have awakened her. *It was their wedding night.* Seemed like a bad way to start a marriage.

You mean like keeping important facts from your wife, like where the two of you would be living?

She hated to admit that she was still upset about that and other surprises her husband had sprung on her. She told herself that she'd known what Ethan was like before she'd married him. Frowning, she wondered, though, if that was true. Maybe she'd seen only what she'd wanted to. Or what he'd wanted her to.

Telling herself to smile as the car pulled up beside Ethan's expensive sedan, she went downstairs and stepped out onto the slate landing, anxious to see her husband and get this marriage started off on a better foot. She would make the best of it, including living in this house. With Ethan here, the house wouldn't feel so cold and alien to her. At least she hoped that was true.

With the sun's glare on the windshield, she couldn't make out who was in the vehicle. So she was surprised when the driver's-side door opened but the passenger side didn't. Only one person climbed out—not her husband.

The man wore mirrored sunglasses and a baseball cap that shaded his face. His blond hair curled at the back of his cap. His lips also seemed to curl as he looked at her. She stared at him, thinking again that he must be the caretaker because he would have had to know the pass code to get through the gate at the bottom of the mountain. But dressed in a blue-checked shirt, new jeans and red tennis shoes without socks, he definitely wasn't a local.

He pushed back his cap and lowered the sunglasses, assessing her from a pair of startling blue eyes. He had a toothpick sticking out of the side of his mouth. He removed it and broke into a broad smile, only then reminding her of someone. "The new Mrs. Ethan Baxter, I presume?"

"Was there an old Mrs. Baxter?" she asked, bristling at his mocking tone.

He merely laughed and looked toward the house. Then he considered the toothpick he still held before breaking it in half and tossing it into the nearby grass.

"What an ugly, pretentious pile of rock and glass,"

he said, taking in the house. "So how much do you hate it so far?"

Definitely not the caretaker, she thought. Or if he was, not for long if Ethan heard the man's opinion of Mountain Crest.

"And you are…?" she asked pointedly, having a bad feeling in her stomach as she realized who it was he reminded her of.

"Sorry," he said, his gaze returning to her. "Jet. I thought maybe Ethan would have mentioned me." He added, "Jet Baxter, your husband's younger brother. You know, the handsome, smart one."

DREY STILL COULDN'T help her surprise. Ethan had never mentioned that he had a brother. He'd talked about his father and grandfather, who'd started the Baxter family empire. His mother had died when he was young so he'd said he didn't really remember her. He'd been raised by a nanny who his father had later married.

Ethan hadn't liked talking about those years so she hadn't pressed. It never dawned on her that he might have had a sibling. The more she looked at the man standing before her, the more she saw a resemblance between him and Ethan. Jet was taller and slimmer, but he had Ethan's blond hair and blue eyes and when he smiled… Still, this man could be just about anyone.

"I assume you have some form of identification?" she asked.

He chuckled but reached into his pocket for his wallet and, flipping it open, climbed up the steps, stopping several below her, so he could show her his New York driver's license.

Jet Baxter. On closer inspection, she could see that he was ten years younger than Ethan, which meant he could be the son of their father and the nanny turned wife. Which could explain why Ethan hadn't told her about Jet. Or was there more to the story?

"So big bro never mentioned me," Jet said as he tucked his wallet back into his pocket.

It appeared they were both wondering why. "I take it that the two of you aren't close or I would have met you before the wedding—or at least *at* the wedding," Drey said.

He looked down as if chastised. "I guess I'm as close as anyone to Ethan." He raised his head and grinned. "He's... Well, I guess I don't have to tell you what he's like."

Actually maybe he did, she thought, but said nothing, not wanting to admit how little she felt she knew about her husband given last night and even this morning. The man could have at least left her a note, texted her or called to let her know where he was and apologize.

"Sorry about missing the wedding," Jet was saying. "I ran into some trouble. Car trouble." They both glanced at his expensive red sports car. "So where is he?" he asked, looking up at the house again. "I wasn't expecting a hero's welcome, but at least he could come out and say hello." He laughed as if he was joking, but his tone said otherwise.

Yes, where *was* Ethan? That was what she had

hoped to ask him. "You haven't seen or heard from him last night or today?"

He shook his head, his gaze shifting from the house to her. "Why?"

"I haven't seen him myself." She hated to admit that he hadn't joined her on their wedding night unless she had to.

"You sure he isn't here somewhere? His car is here and given the size of this monstrosity he built for himself... Sorry," he said with a shrug. "I shouldn't be talking that way about your husband." *Or your brother*, she thought. "I suppose we should try to find him. I can't imagine he would have gone far. He didn't leave a note?"

She felt the pinch of his words but wasn't about to admit now that she hadn't seen him since he'd sent her up to bed and promised to join her. Jet seemed to be enjoying this too much. "I looked around the house but I couldn't find him."

Jet considered that for a moment. "I can't imagine that he took a walk. When was the last time you saw him?"

"He was already gone when I woke up."

Jet's gaze swung back to her. "Seriously?" He looked worried. "I think we'd better search the place."

Drey realized she was actually relieved to have someone to share her concern with—even Ethan's bitter brother. Jet clearly had a chip on his shoulder when it came to his big brother. But Jet's expression mirrored her own growing concern. And the truth was, she was glad for the company right now.

Even in the daylight there was something about the house that made her uncomfortable. All that reflective glass reminded her of mirrored sunglasses. It could see her, but she couldn't see... See what? See what was inside waiting for her? Drey knew it was ridiculous. She wasn't the kind of woman to be afraid of an inanimate object like a house, although when she was young she loved spooky books with haunted houses and evil lurking behind every door.

She and Jet started on the first floor, checking each room before moving on to the next. They each took half of a level and met again in the middle. When they finally reached the kitchen floor, Jet paused in front of the refrigerator. "Mind?" he asked as he opened the door and pulled out a beer. "You?"

She shook her head and glanced at the clock, thinking it was still morning. It was almost eleven. She'd lost half the day already. No wonder she felt confused. She watched him pop the top and take a long swig. "Rough night?"

He licked his lips and chuckled. "I drove all night to get here after I got the car fixed. I'd hoped to make it before the wedding reception ended." He shrugged.

Had his brother really invited him? Wouldn't Ethan have mentioned his disappointment that his brother hadn't made it? Or maybe show some concern?

Jet must have seen from her expression what she was thinking. "You think my own brother wouldn't invite me to his wedding?" He laughed. "I'm sure it gave him pause, but I'd promised to be on my best behavior."

She honestly didn't know if Jet had been invited. Ethan had insisted on handling the guest list and seating arrangements of people she didn't know. Her handful of friends had been relegated to a corner in both the church and the reception.

With a start she remembered something she'd completely forgotten. Ethan had gotten a text last night as they were leaving the reception. He got so many texts and phone calls, that it hadn't really registered at the time. But in her side mirror, she had watched him frown at his phone. He'd looked upset before pocketing it again.

"Did you text him last night?" she asked now.

Jet seemed surprised by the question. "And disturb him on his wedding night?" He laughed. "Not a chance. He knows me. I'm often late. I'm sure he expected me to show up today. That's why it's odd that he's not here."

"I'm surprised he didn't try to reach you," she said. "I would have been worried if I'd known you were coming and didn't make the wedding. You're his brother."

Jet shook his head as he leaned back against the kitchen counter. "He really didn't tell you about me. I'm not surprised. We have different goals in life." He shrugged again. "So it goes without saying that we don't have that much to talk about."

"You're not involved with the family company?" she asked.

He smiled. "Actually, I am. In a lesser way than big brother, but I'm part of the Baxter Inc. team." He pushed off the counter as if her question had stirred up a sore subject. "I suppose we'd better take a look upstairs."

She didn't like the idea of being alone in the master bedroom with Jet. He had a way of looking at her that unnerved her. "I've already checked the master suite. You're welcome to check the guest rooms on the next floor while I get something to eat. I haven't had breakfast, or I guess now, lunch."

"Thanks, I could use a bite," he said and quickly added, "if you don't mind. I didn't take the time to stop and eat." He frowned as he watched her head for the refrigerator. "I would have thought Ethan had a staff by now. Odd, since he had a huge staff for the New York City penthouse and it wasn't a quarter of the size of this place." With that he disappeared up the stairs.

Drey stood for a moment watching him go, hating the way he kept undermining Ethan. And making her question her husband, as well. She tried to call Ethan. The call went straight to voice mail just as it had the other times she'd tried the number when they'd been searching the house.

With a sigh, she told herself that she hadn't planned on making them both breakfast. She'd been hoping that after not finding his brother, Jet would leave.

As she opened the refrigerator, unlike Jet, she had no idea what she would find. She thought about how easily he'd reached in and pulled out a beer. Apparently, he knew his brother well enough to know that it would be stocked. But the way he seemed to make himself at home made her wonder if he hadn't been in this house before.

She saw that there were eggs, English muffins, a slab of ham along with what looked like sandwich fixings, several bins filled with vegetables, including potatoes, and a couple of rib eye steaks.

Ethan had planned ahead, which relieved her some. He hadn't planned to leave. Which meant that he would be back as soon as he could. She tried to relax, telling herself that there was nothing to worry about. Wherever Ethan had gone, he would be returning soon, probably with flowers and an embarrassed apology. It wasn't the first time he'd forgotten to tell her his plans.

She had two pieces of ham warming, along with two English muffins in the large toaster, when Jet returned. She planned to fry them each an egg for a quick breakfast sandwich. Her stomach was still queasy from last night.

In truth, she wasn't up to a long leisurely meal with Jet. She had a bad feeling that Ethan wouldn't like him being here. As he came into the room, she glanced at him, although she knew he hadn't found Ethan. She'd already checked the floor directly above them. Something in his expression, though, made her freeze. "What?" she asked suddenly even more worried.

"Did you check the elevator?"

CHAPTER FOUR

BILLIE DEE STARED at her fiancé. "Henry, what does this mean?"

"That your daughter is looking for you," he said.

"Why do I feel like there's a *but* coming?" she demanded.

He stepped to her and took her shoulders in his big hands. "It's a step, okay? The good news is that she's alive and interested in her birth mother."

"I'm waiting for the bad news."

"When she received notice that the DNA sample was definitely a match, she had the option to contact you at that point."

"She didn't." The cook pulled away to move to the stove. Picking up the large spoon, she stirred her chili. Cooking had gotten her through more hard times in her life than she wanted to recall. "Maybe she just needs a little more time."

Henry said nothing. It had been twenty-six years. How much time did her daughter need?

"This is good news," he said, coming up to wrap his arms around her. "Of course she is leery. She knows nothing about you. It's a step, honey. A step in the right direction."

She smiled, leaning back into him, knowing he was as disappointed as she was. He'd been trying to get her to the altar for months now, she thought, glancing down at the beautiful engagement ring on her finger.

But he seemed to know that she didn't want to set a wedding date just yet. But could she keep holding out in the hope that her daughter might be there? It was foolish, but she couldn't help it. Giving up her daughter had been the hardest thing she'd ever done. But she'd had no choice. Unfortunately, her daughter didn't know that.

"How're Ashley Jo's cooking lessons coming along?" Henry asked, changing the subject.

"She's doing really well." The young woman was a bright spot in Billie Dee's days. Her daughter's age, Ashley Jo was so much like her daughter that sometimes… She shook away the thought.

"By the way, this came in the mail," he said, removing his arms from around her to pull a letter from his jacket pocket.

She wiped her hands on her apron as she turned and took the envelope. The moment she saw the return address, she knew immediately what it was. Her gaze shot up to Henry's. He was grinning.

"It might not be good news," she told him. "Just because they sent me a letter doesn't mean I won the recipe contest. You're as bad as Ashley Jo thinking I'm more of a cook than I am."

"Quit going on and open the letter!"

Billie Dee took a breath and ripped open the envelope. As she pulled out the letter and unfolded it, she didn't dare breathe. Not that she wanted to do well for herself. She didn't want to let Ashley Jo down. Her gaze quickly scanned the words on the page. She could feel Henry holding his breath, as well.

As she looked up, she saw Ashley Jo standing in the doorway. She seemed to have frozen in place.

Billie Dee broke into a smile, her heart rising like a hot-air balloon. "I won."

Henry and Ashley Jo cheered. Henry picked her up and spun her around as she laughed and cried for him to put her down. The moment he did, she turned to Ashley Jo. "This is all your fault," she joked.

"Didn't I tell you?" the young woman said and hugged her. "You're the best cook ever. So what are you going to do with all that money?"

Billie Dee knew exactly what she wanted to do. "I'm going to hire a private investigator to find my daughter."

Ashley Jo started. "Your daughter?"

Tears in her eyes, she said, "I was forced to give up my baby twenty-six years ago. Henry just told me that she is at least a little interested in who her birth mother is. I want to find her. I need to find her." She began to cry. Henry took her hand. "She needs to know that I love her. Have always loved her."

THE SUN BEAT down hard. Hawk wiped the sweat from his forehead with the sleeve of his shirt and looked down the line of fencing they'd strung. His arms ached just enough that he knew he'd never strung this much wire in all his years working the ranch. He felt good, satisfied by the hot, tired feeling—and the day was far from over.

Cyrus tossed him a bottle of water. He took a long drink, tilting back his head and letting the cold liquid run down his throat in large gulps before pouring some over his head. It ran into his eyes, down his neck to his open shirt and over his sun-browned chest before puddling just north of his big silver belt buckle. He wiped his face again with his sleeve.

"You trying to kill yourself?" Cyrus asked as he took in the length of fence his brother had strung.

"I'm fine." He felt Cyrus's gaze on him.

"Lillie believe that?" he asked.

He merely grunted. He should have known that his brother had seen Lillie drive up to the ranch house last night. It didn't take much to know what she was doing there. Their matchmaking sister. He shook his head at just the thought of her.

"You know that if I ever do settle down with some woman, Lillie is going to come after you next," Hawk said. "She's relentless. She'll have you married within weeks after I tie the knot. Mark my words." He took another drink and swallowed. "Be afraid. Be very afraid."

His brother ignored his attempt to try to change the subject. "We goin' to talk about this?" Cyrus asked.

"Nope."

"Maybe you should take a break."

"I am taking a break." He took another swig of the water and then capped the bottle before tossing it back to his brother.

"I meant a break away from the ranch, away from

Gilt Edge, hell, maybe even away from Montana for a while."

"I would never leave Montana, especially in the summer," Hawk said truthfully. Only a fool would think that there was a better place to be this time of year, he thought as he breathed in the sweet scent of the sun-filled pines.

"There's that bull we've been talking about buying down by Denver," Cyrus said as if Hawk hadn't spoken. "Maybe you should go pick it up. You could make a vacation out of it."

"I don't need a vacation. You want to buy the bull? It's fine with me, but you can make the trip to Colorado. I'm staying right here—just like I told Lillie."

Cyrus groaned. "I don't get it."

"It's not yours to get."

"If you're hurting this bad, why in the hell did you let her go?" His brother sounded angry. No one in the family had understood because they didn't have the facts. And they weren't going to get them either. Like him, they were just going to have to accept that he and Drey were never happening. They weren't meant to be. They'd hurt each other too badly all those years ago. There had never been a path back. At least not for him.

"What is wrong with you?" Cyrus demanded, seeming to grow even angrier. "You had every chance to make things right with Drey since she came back to town after she graduated from college. Is it your mule-headed stubbornness? Or are you just plain too full of yourself that you'd rather suffer than be happy with someone who isn't perfect like you?"

Hawk jerked off his straw cowboy hat and raked back his dark hair. These were fightin' words. There was a time that the two of them would be going at it in the dirt over a lot less. But he didn't blame his brother or the rest of his family for being angry with him over Drey. They all loved her. She was damned close to family. They also wanted her to be happy as much as they did Hawk.

No, this was his doin'. He'd put his whole family through this and he wasn't about to take a punch at his brother, even though he would welcome a fistfight right now with anyone else.

"Do I look like I want to talk about this?" he demanded, holding his ground. "The subject is closed. Drey's married. End of story." He slammed his hat back down on his head and grabbed the end of the barbed wire in his gloved hand. "We stringing this wire or not?"

Cyrus cursed under his breath but gave up. At least for the moment.

Hawk felt the bite of the barbed wire through his glove, but it was nothing like the near-lethal blow Drey had delivered all those years ago. He'd never told anyone. Nor, it seemed, had Drey. It was their dark secret. Bringing it to light now would only open those horrible old wounds and Hawk didn't feel all that strong as it was at this moment.

THE ELEVATOR. Why hadn't Drey thought of that? Hadn't Ethan said he was having problems with some of the remote-control devices in the house? What if he'd gotten on the elevator and—

She watched Jet step to the wall next to the elevator. He hesitated a moment before he pushed the button and stepped back. She could hear a whirring sound deep in the bowels of the house as the car began to climb. Ethan had said it was a state-of-the-art elevator. She recalled him mentioning that he'd been forced to get someone out of Germany to design it. The glass car had to balance perfectly as it rose. He'd wanted everything to appear to cling to the side of the mountain— and he didn't want the elevator to be obtrusive. That's why it wasn't seen from behind the wall panels when it wasn't in use.

"Just like the house," he'd said of the design.

That had made no sense to her since all that glass lit at night had looked like an airport landing strip. Even in the daylight with the sun glaring off the mountainside of glass, there was no way the house wasn't obtrusive. Not that she would have argued the point with Ethan, who was clearly proud of his design.

She could hear the elevator approach and looked toward the wood panel that hid it. The elevator stopped. The panel began to slide open. Drey held her breath. She expected to see Ethan lying on the elevator floor. Dead. He was too young for a heart attack. And she couldn't imagine what inside the elevator could have killed him. Maybe an electric short. And since it had been only the two of them in the house alone last night…

Empty.

She let out her breath as a wave of relief washed over her. No dead Ethan. No Ethan at all.

Jet shrugged. "Well, it was a thought," he said as he came over to where she was about to fry the eggs. "Need any help?"

"No, I have it." He was too close in this massive stainless steel–coated kitchen. "You can find some plates and silverware."

"Sure," he said.

Out of the corner of her eye, she watched him try one cabinet, then another, before he found the plates. So why did she still feel as if he was only pretending not to know where anything was?

Why don't I trust him? He hadn't given her any reason. So why was she leery of him? If there was anyone she should be doubtful about right now, it was her husband, she thought with an inward shudder since she still hadn't heard from him.

That thought didn't sit well as Drey cracked two eggs into the skillet. Jet found the silverware on his third attempt. "Voilà," he cried. "Are these solid gold? They feel like it."

She listened to him humming to himself as he set the small table in the sunroom off the kitchen. Then she heard him over by the bar, no doubt making himself a drink. He'd definitely made himself at home, she thought uncharitably. She couldn't help being out of sorts. Her husband had abandoned her on their wedding night and was now missing. His brother—at least according to Jet anyway—had shown up out of the blue. And now she was in a huge, strange house all alone with a complete stranger.

Don't be silly, she told herself. She'd seen Jet's driver's license; he knew how to get through the gate to drive up to the house. Obviously he was who he said he was. She had no reason to be so suspicious, let alone…uneasy.

When the eggs were done along with the ham, she took the breakfast sandwiches over to the small table where Jet had placed the dishes and silverware. He seemed to be studying the underside of one of the plates as if trying to determine its value as she put the food on the table and sat down.

"Here." Jet handed her a drink. She saw that his beer bottle was empty. He'd certainly put that away quickly enough.

"I don't drink alcohol," she said and pushed the drink away. "Thank you anyway."

"There's no alcohol in it. Ethan told me that you don't partake. This is my no-alcohol specialty, lots of fruit juice." Before she would argue, he added, "You look like you are going to jump out of your skin. Not that I blame you. This house gives me the creeps, too. It's so damned…big. All this glass and marble. And what's with all the white?" He shuddered. "On top of that, Ethan has done one of his disappearing acts. This is nothing new for him. Some business meeting must have come up. But you can trust me, so stop looking so suspicious like you think I might try to poison you." He chuckled and held up his hands as if to say he had nothing up his sleeve.

She knew he was right about her state of mind, but she wasn't sure he had nothing to hide. But he was right about one thing. What she needed was to feel better and not be so jumpy. Maybe some food would help. Unfortunately, she had no appetite. She picked up the sandwich, forcing herself to take a bite.

Across the table from her, Jet was devouring his sandwich, chasing bites with a slug of his drink. She took another small bite, her stomach roiling. Why had she bothered to cook it? She was too upset to eat a thing. Jet had said this was one of Ethan's disappearing acts. So he did this a lot? If Jet worked for the same family company, he would know. But she and Ethan had gotten married only yesterday. Why wouldn't he have left a note or texted her or called once he got to his meeting? She tried to call him numerous times, only to have the call go straight to voice mail.

She said as much to Jet.

He shrugged. "He's Ethan. He doesn't think about other people. I can tell you're worried, but he's fine. He could show up at any moment with flowers, a bottle of expensive wine and a humble apology."

Wasn't that what she'd thought herself? Because he'd done it before. And he was always sorry. And he always forgot she didn't drink wine. Still this time felt different. She picked up the drink Jet had made, took a sniff and then a sip.

Her body seemed to be vibrating, her head throbbing and her stomach still upset from last night. Not that she thought fruit juice was the answer as she took another sip. But right now, anything that could relieve some of her tension and take her mind off Ethan and being here alone with his brother in this house…

She could feel Jet watching her. She took another sip. It was a bit odd, but it wasn't bad. She had no idea what his specialty drink was, but within seconds she began to relax. Jet was right. She hadn't been poisoned and maybe the fruity drink did help. Or was it just thinking that maybe she could trust Jet since she didn't taste any alcohol.

He grinned over at her. "What did I tell you?"

She had to smile. "You were right. It tastes good, refreshing."

"I'm sorry Ethan didn't tell you I was coming. If my being here is a problem…" Jet was studying her.

She wanted to say that it was. While she didn't want to be alone in this house, she didn't want to share it with Jet. "So you're…staying?"

"If you don't mind. Just until Ethan returns, which will hopefully be this afternoon. Don't worry. As soon as he gets back, I'll clear out. I won't interrupt your honeymoon."

No, Ethan had done that.

"In the meantime, I promise to stay out of your way. I believe there is a lower floor, a parking garage of sorts, with staff quarters. If he isn't back by tonight, I'll just bunk down there. You won't even know I'm in the house."

If Ethan wasn't back by tonight? She took another sip of the drink, telling herself that of course he would be back. But what if he wasn't? She could just imagine what Ethan would say when he returned to find his brother staying in the staff quarters.

"You should stay in one of the guest rooms," she said, knowing she had no choice but to extend the invitation. The house was huge. Jet was right; they wouldn't even have to see each other. And Jet was family, even though Ethan had never mentioned his existence to her—or told her that he might be stopping by after the wedding.

Jet chuckled. "I'd feel better below on the ground level. This house makes me feel like it's a spaceship that could take off at any moment."

She laughed since she could see what he meant.

"Don't worry, I'll let my brother know I insisted on staying down there. It isn't like the rooms are in the dungeon. They're a hell of a lot nicer than a motel. Trust me, Ethan wouldn't want me using the guest towels anyway. I believe he said the staff have their own kitchen. Thanks for breakfast, though. It really hit the spot. I'm sure the staff Ethan hired will be showing up soon. Ethan wouldn't want you cooking and cleaning. Not his *new* bride."

This time, she didn't imagine the way he said *new*. "Was there an *old* bride?" Drey asked, hearing the same thing in Jet's voice that she'd heard earlier, the first time he'd mentioned Ethan's new wife.

Jet grinned. "Sorry, not my story to tell."

"Ethan was married before?" she asked in surprise.

Jet met her gaze as he rose to refill their drinks. "There is a lot he didn't tell you, apparently. I'm sure he'll fill you in when he returns."

If he returns. That thought did nothing to help matters as she listened to Jet return to the bar.

"That drink help a little?" he asked from behind her. "You looked like your blood sugar was a little low."

She had to admit that it had. She was surprised that she'd finished it. She felt as if she was stepping off a high wire, the tension in her body starting to ebb away. Maybe there wasn't anything to worry about. Ethan was just being...Ethan. At least according to his brother.

She didn't feel strung quite so tightly now. But while the food and juice had helped, she now felt closer to tears than she had all day. Jet being kind to her made her predicament only worse. Her husband had abandoned her on their wedding night. Who did that without leaving a word?

Drey took another bite of her sandwich. Jet seemed to think that his brother was an inconsiderate jerk. But what if Ethan was in trouble? Maybe she should have called the sheriff the moment she found Ethan gone. What if she was losing valuable hours needed to save him? She said as much to Jet, who laughed.

"Your blood sugar must have been lower than even I thought," he said as he returned with two more of his specialties. "You look like you're feeling better. As for my brother, I wouldn't be surprised if Ethan had one of the company helicopters take him to the airport. He mentioned that he was going to have one nearby since he was giving up his New York City penthouse."

She'd heard that Colt McCloud, a cowboy she'd

gone to school with, had started a helicopter service right outside of town. Colt had been an army helicopter pilot. So maybe what Jet was saying could be true.

It appeared that Jet knew Ethan better than she did. He knew that the penthouse had been sold. Maybe it was true that old saying about the wife being the last to know. She knew the saying referred to extramarital affairs. Now, there was a thought. Had Ethan left her on her wedding night to be with another woman?

Jet slid her second drink across the table to her. "So you have no idea where your brother could be?" she asked as she took another bite of her sandwich.

"Where Ethan might have gone? Not a clue." He sat down. He'd gotten himself a toothpick. It now stuck out of the side of his mouth. He'd finished his breakfast and now leaned back in his chair, looking more like he belonged here than she did.

"Seriously, are you sure we shouldn't call the sheriff?"

"Seems a little early for that, don't you think?" he said around the toothpick. "You know my brother. He'd be mortified. Are you sure he didn't leave a note or a text where he's gone and you just missed it? I'm sure it's business related since he eats and sleeps making money."

She checked her phone, not for the first time. Nothing. She saw no reason to try to call again since she'd left a half dozen messages. "I didn't see a note. I'll check again. Maybe I just overlooked it."

"Maybe. Ethan can be forgetful, but it could also be that he knew I would show up so he wouldn't have to worry about you being alone. You have nothing to be sorry about. This is all on my brother."

She took a sip of the new drink. Whatever he put in it, she liked it because it wasn't too sweet. Just a sip or two, she thought, enjoying the languid feel of her body as she began to relax even more. Jet was right. Her blood sugar must have been very low.

"What was Ethan like when he was young?" she asked as she pushed her half-eaten sandwich away.

Jet chuckled. "You aren't going to believe this, but he was a lot like he is now. Always driven. Always very serious. He was our father's favorite, of course. Mom loved me more."

"Your mom? Ethan told me his mother died and your father married your nanny?"

Jet let out a bark of a laugh. "Is that what he told you? He always wished that we had different mothers. No, we are true siblings right down to our blood. The nanny came later but even she tried to balance out the love and did a pretty good job of it. Mom didn't die until I was seven. I guess Ethan doesn't have as good a memory of her as I do." He sounded less bitter and she liked that. "You should eat more," he said, seeing that she'd left half of her sandwich.

She shook her head and felt a little dizzy as she watched him chew on the toothpick in his mouth. Mostly she felt overly tired. She could hardly keep her eyes open.

"Another place we haven't looked is the parking garage," he said. "I don't know why I didn't think of it. Ethan keeps an extra vehicle down there. He could have taken it somewhere."

"I thought you'd never been to this house before," she said and hated how suspicious she sounded.

He smiled and didn't seem to take offense. "It's my first time seeing the real thing, but Ethan had a model built of it before construction started. He kept it at the office. Of course he had to brag about all the different levels, the unique design he'd come up with himself." He shook his head as he removed the toothpick, broke it in half and dropped it onto his plate. "I call the place Ethan's Ego. He told me about the vehicle he planned to leave here. An SUV since his expensive sedan just won't do come winter. Sorry, I did it again." He held up his hands in surrender. "I love my brother but you have to admit, sometimes he's too much. I would imagine the wedding was quite the event. Sorry I missed it." He didn't sound sorry as he stood to take his plate and dirty glass away. "I'll quit complaining about my brother. Truth is, I'm a little worried. We'd better hear from him today."

She agreed and was shocked to realize that she'd finished the second drink he'd made her. He picked up her glass to make her another one. "No more for me," she said as he returned to the bar.

Getting to her feet a little unsteadily, she took her plate over to the sink and scraped the contents into the disposal. Just the smell of the sandwich was turning her stomach. She kept thinking about what he'd said about his brother. He kept saying, "You know how Ethan is." If half of what Jet had told her was true, she didn't know her husband at all, she thought as she leaned into the counter for support and looked around for the disposal switch.

Her cell phone rang, making her jump. Pulling it out, she prayed it was Ethan. As upset as she was with him and this new situation she found herself in, she wanted to hear his voice more than anything. She also wanted to hear his explanation for disappearing on her.

But it wasn't her husband.

Disappointed, she looked up and caught a fleeting expression on Jet's face. "Ethan?" he asked.

She shook her head, trying to make sense of what she thought she'd seen on Jet's face. He'd almost looked as if he'd known it wouldn't be his brother. Did he know where Ethan was and why he hadn't called? Was that the real reason he was here? The reason she'd gotten the impression he'd known it wouldn't be Ethan on the phone? She could feel the effects of the past few days. A mistake not to eat more probably since it was so late in the day. But maybe her bigger mistake was marrying Ethan.

"A friend. I need to call her." But she didn't move. She leaned against the kitchen counter, feeling sick and trapped and resentful of both Ethan and his brother for putting her in this position. She felt anger bubble up in her, mixing with her mental and emotional exhaustion. There was nothing keeping her here. She could leave. Just walk out and let Ethan wonder where she'd gone for a change.

Except she didn't even have a car. And where

would she go? She'd given up everything to be here right now—her apartment she'd loved, her furnishings, her life, even her vehicle. Tears burned her eyes. She brushed at them. Where the hell was the stupid disposal switch?

Jet stepped over and flipped a switch she hadn't seen until that moment.

Instantly, the disposal began to make a horrible sound.

He hurriedly turned it off. "What the hell is in there?" he asked, looking at her.

"That's the first time I've used it. All I put in was my sandwich." At least that's all she thought she'd put down the drain.

"Your sandwich shouldn't make that sound. Let me take a look. You sure that's all you put in there?"

She stepped back to give him room and realized that she was light-headed and even more unsteady on her feet. Clearly her emotions were making her sick.

His gaze locked onto her as he reached in and felt around. She held her breath, hoping she hadn't accidentally dropped a piece of the silverware down the disposal. Like Jet had said, the set was heavy enough that it could be solid gold.

Suddenly Jet's hand stopped moving. She saw him grimace in distaste.

"I hate to think of what this might be," he said as he slowly withdrew what he'd found—and then quickly dropped it into the sink with a curse. "Oh God, is that what I think it is?" he exclaimed, taking a step back.

CHAPTER FIVE

DREY COULDN'T SPEAK. She stared at what appeared to be a thumb. It was large with tiny hairs sprouting out of it. There was a slice across it—no doubt from the disposal blade. It was large enough to be a man's.

"Is it real?" she cried and took a step back.

"I'm not sure."

As she pushed off the counter and took another step, she swayed, suddenly feeling her legs want to give out under her.

"Easy." Jet grabbed her arm. "Are you all right?"

She was unable to take her eyes off the thumb lying in the sink. Because of the cut across the top she couldn't be sure, but it could have been Ethan's. She knew that didn't make any sense. If Ethan had accidently cut off his thumb...

"I'm no doctor, but if that's a real thumb, shouldn't there be blood?"

She had no idea. "It's not Ethan's."

"Of course it's not Ethan's. Why would you even say that?" He sounded upset. "But as bloodless as it is and sliced open right behind the nail, I wouldn't even be able to identify it if it was. How the hell did it end up in your disposal?"

Now it was *her* disposal? Her head was spinning. "You have to do something with it. Take it to the sheriff. If it's human…"

"Okay, let's slow down here. Imagine if I take it to the sheriff and it's *not* human. It doesn't even look real. We call the sheriff, get him up here and it turns out to be a joke… I'm sure the locals already think Ethan and this house are a joke. You really want to go through that? Maybe more to the point, do you want to put him through it?"

How would he know that the locals made fun of Ethan and the house? She felt as if she was going to be sick to her stomach.

"I think this is just a prank."

"What if it's not?" she cried, remembering the workers who'd gotten hurt on this job. What if the thumb belonged to one of them?

"I say we wait until Ethan comes back, let him decide if it should go to the sheriff. If it's just a joke, then Ethan won't have our heads over it. Ethan gets here, and we'll let him handle it," Jet said.

The more she looked at the thumb, the more she couldn't be sure it was real. "What will you do with it?" Her words seemed to slur. "You can't just leave it in the sink."

Jet sighed. "I suppose we can't put it in a baggie in the fridge, huh." She shuddered. "How about the freezer? I think it's empty."

When had he looked in the freezer? She must have turned away, because when she looked in the sink again, it was empty and Jet was zipping a sandwich bag shut. He opened the freezer, tossed the parcel in and slammed the door. Making a show of brushing his hands together, he said, "Now it's all up to Ethan. 'Welcome home, brother. Oh, by the way, there might be a human thumb in your freezer or not.'" He laughed, but she didn't see anything funny about it.

She heard the whir of the disposal as Jet finished pulverizing her sandwich and washing it down the drain. She must have looked as if she was going to cry because she sure wanted to.

Jet touched her arm, startling her. "You look exhausted. Maybe you should lie down for a while. If I hear from Ethan, I'll call you."

She nodded. Her legs felt like rubber. She let him lead her over to the elevator since the thought of climbing all those stairs seemed impossible right now. He pushed the master-suite button for her. She stood there looking at him as the door began to close.

"Are you going to be all right?"

She didn't have a chance to answer as the panel door closed and the elevator began to move, making a whirring sound. When it stopped and the door slid open, she stepped out, feeling confused and disoriented for a moment until a panel in the wall of the master suite opened into her enormous bedroom.

She hadn't been aware of the hidden elevator room, she thought as she stumbled. The door closed behind her, becoming a wall again. She realized there was a small screen at the edge of the wall that she'd hadn't noticed before. She would never have guessed that the elevator was behind there.

Feeling woozy, Drey had barely gotten the thought out when she heard the whirring sound and realized Jet must have called the elevator back down to the kitchen. Her mind seemed fuzzy and yet she still wondered why a man as healthy as he looked wouldn't take the stairs.

Not that it mattered, she told herself as she moved toward the bed, thinking she just needed to lie down. She felt light-headed and at the same time, her body felt leaden.

Just the sight of the large bed with its expensive sheets and comforter looked like an oasis in the desert. All she wanted to do was crawl up on it and rest for a little while. By then Ethan would be back.

But first, she had to call Lillie back. She and Lillie Cahill had been friends for years despite the fact that Drey and Hawk had broken up after being high school sweethearts and dating through college.

Thinking that fresh air might do her good, she stumbled toward the balcony. Maybe this house was suffocating her. She reached the sliding glass door that opened onto the small balcony and fiddled with it until she realized it was already unlocked. She flung the door open and staggered out, nearly going over the railing.

She hadn't realized how high she was from the ground. For a moment, she teetered at the edge of the balcony railing, the dizzying drop making her head swim. She lurched back and dropped into one of the two small deck chairs as she pulled out her cell phone. She couldn't remember ever being this exhausted. Jet had sworn there was no alcohol in her drinks. She would have tasted it if there had been. She couldn't explain how light-headed she felt.

Closing her eyes, she listened to it ring, her mind whirling. She had to calm down. Her heart was pounding. She couldn't keep worrying about Ethan and at the same time, being furious with him. She had to get some rest so she didn't feel so emotionally wrung out. But she knew it was more than that. More than even finding a thumb in the disposal. She'd made a horrible mistake marrying Ethan.

Lillie answered.

"Lillie," Drey said into the phone and burst into tears.

THE NEXT MORNING, at the sound of an approaching vehicle, Hawk instantly regretted not getting his horse saddled sooner. "I don't want to hear it," he snapped as he heard his sister get out of her SUV and head toward him. He kept saddling his horse, telling himself if she wanted to talk about Drey, he would be forced to ride off and leave her standing in the barn.

"I'm warning you, Lillie," he said at the sound of her hurried steps. "If this is about Drey—"

"You have to listen to me," Lillie cried, grabbing his shoulder and spinning him around to face her.

"Lillie—"

"Drey's miserable. She called me yesterday afternoon bawling her eyes out. She sounded drunk. Drey, who I've never seen drink more than a glass of wine.

Drunk! She's made a terrible mistake. As if that isn't bad enough, her husband has disappeared."

Hawk growled under his breath. He bit off each word, suspecting all of this was a vast exaggeration. "I'm sure her husband has not disappeared."

"On their wedding night." She lifted a brow. "Before—"

"Damn it, Lillie. I don't want to hear any of this. It's none of my business."

"Now Ethan's creepy brother, Jet, has moved into the house. She's scared of him. I could hear it in her voice before she…passed out."

Hawk shook his head as he turned back to finish saddling his horse. He didn't want to hear any of this, but try as he might, he couldn't imagine Drey drunk-dialing his sister—let alone passing out. If she really had admitted that she'd made a mistake, well…it was just the alcohol talking. And if her husband really had left her on their wedding night, well…that was none of his business. Whatever had happened, he had no doubt that they would patch it up and, along with her hangover, Drey would regret calling his sister.

"I'm riding away now," Hawk said firmly to Lillie. "When I return either you aren't here or you don't mention any of this to me again. I can't make it any clearer than that. Have you heard the expression 'made her bed and now has to lie in it'?"

"You can't mean that. This is *Drey*. Even if I believed for a moment that you don't love her anymore, you can't just abandon her now."

"I'm dead serious, little sister. Unless you really

want to piss me off." He swung up onto his horse, spurred the gelding and didn't look back.

The only sanity he'd had in the past forty-eight hours was either working or riding his horse up into the mountains. Not that Drey had ever been far from his thoughts. Trying not to think about her was thinking about her. It made him furious with himself. Then to have Lillie twisting his ear about her...

He told himself that his sister had to be exaggerating about the phone call. He could remember Drey crying only a few times in the years they were together. She really must have been drunk, something he'd never seen, couldn't even imagine. On top of that, she hated to cry, seeing it as a weakness and Dierdre Hunter hated seeming weak more than she hated to cry. He'd admired her strength and determination and even her weaknesses—at least until they came head-to-head with his own weaknesses.

Hawk rode out to where he was meeting his brother for another backbreaking day of stringing barbed wire fence. He couldn't wait. Anything to get his mind off Drey.

DREY WOKE CONFUSED, head aching. She tried to sit up. Morning sunlight and the scent of pines poured in through the open balcony door. She shivered, surprised to find herself lying across the bed, fully dressed, her phone lying on the duvet next to her. She frowned, trying to remember what had happened. How many hours had she slept?

Was it possible she'd lain down yesterday afternoon

and was only now waking up? She dropped back onto the bed and closed her eyes, wishing she could sleep forever if it would keep her head from pounding. Yes, she was exhausted but...

She opened her eyes. She didn't need to look around the room to know that Ethan was still gone. Had he returned, she was sure he would have awakened her. She sucked in a breath as she felt that ominous weight on her chest and was struck with another terrifying premonition. *She would never see him alive again.*

At the squawk of a bird on the balcony deck outside, she started. She was sick of these premonitions. Worse, sick of the worry and anxiety she'd felt since even before the wedding. Where was her husband?

Turning, she saw a crow staring at her from the balcony with its beady little dark eyes. The bird flapped its silken ebony wings at her and hopped to the chair closest to the open door. Wasn't there some superstition about crows and death?

She shivered as she swung her legs over the side of the bed and tried to sit up. When had she opened the balcony door? And she'd left it open?

The bird cawed at her and hopped closer. "Oh, no you don't," she said, struggling to her feet, determined to chase the bird off and close the door. She swayed for a moment. Why couldn't she remember leaving it open? Unfortunately, all of yesterday afternoon and night was a blur.

Dizzy, she had to hang on to the door handle for a moment. The bird didn't look the least bit afraid. Instead, it appeared to be challenging her. She wasn't up to a challenge this morning. She started to close the door, when she saw something on the balcony floor under one of the chairs.

She blinked, the headache splitting now. The crow hadn't moved. It seemed determined to get into the house. She stepped back to the bed, grabbed her pillow to shoo it away and returned to the balcony. She used the pillow to chase the crow away from the doorway and bent down to pick up the cell phone that lay next to the wall under the chair. The crow hopped along the railing, finally taking flight, but not before looking back at her. She met those beady eyes... If she was the superstitious kind...

Dropping into one of the balcony chairs, she stared down at the device in her hand. A sliver of a memory came back to her of being out here on the balcony on the phone yesterday. With a curse, she remembered talking to Lillie Cahill. She felt her face flush with embarrassment. Recalling it all, she couldn't believe that she'd broken down on the phone—and to Lillie. The last person she wanted to know about her problems because her friend would go to Hawk and he would be delighted to hear it. She was sure that he still felt she deserved whatever mess she made of her life. Well, she'd done it up proud this time.

But as she looked closer at the phone, she realized it wasn't hers. Hers had been next to her on the bed when she'd awakened this morning. It was still there, she saw as she looked back into the bedroom.

Suddenly she felt as if she was going to throw

up. *This is Ethan's phone.* Her heart began to pound harder as she realized what that meant. No wonder her calls had gone straight to voice mail. This also explained why he hadn't called her.

She frowned. But how had it gotten out here on the balcony unless…he'd been out here. He had come to their bedroom. But then where had he gone—*without* his phone? That was unheard-of. He would never have left it behind. Couldn't. He would be completely lost without it.

And yet apparently he had. She rubbed her forehead with her free hand, trying to make sense of it as she stared at the phone, uncomprehending. If he'd dropped his phone when he was out on the balcony… Had she slept so soundly on her wedding night that she hadn't known he'd been out here at some point?

Or had he come back yesterday, found her passed out again and come out on the balcony for some reason? To make a phone call?

That seemed unlikely. She shivered from the cold morning air and pushed herself up out of the chair to go back inside. She closed the door and swiped the surface of the phone. The log-on screen appeared, but she didn't know his backup pass code to unlock it. Ethan, she recalled, used his thumbprint.

Her head ached worse as she tried to make sense of this. His phone was locked. But if he'd misplaced it, wouldn't he have tried to call his phone to find it? Wouldn't she have heard it ringing out on the balcony?

A chill ran the length of her spine. She hugged herself as she had a horrible thought. The thumb in the freezer. Her pulse thundered in her ears. Had that been real? Or had she dreamed it? She'd had such strange dreams lately. Even worse ones since passing out on the bed that she couldn't be sure what was real.

But if there was a thumb in the freezer, she had a bad feeling it was Ethan's. She would know it was his if it could open his phone. The thought made her shudder. It was crazy. Ethan was fine. His thumb wasn't in the freezer. He'd just gone to New York or somewhere on business. He might already be back.

She shoved his phone into the pocket of her jeans. She needed a shower but she didn't want to take the time. Right now, she had to know if Ethan had returned. Even as she thought it, she knew better. He would have awakened her. Or at least tried. At this point, she didn't know what to expect from him. He could have gotten in late and, thinking she'd had too much to drink, really slept in one of the guest rooms this time. Jet must have slipped alcohol into those drinks for them to affect her the way they had.

Pocketing her own phone as well, she hurried downstairs. All of the doors to the guest bedrooms were open. None of the beds looked as if they'd been slept in. She fought the feeling of déjà vu. Was this how each of her days would begin? Her looking for her husband, wondering where he'd gone this time?

At the kitchen level, she slowed. The house felt deathly quiet. She wondered where Jet was. She peered in, relieved to see that the kitchen was empty. No Jet.

Drey hesitated. Her movements felt surreal as if

still in a dream. She was sluggish, slow-thinking, her head pounding, her mind dull. All of this felt like a nightmare that she couldn't wake up from. Since meeting Ethan, she'd often felt as if her life was no longer her own. Like now as she sleepwalked toward the refrigerator, headed somewhere she didn't want to go, doing something she didn't want to do. Something so crazy...

She stopped in front of the appliance, but for a moment she couldn't bring herself to open the freezer door.

Taking a deep breath and letting it out, she grabbed the handle and jerked the freezer side open and blinked.

The plastic bag with the thumb in it was gone.

CHAPTER SIX

Drey stood in front of the refrigerator, the freezer door hanging open, for a full minute. The thumb was gone as if it had never been there. She'd dreamed it? What a horrible, crazy dream if that was true.

But on closer inspection, she could swear that the plastic bag with the thumb in it had left a mark in the frost on the freezer shelf. It *had* been there. The mark wasn't conclusive, but her memory of Jet pulling the thumb out of the disposal was so clear, it had to have happened.

Jet. Maybe he'd changed his mind and taken the thumb to the sheriff. He'd made it sound as if he was going to do something if Ethan hadn't shown up yesterday.

Her feet were already moving before she made the decision. She rushed down the stairs to the first level. At the end of the hallway, she found the stairs down to what Jet had said were the staff quarters.

She checked one room after another. Empty. Maybe Jet had left for good, leaving the way he had shown up—without any notice. It made no sense given that he'd said he would stay until Ethan returned and then leave. No more sense than the fact that Ethan had also disappeared.

In the last room, she threw open the door to find Jet's suitcase open on the bed. *He must travel light*, she thought, seeing the small carry-on suitcase and a laptop computer on the bedside table next to it.

She tried to catch her breath, not sure if she was relieved or not to realize he hadn't left. For a moment, she simply leaned against the door frame, trying to calm down. Her heart was racing. Jet had taken the thumb to the sheriff. It was the only thing that made any sense.

So why did she still feel scared? She should be relieved. Jet had left without saying anything—just like Ethan had. But then again, she'd been lost to the world both evenings.

Was it possible Ethan had returned and the two of them had taken the thumb to the sheriff? She realized she hadn't looked out to see if Jet's car was still out front.

Turning back toward the upper part of the house, Drey noticed stairs down to what Jet had said was an underground parking garage. She took them, dropping into the cold concrete darkness. There appeared to be space for parking a half dozen cars. There was an unfamiliar vehicle in one of the spaces. She walked over to the white SUV and tried the door. It opened.

Peering inside, she saw that the keys were in the ignition. Jet had mentioned that Ethan had left an extra vehicle here. She reached in to open the glove box and pulled out the registration. It was registered to Ethan

Baxter. She put the registration back and closed the glove box as she exited the SUV.

She was shocked by how little she knew about her husband, his plans, this house, his business. She stood for a moment, overwhelmed by all of it. Her head still hurt and she didn't feel well. Nor was she looking forward to that climb upstairs. She considered taking the elevator but couldn't bring herself to get into that box. Clearly Jet didn't have that problem.

After Jet had poured her into the elevator and sent her to the master suite yesterday, she remembered hearing the elevator leave again. He'd probably used it to bring his things in from his car. She suspected that as much as he complained about his brother, he liked his house and all Ethan's high-tech gadgets.

That thought made her even more uneasy about his staying at the house. How long would he stay if Ethan didn't return? If only Ethan would come back. She checked her phone to see if she'd heard from either brother. She hadn't.

Jet could have simply gone into town to get something to eat. Or even to look for Ethan. Or taken the thumb to the sheriff because someone had taken it.

She didn't want to think about Jet's return with the sheriff in tow—or to tell her that the thumb had been a joke and now everyone in the county would know.

Drey started up the stairs, feeling lost. She'd quit her job as a librarian in Gilt Edge for Ethan because she thought she was going to be living in the Big Apple. Now what was she supposed to do with her time in this house if Ethan was going to be gone a lot?

She knew the best thing she could do was keep busy. She headed for the bedroom, scaling the stairs. As she did, she felt too aware of the cold quiet that hung in the house. Once in the master bedroom, she went to work putting away her wedding gown in the box that would be sent to some storage place. The gown would be kept dry and clean and at the right temperature until her daughter could wear it, Ethan had said.

At the time, Drey had been touched by his thoughtfulness. Also she'd liked the idea of thinking that far ahead. But with Ethan missing… She'd begun to think of his absence as permanent and wondered how long she should wait before she called Sheriff Flint Cahill. Maybe Jet had already taken care of it.

Inwardly she groaned. Even if Lillie hadn't already told Hawk, the news would travel like a wildfire once Ethan was reported missing. Sheriff Flint Cahill was like family to her—just like Lillie and her twin brother, Darby, as well as Cyrus. Their other brother, Tucker, hadn't been around when she and Hawk were in love. Now that he was back, she'd seen him only in passing—long enough to recently wish him happiness at his wedding reception at the Stagecoach Saloon, which Lillie and Darby owned.

She hated to think that pretty soon everyone would know that her husband had left her on her wedding night. She cringed, embarrassed and growing angrier. She and Ethan were definitely going to have a talk about this when he got back. He wasn't going to treat her this way ever again.

Tears burned her eyes and all the fight went out of her. Her head ached. When was she going to admit that she'd made a mistake? She probably had to Lillie on the phone yesterday. She groaned at the thought.

It didn't take long to straighten up the bedroom after downing a couple of aspirin for her headache from the container in the bedroom. Jet seemed to think that Ethan had hired staff that would be arriving at any time. She hated the thought. It was bad enough being alone in this house with Jet without adding more strangers.

At loose ends again after showering and changing clothes, she thought about making something for a late lunch but couldn't face the kitchen right now. She remembered the SUV in the parking garage. She missed her own vehicle. Ethan had insisted she sell her small old pickup. She'd agreed—at that time still thinking they would be living in New York City.

Now she yearned for something familiar. Something that was truly hers. Grabbing her purse, this time she took the elevator, just wanting to get out of the house as quickly as possible. Once inside the SUV, she hit the remote opener and watched the large garage door slowly open.

She started the motor and drove out of the cold darkness, anxious for the feel of sunshine and freedom. The moment she was through the gate at the bottom of the mountain, she began to relax. She still felt as if her head was full of cotton.

She hadn't gone far, though, when she saw Jet's red sports car streak past. She thought about where he'd been and what he might have learned that he was racing back to tell her. There hadn't been anyone in the passenger seat so Ethan still wasn't back. If he'd been to the sheriff, he might have reported his brother missing. She didn't want to think about it. As warm as the summer sun felt pouring in through the windows, she shivered and kept driving.

No MATTER HOW hard Hawk worked, he still couldn't get it out of his mind. What if Drey was in serious trouble? What did anyone know about this Ethan Baxter? Except that according to the grapevine he was overbearing, demanding, obnoxious and generally what you would expect from some rich guy who had bought a piece of Montana and had no intention of being part of the community.

Hawk had wanted to cut the guy some slack, hoping to be wrong about him. But everything he'd heard had made him sorry that Drey had chosen Ethan Baxter to move on with. Hell yes, part of it had been jealousy. As large as the Cahill Ranch was, his family knew nothing about real wealth. Certainly not the kind that bought New York City penthouses or built a shire like that glass-and-rock monstrosity on the side of the mountain.

It didn't help that Hawk could see it if he crossed into the forest service property adjacent to the Baxter property. Drey was so close now and yet...

Back at the ranch, he unsaddled his horse and headed for his pickup. Every step of the way he mentally kicked himself. *Stay out of this. It's none of your*

business. You're a damned fool for getting involved.
That was his mantra all the way into town.

As he pulled up in front of the sheriff's office, he almost didn't park. But he'd come this far. And if Drey really was in trouble…

Cursing himself, he got out and pushed through the door. He merely waved to the dispatcher, who nodded that his brother was in. The sheriff's office was down the hall, the door standing open. He walked in and stopped, still cussing under his breath.

"Can I do something for you?" his brother Flint asked, humor in his expression. "You look upset."

Hawk took a deep breath, let it out and stepped farther into the room to stand over his brother's desk. "Look, I can't tell you how much I hate to ask you to do this. But Lillie is worried about Drey."

"*Lillie* is, huh?" His brother grinned.

He tried not to turn and leave. Biting his tongue for a moment, he finally said, "I hate doing this enough without getting any crap from you over it."

"Sorry, please proceed."

"I don't know if Lillie talked to you about Drey, but apparently her husband is missing. He might already be back and there would be no cause for concern, but I know Drey and if she is as upset as Lillie said she was, well, just in case…"

"You want me to look into Ethan Baxter."

He felt a flood of relief. At least he wasn't going to have to spell it out for his brother. "If you could just make sure that she hasn't gotten herself into somethin' bad."

Flint nodded. "I'll make a few inquiries off the record."

"Thanks. And, Flint, I'd prefer this stay between the two of us."

His brother smiled. "You got it."

CHAPTER SEVEN

DREY HAD PLANNED to go to the Stagecoach Saloon. She remembered when Lillie had fallen in love with the original stagecoach stop's stone building. She had worried that it would be torn down if she didn't save it, so she'd bought it. It had been her twin Darby's idea to make it into a bar and café. The place had taken off, especially since their Texas cook, Billie Dee Rhodes, had come into the picture.

She could just taste a big bowl of Billie Dee's shrimp gumbo right now, she thought, as she headed down the road toward the saloon. But as she neared it, she realized she wasn't up to facing anyone. Even if Lillie hadn't told anyone in her family, Drey knew she couldn't put up a front. She wasn't a happy, blissful new bride. And right now she didn't have what it would take to pretend to be one.

Worse, she might run into Hawk Cahill. In the mood she was in, seeing her former lover was the worst thing she could do. Hawk would know. One look at her and he would see how upset she was. That's if Lillie hadn't already told him.

After going on down the road, she finally stopped at the In-n-Out, ate a burger and fries in the car, tossing away most of both, and drove back to the house. She still had an upset stomach and her head felt filled with cotton.

When she was almost to the gate, Ethan's cell phone buzzed, startling her. She'd forgotten it was still in her pocket. She pulled over to the side of the road, drew it out and tried to answer it. *Still locked.* But to her surprise a partial message showed up on the screen.

Where the hell are you? It's insane here. I thought you were coming in? Ethan, this is starting to look—

That was all there was and after a moment even that disappeared from the screen. Coming in? To the New York City office? So at least someone knew he had planned to be there. Maybe he was just running late.

She pocketed the phone again, thinking about what Jet had said about his brother. He was all business. Still, it hurt. This was some honeymoon. It did sound like whatever was going on was serious, though. Maybe it wasn't Ethan's fault.

Shifting the SUV into gear, she was angry with herself for making excuses for the man. He should have left her a message. He should have called. So he didn't have his cell phone. He still could have borrowed a phone to call to let her know he was all right.

She called his office in New York. But the woman who answered said that Ethan was on vacation and not expected in.

"Are you sure there wasn't a meeting he was supposed to attend today?" she asked after explaining who she was.

"If there was, it wasn't on his calendar, Mrs. Baxter."

She drove toward the house, telling herself he could have had something come up unexpectedly just as Jet has said.

At the gate into the property, she froze for a moment. Did she know the code to get back in? Panic had her heart racing. Then it came to her. The night of their wedding, Ethan had told her the code and said he would write it down for her. He hadn't, but fortunately after years of working as a librarian, she had a knack for remembering numbers.

She keyed in 102937. The gate slowly swung open and she began to breathe again. Being away from the house had helped a little. She still felt off balance. When she reached the house, she found the garage door was open. She could see Jet's sports car in the cold darkness under the house.

For a while, she'd forgotten about passing him on the road. Had he been to the sheriff? Had he taken the thumb they'd discovered in the disposal? She wasn't sure she wanted to know what he'd found out.

Parking beside his car in the underground garage, she climbed out and was startled when she heard Jet behind her. She swung around, trying hard to hide her sudden fear of being down there with him.

"What did the sheriff say?" she asked, sounding breathless.

Jet blinked. "The sheriff?"

"Jet, where is the thumb we found in the disposal?

I looked in the freezer but it's not there. I thought you must have taken it to the sheriff." He gave her a confused look. "Was that you I passed on the road?"

She took a step toward the elevator because it was the quickest way out of the basement. It felt so cold and dark down here. Earlier she'd thought she had dreamed the thumb in the disposal, but seeing Jet, she was sure it was a memory. Just as she was sure the frost impression had been a thumb. Why was he acting like he was confused?

He opened the elevator door for her. She stepped in and swallowed as he joined her.

"Did you talk to the sheriff about Ethan? What about the thumb you took from the freezer?"

He pushed the elevator button. "A thumb? In the freezer?"

"Don't pretend that you don't remember. You're the one who reached in and got it out of the disposal. It was your idea to put the thumb in the freezer until Ethan returns."

Jet chewed at his cheek as the elevator began to rise. She saw that he'd pushed the button for the kitchen–dining room level. "When did this happen?"

She felt her face heat with anger. "Yesterday after I made the two of us something to eat."

The elevator whirred as it moved upward through each level.

Was he just teasing her? "Stop acting as if you don't know what I'm talking about. I made egg-and-ham sandwiches—"

"Drey, I remember. When I got here, we searched

the house looking for Ethan. We had a meal together. I cleared the dishes. You were exhausted from worry about my brother. I called the elevator for you so you could go up and lie down. I didn't talk to you again until just a few moments ago."

She took a step back, suddenly feeling trapped in the elevator with him. "Why are you doing this?"

He shook his head as the elevator stopped, the door opened and he stepped out to hold the door for her.

She stormed out, heading toward the kitchen counter. "Are you going to tell me that you didn't make me two drinks, your specialty, as you called them?"

"No, I did make you two drinks. But after that—"

"We found the thumb in the disposal. You bagged it. You opened this drawer…" She grabbed the drawer to reach in and show him where he'd gotten the plastic sandwich bag. But when she looked, the drawer was full of dish towels. No plastic bags. She closed it and opened the one next to it, thinking maybe she'd been off one drawer. No bags.

Her heart began to pound. When she looked up to find him standing in front of her, all she saw was sympathy in his gaze.

"You put something in my drinks." Her voice trailed off as she looked around for their glasses. There might be a residue in her glass that would prove… No glasses on the counter by the sink. She stepped to the dishwasher and pulled it open. Empty. "Why else would you run the dishwasher but to hide the evidence? You drugged me."

He laughed. "I'm sorry, but that's crazy. I ran the

dishwasher and put everything away after you went upstairs, trying to be a good houseguest," Jet said reasonably. "The last time I saw you, I put you in the elevator. You looked dead on your feet."

She was shaking her head.

"Okay, look, there was nothing in the drinks I made you but fruit juices—and maybe just a little vodka to help you relax." He held up both hands. "I'm sorry but you were wound so tight... I guess the drinks were stronger than I led you to believe. My bad. I'm assuming you've been asleep all this time?" he asked.

"I saw the thumb," she said stubbornly.

"Drey, it must have been a bad dream."

Drey? He called her Drey. How did he know about her nickname? Would Ethan have mentioned it? She stepped away from him to go to the freezer. "No," she said, shaking her head as she opened the freezer door, ready to point inside at the impression in the frost that the thumb had left. But like everything else, it was gone. "There *was* a thumb." She could remember it clearly. The hairs spiking out of the knuckle. The bloodless gash from the disposal blade.

"If we really had found a thumb in the disposal, wouldn't we have taken it to the sheriff straightaway?"

That was exactly what she had wanted to do, she thought as she slammed the freezer door and turned toward him. "You were the one who said it might be a joke and..." He was staring at her with concern. She thought of how late she'd gotten up again. She had been exhausted from all the emotional turmoil, the wedding, the news that they would be living in this house. Had it just been a bad dream? But it had felt so real, standing here, she and Jet, discussing what to do with the thumb from the disposal.

She took a breath and let it out slowly. He was lying for some reason. She began to tremble inside. She was in danger as long as he was in this house with her. "Pretty crazy dream, huh?"

"I'd say." He laughed again and seemed to relax. "You had me worried there for a moment."

"You said the thumb looked nothing like Ethan's but I…" She shook her head.

"You thought it was Ethan's thumb and we didn't go to the sheriff?" He sounded incredulous.

"I know how it must sound." And to think she'd come down here earlier to see if the thumbprint unlocked Ethan's phone. She'd been so sure it *would* open the phone. She pulled Ethan's phone from her pocket. "I found Ethan's phone."

"Really?" Jet seemed as startled to see it as she had been. He took a step toward her. "Where did you find it?"

"On the balcony off our bedroom. It must have fallen out of his pocket when he was out there." She frowned, still wondering when he'd been on the balcony outside their bedroom. She felt so confused, a constant ache in her head as if she had a hangover. She hadn't tasted any alcohol in the drinks Jet had made her and wasn't sure that was what he'd put in her drinks. Another lie? "I tried to unlock it…"

Jet let out a chuckle. "Which explains the dream you had, don't you see? You needed Ethan's thumbprint. See? Mystery solved." His gaze softened. "Don't be too hard on yourself. You're under a lot of strain right now. The whole new bride and all that. It's understandable. I don't want you worrying about Ethan, though. I told you that business always comes first with my brother and since he lost his phone... He'll turn up, I promise. Can I see his phone?"

She hesitated before she handed it over. But the phone was no good to her without the thumb. "Like you said, it takes a thumbprint to open it." He'd already known that, though, didn't he?

"I know my brother. He'd have a backup pass code, as well. Let me fiddle with it. Maybe I can find out if he had a meeting he'd forgotten about and had to fly off to New York."

"Actually, the phone rang earlier. I saw part of the message someone sent. It seems he was expected at a meeting somewhere but he hadn't shown up. I called his New York office. They haven't seen him and there are no meetings scheduled. Don't you think it's time we notified the sheriff?"

"Let me try to get into his phone first," Jet said.

She stared at him, one clear thought in her dull brain: if the thumb had been Ethan's and Jet had taken it, he would be able to open the phone. She shivered, hugging herself at the crazy thought that felt so true. She tried not to look at Jet for fear he would see that she didn't trust him.

"I'm going to go lie down for a while. You're right, I've been under a lot of strain. I think it's getting to me."

He studied her openly and at that moment, he definitely looked like Ethan. She could feel him searching for something? The truth? Then he grinned and he was all Jet again. "Have you had anything to eat? I could make you a drink if it would help you relax."

She felt a chill. "Your specialty?"

Jet smiled. "Hair of the dog, so to speak. No alcohol this time, I promise."

"Thanks, but I'll pass. Maybe just a bottled water if there is any." She opened the refrigerator, not surprised to see that her favorite brand was in the door. She hadn't noticed them earlier.

Jet shrugged as he went to the bar to make himself a drink. "I hope you get some rest. Don't worry about anything. And, Drey?" She stopped to glance back at him from the stairs. "Sweet dreams."

CHAPTER EIGHT

"GIGI'S," GEORGIA ANNE BUCHANAN said into the phone as she stepped down a hallway at her Houston restaurant away from the kitchen noises.

"Why aren't you answering your cell phone?" Ashley Jo could hear the clatter of dishes in the background and realized the restaurant was getting ready to open for dinner. She often forgot the difference in time zones.

"AJ? I have been worried to death about you. Where have you been?"

"I told you I was going to be gone for a while, had some business I needed to tend to."

"What's going on?" her best friend asked, stepping out the back door so she could hear better. "If you're in trouble—"

"I know you said you didn't want this…"

"AJ, what have you done?"

"I found your birth mother."

Silence.

"I know you said you weren't interested, but I had to find her. I had to find out what she was like because I love you like a sister…"

"Honestly, I can't talk to you right now."

"She's delightful. You would love her—"

"AJ, I'm going to hang up."

"She's been looking for you. She's going to hire a private investigator to find you. I'm so sorry, but once you meet her…" Ashley Jo realized that her best friend had just hung up on her.

She disconnected, telling herself she'd done the right thing. Gigi needed to know her birth mother—now more than ever.

But what if she didn't come around?

She put her face in her hands for a moment, fighting tears. Since coming to Montana and finding Billie Dee, she'd fallen in love with the older woman. She could see so much of Gigi in her. Yes, she'd overstepped. But her friend needed her birth mother no matter what she said. The two had so much more in common than either of them would have guessed. And last year, Gigi had lost both of her adoptive parents. She'd been having a terrible time since.

No tears, she told herself as she took a deep breath. Gigi would come around. In the meantime, all AJ could hope was that the private investigator Billie Dee planned to hire wouldn't find Georgia Anne Buchanan. At least not yet. Her friend would balk even worse if a complete stranger contacted her about her birth mother. And to think this was all because of the prize money from the contest Ashley Jo had insisted Billie Dee enter. She'd never thought the cook would want to use her winnings to hire a PI to find the daughter she'd been forced to give up all those years ago.

She looked up to see Darby Cahill come through the door.

"Everything all right?" asked the co-owner of the saloon—and the twin brother of Lillie Cahill.

"Just having one of those days."

"Already today?" Billie Dee said as she came into the bar part of the Stagecoach Saloon. The cook smiled at her, making AJ feel even worse.

"Did you hear?" AJ asked, smiling back at the cook before turning to Darby. "Billie Dee won the recipe contest!" There were more high fives, more cheering, more back slapping. She watched from the sidelines, keeping a smile on her face.

She would call Gigi back tonight after the restaurant closed. Maybe after putting her feet up with a glass of wine her friend would be more ready to hear what she had to say. She could only hope.

DREY CLIMBED THE stairs to the bedroom, trying not to run. Nor did she turn around, knowing that Jet would be watching her. Jet was a liar. She was sure of it. Worse, he wanted her to believe that she'd dreamed the entire thing.

Either that or she was losing her mind because she'd seen the thumb. Worse, even then she'd feared it was Ethan's. Now Jet had it. He could unlock Ethan's phone. She shuddered.

Doubt made her weaken her resolve. What if she was wrong about all of it? She'd had awful dreams lately, some of them hanging over her all day. She wanted to lie down because she felt sick. Not that she needed more sleep. It made no sense. She felt as if all she'd done was sleep. To keep from worrying while she waited? But her head ached and she felt groggy. Was it exhaustion? In her bathroom, she opened the medicine cabinet and shook out a couple of aspirin from the bottle and downed them with the water she'd brought up from the refrigerator.

It wasn't until she was back in the bedroom that she noticed another control panel next to the one that opened to the elevator. She went to it, pressed, and the wall opened to reveal a small bar complete with a refrigerator and ice maker. Ethan had thought of everything, she thought.

There were several bottles of champagne in the refrigerator portion, along with soda pop, beer and more of the sparkling water she liked. She closed the door, having already gotten a bottle from the kitchen. As she walked back over to the bed, she wondered, was this to be her life—spending so much of it sleeping out of boredom or mental exhaustion?

Just the thought of Ethan made her furious. Not to mention Jet. She couldn't get the so-called dream off her mind. It was too detailed, but then again weren't most of her dreams? The big question was why would Jet lie? What would he have to gain? It made no sense.

She sat on the edge of the bed, feeling foolish, embarrassed and lost. She was out of her element, adrift without Ethan here. Since meeting him, he'd taken care of everything. She hadn't even had to think about what to do next. So why did that not seem like such a good thing now? She shook her head and took a long drink of the water.

Her gaze went to the panels that hid the elevator and bar. Was there any way to lock the elevator so no one could come up? She rose to walk to it. She could lock the double doors into the bedroom from the stairs, but the elevator… She didn't like the idea that someone could come up and, at the touch of a button, be in her bedroom. Was that what Ethan had done the night he lost his phone out on the balcony?

He'd come up to check her, gotten a call, stepped out on the balcony and… And then what? Dropped his phone and then left?

She shivered, feeling scared. What was it she thought she had to fear, though? The thought made her laugh. Her husband was missing. She'd either had a man's thumb in her disposal or she'd had a very disturbing dream. She was alone with a stranger who she didn't trust in her house. And right now she was about to lock herself in her room.

Her cell phone rang as she closed and locked the bedroom doors. She expected it would be Lillie and she wasn't sure she was up to talking to her. But when she checked, she didn't recognize the number. Something told her to pick up anyway. "Hello?"

"Drey, it's Jet. I hope you weren't already lying down."

"No, what?" She wasn't in the mood for chitchat. She rubbed her temple, feeling oddly dizzy again. Maybe she was catching something.

"Ethan just called me. Apparently he's been having

trouble getting through to you since he lost his phone and had to borrow a phone and, like a lot of international calls—"

"Where is he?"

"Mexico City. At least that's where he said he was. He said there was an emergency at one of the plants down there. I didn't know we even had plants down there, but anyway, he had to leave right away and he wanted me to tell you that he feels really bad about it, but that he would—"

"Why didn't he call me himself?"

"I told you, he said he was having trouble getting through. More than likely, he didn't want to take the time to apologize. With me, he can be brief and won't hurt my feelings."

She tried to feel relieved, but all she felt was sick to her stomach and angry. "Still, if he could get through to you—"

"I told him I was staying here. He told me go stay at the hotel in town and leave you alone, so that's what I'm going to do first thing in the morning. He also told me to tell you to change the pass code on the gate at the bottom of the mountain. The book, he said, is in his nightstand to tell you how to do it."

"This sounds like a pretty long phone call."

"I'm just telling you what he said. I thought you'd be relieved with me gone."

She didn't deny it. So she said nothing as she sat down on the side of the bed because her knees had gone weak. With relief? Or the dull throb in her head as if she'd had another couple of Jet's specialty drinks?

"Anyway, he said he would make it up to you when he gets back. A real honeymoon anywhere in the world you want to go. You know my brother. He'll pull out all the stops to make it up you. It's what he does best."

That did sound like the Ethan she knew. She reached over and opened the drawer on his nightstand. Sure enough, there was a notebook called Mountain Crest Codes. So why was she still having trouble believing Jet?

"Did he mention when he'd be back?"

"Sorry. Sounded like it would be a few days. I know this isn't what you want to hear, but it's got to be a relief. I know it was for me. Ethan just being Ethan. Look, if you want me to move out tonight—"

"That's not necessary. Thank you for letting me know." She disconnected and lay back on the bed. Her relief chased away some of her disappointment. But she wished Ethan had called her instead. She needed to hear his voice. But also she wanted to ask him why he'd never mentioned his brother, Jet. There were a lot of things she wanted to ask him. But it could wait until he got back. What were a few more days in the grand scheme of things?

She'd barely disconnected when her phone rang again. She thought it might be Ethan calling her. It was Lillie. "Hi."

"Are you all right?" Her friend sounded worried, making Drey feel even guiltier for calling her in the state she'd been in.

She let out an embarrassed laugh, feeling worse

now that she'd heard from Ethan via Jet. "I'm sorry about calling you yesterday."

"So things are better? Your husband came back?"

"No. But I just heard from him." She saw no reason to get into the specifics. "He was called away on business. One of the company's plants in Mexico City."

"So you don't have to worry anymore." Did Lillie sound disappointed?

"No," she said, hoping that was true as she thought about Ethan's brother. Worse, the thumb she was convinced had been real. But it hadn't been Ethan's; it couldn't be since he was in Mexico City, not bleeding to death somewhere. The thought made her shudder, because now she really did have to wonder if she was losing her mind. "Everything is fine."

"Oh, Drey. What about his creepy brother?" Lillie asked as if reading her mind.

"Jet?" For a moment she almost voiced the crazy thought that had been running around in her head. *He drugged me last night, and now he's trying to make me think that I'm crazy and I can't even be sure he really talked to Ethan.* "He's going to be moving to the hotel tomorrow morning."

"So you'll be alone in the house? I think you should come stay with me."

"I'll be fine." She'd bailed once on a relationship years ago, running away instead of staying and fighting for it. She wouldn't make that mistake again. Anyway, she was a married woman and this was now her home.

"I need to stay here. It's only a few days until Ethan returns. I was worried and afraid something had happened to him. In fact, I was planning to go to Flint if I didn't hear something today. Now that I know Ethan's all right…"

"You have to be furious with him for worrying you like this."

"His brother says that he's always been like this. He gets business on his mind and that's all he can think about at the time," she said.

Lillie made a sympathetic sound. "But it's your *honeymoon*."

Moving to the balcony, feeling as if she needed fresh air, she opened the door to step outside while talking to her friend. She started to drop into one of the chairs, but saw movement in the nearby pines and caught a whiff of cigarette smoke. Jet?

She stepped back inside and closed the door. How long had Jet been out there? Was he watching her room? Not with the tinted windows that allowed her to see out, but him to be unable to see in—except when she had the glass door open to the balcony. She would have to remember that, she told herself.

"I'm glad you called, Lillie, but I'm fine, really. I'm sure Ethan will be home soon and I can handle his brother." She'd never been less sure of anything as she disconnected. But Jet would be gone in the morning and once she changed the pass code on the gate into the house… And she always had her gun, she thought, remembering seeing it among her personal items that had been moved to the house.

CHAPTER NINE

IT WAS DARK by the time Hawk turned his horse back toward the ranch. His body hurt from an impossibly hard day's work, but his mind wouldn't rest.

He couldn't bear the thought of Drey being miserable. Or even unhappy. And yet he'd made her that way for years. They'd made each other unhappy until she'd had enough and decided to strike out and have a life for herself with someone else.

Hell, he admired her for that. He wanted the best for her. At least that's what he kept telling himself. But what if she wasn't happy? What if her husband had really left her alone? Or maybe worse, in that house with his brother?

He drew up short as he realized where he'd ridden. Through the pines he could see that all the lights were on at Mountain Crest. Such an odd-looking place, so much glass and yet he couldn't see anyone moving behind it. That apparently was the idea.

An in-your-face house from a man who supposedly wanted privacy by building up here on the side of the mountain so he could look down on the rest of the world. Hawk shook his head, knowing he wasn't being fair. He knew nothing really about Ethan Baxter except that he was rich and he had Drey.

He told himself that he should ride on, but he found himself studying the place, wondering if even half of what Lillie had told him might be true. Was Drey in that house, miserable, scared?

There was only one car parked out front: an expensive sedan. He'd seen in the local paper that her old pickup had been for sale. He'd actually thought about buying it—for old times' sake. The idea was so ludicrous he'd felt more like a fool than usual. Kind of like he felt sitting here on his horse staring at the house where Drey now lived.

Had her husband returned? Probably. Which meant everything was all right now—just as he had suspected would happen. False alarm.

Something moved along the side of the house. He saw Drey step out on the balcony on the top floor. She was on her cell phone. He couldn't hear what was being said, but he could read her body like a neon sign. She wasn't herself. He tried to see into the room behind her but his view was blocked. Something told him that she was still alone. No husband. So who did the car belong to? Or maybe her husband had a car service pick him up. Did Gilt Edge even have a car service?

Something else caught his attention. A dark figure moved from the pines and started down the mountainside toward one of the lower entrances. He caught only a glimpse of the man's face, but he was sure it wasn't Ethan Baxter.

Not your rodeo. Not your bull, he told himself. He started to spur his horse, feeling like a voyeur, when suddenly all the lights went out in the house. Like a blink, the whole place went completely dark.

His heart began to race as he waited for the lights to come back on. There had to be a backup generator for a place that cost that much. Ethan Baxter had dropped a pretty penny for this monstrosity.

He felt goose bumps ripple over his skin. The lights hadn't come back on. Something was wrong.

DREY PICKED UP her sparkling water to take another drink. She'd taken a shower and then curled up with a book on the bed, still feeling tired and lost. For so many years, she'd worked. Now she didn't know what to do with herself.

The first two aspirin hadn't done the trick so she'd taken two more. Her brain felt sluggish, her body weak. She couldn't help but wonder if it was more than the wedding, the worry, that nagging, relentless feeling that she'd made a mistake. Those had been aspirin she'd taken, hadn't they?

She knew she was being ridiculous, all these crazy suspicions. But she felt even more foggy than she had earlier. She told herself that she would feel better once Jet was out of the house and Ethan was back. If Ethan ever came back. She couldn't help thinking of that other premonition she'd had. That she would never see him alive again.

Wouldn't Hawk Cahill just love it if her marriage ended before it even began? She shook her head. Ethan had called Jet. Everything was fine. This marriage would work. Or she would die trying to see that it did just to show Hawk that she could be happy with another man, come hell or high water.

The thought reminded her of another awful premonition she'd had when she'd seen this house. She shivered, telling herself she'd been under a lot of strain lately. She'd tried to call Lillie, feeling the need to talk to someone sane. Her thoughts were so random. Some too real. Like that thumb in the disposal. So real and yet… What if she was losing her mind?

But why wouldn't she feel like that? Ethan had thrown her more than a curve. He'd derailed her with his surprises and then his disappearance. How could he do this to her? And calling Jet, instead of her? Did he not realize how awful that was? When he returned, she would make sure he never did this to her again.

She started to lift the water bottle to her lips when she realized there was something in the bottom. Her eyes widened in alarm. Curled at the base of the bottle was what appeared to be a tiny mouse, as if it was asleep.

Drey screamed and dropped the bottle to run into the bathroom to throw up. Had the mouse been in there all the time? She'd left the bottle by the bed when she'd gone into the bathroom to shower. Was it possible the mouse had crawled in there then?

She clung to the sink, throwing up what little was in her stomach. How could she not have seen it before? Had she been so out of it that she hadn't noticed there was something in the bottom of the bottle before now? A shiver of terror moved through her. What was wrong with her?

She gagged again, still sick to her stomach. How much had she consumed? Not much. Maybe a few sips before—

The elevator. Someone was coming. Jet? She'd locked the doors but she didn't know how to keep the elevator from coming up and opening right into her bedroom.

She wiped her mouth and stepped back into the master suite, listening. The elevator kept coming. She hurriedly stepped to the bedroom doors to make sure they were locked. But what would it take to break in here? Why would Jet want to—

The lights went out, throwing her into pitch-black darkness. Drey screamed as something brushed her leg. A cold breeze stirred the drapes at the balcony window. She spun around to see a shadow move across the open doorway of the balcony and screamed again.

In a flutter of movement, the crow Drey had seen earlier on the balcony let out a cry and spread its dark wings. She cupped a hand over her mouth as she stared at the bird sitting on the balcony railing silhouetted against the night. Between the lights going off, the breeze coming in the balcony doorway brushing her leg and the crow—

Her heart was still pounding as she rushed to the balcony door, closed and locked it. She tried to calm down. But then she heard it. The elevator was still coming. How could the elevator still be working with the power out? A backup generator. She recalled Ethan mentioning that it hadn't been working. But if it was working, then why were the lights still out?

She thought she heard a key in the lock at her bedroom doors. Now she felt as if someone was in the room with her. She closed her eyes tightly. *This isn't real. It's just a bad dream.*

But when she opened her eyes, her breath froze in her throat. The double bedroom doors that she'd locked earlier? One of them was standing open. She could see the landing to the stairs.

She worked her way in the pitch blackness to the double doors, locked them, then dragged a chair over. Who had unlocked the doors? Was it possible the doors could have blown open? Not after she'd locked them.

Her head ached and her body seemed to plead with her to simply lie down. Adrenaline fueled her and kept her upright. The elevator was still coming. Jet? Had he heard her scream? There could be only one person on that elevator. Jet. Or had he already been here?

She felt sick again. Moving back away from the doors, she stumbled against the bed and felt around blindly as she made her way toward the bathroom. But before she could find the bathroom doorway in the blackness, she heard the elevator stop on her floor and open on the other side of the wooden panel.

She froze, listening, but heard no movement. She waited for Jet to open the panel into the bedroom. But there was no sound. Who had been on the elevator? If it was Jet and he'd heard her scream, why hadn't he said anything?

Drey listened as she continued to edge along the wall quietly toward the bathroom doorway. Once inside, she would lock the door and find her gun. There had to be a reason Ethan didn't want his brother staying in this house with her.

She took another step toward the bathroom, then another and froze. She'd heard something. *Move!* Her mind raced. If she could reach the bathroom, get the door closed and locked—

The sound of shattering glass broke the untenable silence. She kept screaming as she hurriedly pushed herself along the wall until she felt the bathroom doorway. Just a few more steps and—

Tackled from behind, she fought, but the body holding her was much stronger, much more fierce. Not Jet. But someone larger, stronger—

"Drey, it's me. Stop fighting."

It took her a few breathless moments for the familiar voice to register. Even more for her to trust that she'd heard right. The hold on her loosened. She started to turn when the lights came back on.

She blinked as she stared at Hawk Cahill, uncomprehending. For a moment, she thought she was seeing things. Another hallucination. The sparkling water. Maybe Jet had drugged it, because what were the chances that Hawk would be standing in her bedroom?

"No, no, no." She fought to pull away from him, telling herself this couldn't be real, *he* couldn't be real. If this was another bad dream—

Hawk gave her a shake. "You're all right now. Drey! You're all right."

She stared at him. No hallucination. Hawk was as real as his warm strong hands holding her. Hawk. Standing in her bedroom. The bedroom she should have been sharing with her husband. She felt disoriented as she looked from him to the broken glass near the balcony.

This felt so surreal. She hugged herself, feeling like she was going to throw up again. She wasn't sure what was real and what wasn't. She remembered seeing the mouse and screaming. The hum of the elevator coming up to her floor. The lights going out. Had someone gotten off when the elevator door opened? She had sensed someone in the room with her—someone there earlier *before* she'd heard the glass breaking, before Hawk grabbed her. When she'd heard the key in the door lock and found one of the doors standing open. This had to be another dream.

"You aren't really here," she said in a sob. "You can't be here."

At her words, he let go of her. "I saw all the lights in the house go out. When you screamed…" He glanced around the room. She followed his gaze. Her bedroom doors, the ones she'd locked, were still shut.

She looked toward the panel that hid the elevator. It was open, the glass elevator empty. Had she only imagined someone in the room before Hawk had broken through the balcony window and grabbed her?

"I don't understand what's going on," she said, fighting tears as she looked toward the floor where she'd dropped the sparkling water bottle with the tiny mouse inside. It was gone. Her gaze flew to the table beside her bed. A half-full bottle of sparking water sat on a coaster. Even from where she stood, she could see that there was no mouse in it.

She let out a cry at the realization that she was losing her mind. Her legs no longer held her. She would have slumped to the floor if Hawk hadn't caught her and helped her over to one of the chairs in the sitting area.

HAWK HAD NEVER seen Drey like this. She sat in the large chair, her legs curled up, her arms hugging her knees, her eyes wide as a harvest moon and just as golden. "Tell me what's wrong," he said quietly as he pulled the other chair closer and sat down. That she looked terrified was a given. But what had frightened her enough to leave her in this state? "Drey, what's going on?"

She looked around the room for a moment and then shook her head. "It was just a bad dream." Her voice was small, scared, her body trembling. Worse, she was slurring her words as if she was drunk. Again, given what Lillie had told him. Drey had never drunk more than a glass of wine or a beer. At least the Drey he'd known hadn't.

He rose, went to the bed and pulled off the down comforter. Returning to her, he tucked it around her. She clutched at it, balling the fabric in her fists as she looked up at him, pleading in her gaze.

"You're really here," she whispered. "In my bedroom."

He glanced around and then slowly nodded. This was the last place he'd ever thought he'd find himself.

"So it was just a bad dream?" Nothing seemed to be out of order in the room—except for the window he'd broken to get to her. Had he overreacted? No, he told himself as he looked into her brown eyes and saw the fear still there. Whatever had made her scream, Drey had sounded terrified. This wasn't the woman he knew. Not his Drey. Not strong, determined, self-assured Dierdre Hunter.

He reminded himself that she was no longer his Drey. Her name was now Baxter. The wife of Ethan Baxter. So where the hell was this husband of hers?

"How did you get up here?" she asked in that small, scared voice.

Hawk glanced toward the balcony. "I climbed up the balconies. I'm sorry. I had to break the window. I'll have it replaced."

"You didn't come up the elevator."

He shook his head. It should have been obvious how he'd gotten in. "Where is your husband?" he had to ask.

"Mexico City," she said quietly as she stared over at the nightstand next to her bed.

He could see little of interest there other than a lamp and a bottle of sparkling water.

"You just happened to be in the area and heard me scream?"

He sighed and removed his Stetson. He could see that she was having trouble making sense out of this. Welcome to his world. He had no business being here in this house—let alone in her bedroom she should have been sharing with her husband. "So your husband isn't still missing?"

She turned her attention back to him to groan. "Lillie told you. Of course she did." She covered her face with the comforter for a moment before looking at him again. "He's not missing. He was just called away on urgent business."

"On your honeymoon."

"This isn't my honeymoon. When he gets back…" She shook her head.

"He left you on your wedding night? Left you alone in this house?"

"I'm not alone. His brother, Jet, is staying here."

Yes, Jet, he thought. Lillie had mentioned the brother Drey had called creepy. If the man was in the house, wouldn't he have heard Drey scream? Wouldn't he have come to check on her? "So where is Jet?" he asked.

YES, WHERE WAS JET? Drey looked toward the wall that hid the elevator. She'd thought that was him coming up after the lights went out. But the elevator was there and no Jet. And her bedroom doors were still closed, a chair in front of them. She shook her head and regretted it. She felt dizzy and disoriented. Something was very wrong with her. "Maybe he left."

She looked at the man she'd once promised her heart to forever. Hawk Cahill, her handsome cowboy. The man she thought she could always depend on to be there for her no matter what. And here he was, coming to her rescue. Except it appeared that she didn't need to be rescued at all. Or did she?

"Drey, why were you screaming? I think it was more than a bad dream. Tell me I'm wrong."

She could feel his gaze on her, worried, searching. Could he see how close she felt to the edge? She tried not to look at him, just wanting him to leave and yet wanting him to stay just a little longer. Her heart was still pounding hard in her chest. She felt…scared and embarrassed. She hadn't wanted Hawk to know about any of this. She didn't want him taking satisfaction from her situation, let alone Jet showing up and seeing him here in her bedroom and telling his brother.

"Answer me. What were you so terrified of when I found you?"

"I told you. I had a bad dream. That's all it was," she said, glancing at the sparkling water bottle sitting on the bedside table. That's all it could have been since there was no small creature curled in the bottom. She shuddered, though, remembering how real the mouse had looked. Just like the memory of the thumb.

Hawk leaned toward her and took one of her hands in his two large ones. She felt a tingle all the way down to her toes and when he looked into her eyes like that… She pulled her hand back, reminding herself that she was married to another man.

"Are you sure you're all right?" he asked, his voice low, intimate. He was still looking at her with concern. If he only knew the half of it. But he did know her, that's why he looked afraid for her.

"I've been under some strain, I'll admit, but I'm

fine. You really didn't need to—" She glanced at the glass strewed across the wood floor from the window he'd broken to get to her. So Hawk-like. Woman in distress? Just climb the balconies, break a window and chase away the bad guy.

Had there been a bad guy in this room? Or had this been just another nightmare? Except she hadn't been sleeping. So another hallucination?

He saw her staring at the broken glass on the floor. "I'll have someone come fix the window, if that's what you're worried about. I'll pay extra so it's fixed before your husband returns."

She nodded as he got to his feet. She wanted to beg him to stay. Something was terribly wrong with her. She could hardly keep her eyes open and yet she'd slept so much. And the dreams…

He stood over her, holding his Stetson and looking at her as if afraid to leave her here for fear… For fear of what?

"You know that if you ever need me—"

"Need you?" Tears burned her eyes and she felt her stomach roil. He couldn't come here like this. It wasn't fair. It hurt too much. "Hawk, those days are long gone, aren't they?" If only he would tell her how wrong she was. If only he would take her in his arms, tell her he loved her, stay with her…

"I'm worried about you, Drey."

"*Now* you're worried about me?" She realized she was slurring her words badly. Her brain was shutting down. She could feel it. She licked her lips, her mouth suddenly dry.

When she looked at him, his gray eyes were dark with worry and an emotion she knew too well. If he didn't leave—

"Drey." He took a step toward her and stopped as if coming to his senses. "Don't walk on the broken glass." He touched the brim of his hat. "You have my number."

Oh, she had his number all right.

He left through the balcony door, the way he'd come in. She watched him leave, too tired to get up from the chair. Her chest ached with sobs she didn't dare release. Hawk. None of this could be real. Especially the look she'd glimpsed in his eyes. *No, this, too, must be a dream.* When she woke in the morning, there would be no glass on the floor. No comforter lying on the chair. Hawk Cahill, the cowboy hero to the rescue, would have been only a dream in the middle of her waking nightmare.

CHAPTER TEN

SHERIFF FLINT CAHILL had quit working late after marrying Maggie. Before, he'd put off going home to an empty house. Now, though, he couldn't wait to get home to his wife. And with her expecting...

But tonight he'd been catching up on paperwork since Maggie was over at her mother's putting up chokecherry syrup and jam. She'd called earlier to say that she was running late.

"Not to worry. I have a lot of work to do here. It will give me an excuse to get caught up. Say hello to your mother for me." He'd disconnected and smiled, glad that after all these years Maggie had been re-united with the mother she'd never known until re-cently.

Flint stretched now, thinking he might call it a night. Maggie had promised to call when she was finished with her canning project. He glanced at the clock, half expecting to hear from her at any minute.

The dispatcher called back on the intercom to say two men were headed back. She'd barely finished before two dark-suited men entered his office.

He stood, frowning, even before the two pulled out their credentials. FBI. One of them closed his door.

The other took a step toward his desk. That this was serious was obvious. He felt his heart begin to pound. It wasn't every day that FBI agents showed up in his office.

"Sheriff Flint Cahill?" the one closest to his desk asked.

He cleared his throat. "What's this about?"

"Earlier you made some inquiries about Ethan Baxter?" the agent asked.

Flint thought about the phone call he'd made after Hawk had asked him to do some checking on Drey's new husband. One phone call and two FBI agents show up interested? His heart began to pound even harder. He'd opened a can of worms, he thought as he sat back down at his desk. "I did."

"We need to know why you made that inquiry," the agent said.

The sheriff nodded. "How about you tell me why that would interest the FBI enough to send the two of you to Gilt Edge?"

GIGI HAD MANAGED to get through the day, but by the time she'd closed the restaurant she was exhausted. All day she'd been unable not to think about what AJ had told her. Her best friend had always been impulsive but this was beyond the pale. AJ had actually tracked down Gigi's birth mother?

She'd thought about calling her back and demanding to know what she'd been thinking. But she knew. Her friend thought she was helping.

Groaning, she poured herself a glass of wine and

walked over to the wall of windows that looked out on downtown Houston. She loved this view of her city. That was how she thought of it. Born and raised here, she'd grown up as Texan as a woman could get. Minus the accent, thanks to that finishing school she and AJ had been forced to attend.

She chuckled at the memory of the two of them. They had gotten into so much trouble. If it hadn't been for their prominent parents... Just the thought of her own parents brought tears to her eyes. She took a sip of her wine. It had been almost a year since their deaths and yet she still wanted to pick up the phone daily to talk to them. They'd left an incredible hole in her heart.

And AJ thought she could fill that with some birth mother who'd given her away moments after she was born? Gigi scoffed at the idea. She had no interest in meeting the woman no matter what AJ said. How could her friend even know that she'd found the right person?

Oh, she didn't! Grabbing her phone, she called AJ back. All these months, she'd thought her friend was in Europe taking care of some business for her father's company. So where was she really?

"Gigi—"

"Tell me you didn't steal my DNA."

"If you would just listen for a moment—"

"I don't believe this." She fumed as she walked over to the loft kitchen and refilled her wineglass. "I could have you arrested."

"It's a good thing you're a better cook than you are a lawyer," AJ said with a laugh.

She felt herself begin to calm down. Maybe it was the wine. Or maybe her friend's voice. She missed AJ. "So you're not in Europe, too busy to take phone calls."

"I'm in Montana."

"Montana?" This was worse than she'd thought. "If you tell me that my birth mother is a cowgirl—"

"She's a cook. One of the best. I've been taking cooking lessons from her."

Gigi had to laugh even though it hurt. AJ had been hanging out all this time with this…woman? "You are a hopeless cook."

"I'm actually not doing that badly. At least according to Billie Dee."

Billie Dee. That was her name? It was more than she'd ever wanted to know. "I still don't want to meet her," she said.

"Okay."

Her friend had given in too easily. "What does *okay* mean?"

"Just what I said. You don't need to meet her. But I'm staying here for a while. I like it in Montana."

"You can't be serious. What does your father have to say about this?"

"I might have fibbed about where I was and what I was doing."

Gigi had to smile. This was indeed her friend AJ. No wonder the two of them had gotten into so much trouble in school. "So what are you doing?"

"I'm a bartender at the Stagecoach Saloon in Gilt Edge, Montana."

She let out a snort and almost spewed wine all over the floor. "You can't be serious."

"I'm actually having fun."

"You're a high-priced lawyer."

"Only because I had to be something. You know how my father is. But I have to tell you, being a bartender is a lot less stressful. How is the restaurant business down your way?"

"Busy. Stressful. I envy you your job."

"They might be hiring here, if you're interested," AJ joked.

"I'm not coming up there."

"Okay."

"You're impossible. You're sure this woman is my mother?"

"Your DNA was a perfect match."

"Great. And she's a cook?"

"She just won a contest with her Texas chili recipe."

"She's from Texas?" Gigi asked in surprise.

"Born and raised."

"So what is she doing in Montana?"

"You'd have to ask her that yourself. Gigi, you're going to love her. I promise. I'm half in love with her."

She sighed, dead on her feet. Not even wine was going to revive her tonight. "I have to go. Opening early for a special brunch."

"It's been so good to hear your voice. I would have called sooner but—"

"But then I would have known what you were up to."

"I miss you, Gigi."

She sighed again. "I miss you, too." As she disconnected, she looked again at the view. *Montana?* She could wring AJ's neck. Worse, now it seemed she had a private investigator trying to find her.

HAWK CLIMBED DOWN, swinging from one balcony to the next just as he had earlier. Except this time he mentally kicked himself the entire way. What had he been thinking rushing into that house like that? He knew damned well what he'd been thinking. That Drey was alone. Alone with all the lights out and screaming. Drey in trouble. Drey needing him.

So he'd scaled the balconies to hers, broken a window and burst in to save her. It had made perfect sense at the time.

Except that he had no business watching her house, watching her. No business butting into her life. She was *married*. She wasn't his responsibility and hadn't been for years. What the hell was wrong with him?

Too bad he couldn't shake the feeling that Drey was in trouble. Like there was anything he could do about that. But damned if he hadn't wanted to leave her up there. Not that he could stay with her in that big bedroom of hers.

He dropped to the ground, just wanting off this property as soon as he could get back over the fence. Maybe he should call Lillie, though. He couldn't shake the feeling that Drey shouldn't be alone. Then again, she wasn't alone. Her husband's brother was here somewhere, right?

The moon peeked out of the clouds that had darkened the night earlier. Overhead, the sky filled with sparkling stars. Another beautiful Montana summer night and what was he doing? He cursed under his breath.

She'd heard from her husband. He was in Mexico City on business. And that fear he'd seen in her eyes? Just a bad dream. He slowed as he crossed a stretch of grass beneath her balcony. That terror he'd seen... It had felt like more than a bad dream. The way she was trembling, that look in her brown eyes, the fact that she'd been drinking—or had taken something...

The starlight shone on a glass bottle lying in the grass. He'd almost stepped on it. Looking back up at the balconies, he realized it must have been dropped from one of the floors. Had he expected to see Drey on the balcony? If so, he would have been disappointed.

But he did see movement on the dark balcony beneath hers, as if someone had been watching him and had now stepped back so as not to be seen.

Her husband's brother, Jet? But if Jet had been in the house, wouldn't he have heard Drey scream? Wouldn't he have reached her long before Hawk himself had been able to get to her? Maybe he had been gone, just as Drey had speculated.

Either way, it was none of his business. Cursing again, he reminded himself that Drey was a married woman, having started over with another man in her life. He was the last person she had wanted to see to-night. Or any other night.

As he started to leave, he remembered the bottle on the ground. He'd been taught since he was a boy that you just didn't litter. He reached down and picked it up. It was the brand of sparkling water that had been on Drey's nightstand. He frowned, thinking it wasn't like her to throw the bottle off the balcony. At least when she was sober.

That's when he saw that there was something at the bottom of the bottle.

Gingerly, he held it up to the starlight. A small dead mouse was curled against the clear glass at the bottom.

CHAPTER ELEVEN

DREY WOKE CURLED in a chair, head aching and confused. What was she doing here? She pushed off the comforter and started toward the bathroom. Her head felt foggy, but pieces of a dream seemed to float around her.

She glanced toward the balcony. There was glass all over the floor from where the window had been broken. She stopped in midstep. It hadn't been a dream. Hawk Cahill had really burst into her bedroom to save her.

Groaning, she wanted to cover her head with the comforter and lose herself in sleep again. Her cowboy hero. The one she'd fallen in love with so many years ago. She'd given him her heart and the bastard had kept it and for the life of her, she hadn't been able to get it back.

Watching her step, she continued to the bathroom, hating that moment of honesty. Even admitting it to herself felt like a betrayal. She loved Ethan. Just not the way she'd loved Hawk most of her life. But she hadn't expected to. Hawk had been her first love. Everyone knew how intense first love could be.

So it hadn't been a dream. She used the toilet and

then opened the medicine cabinet for aspirin for her headache. Shaking two into her hand, she suddenly stopped. These didn't look like the usual aspirin she took. She thought about how out of it she'd been last night and, taking the two aspirin with her, walked into the bedroom.

She stopped to look around the room, pieces of memory floating in and out. Hawk had said he'd heard her scream and come to her rescue only to find out that she didn't need rescuing. Or did she? she wondered as she glanced at the bottle of sparkling water sitting on her bedside table.

Even now, as she looked at the bottle, she couldn't help remembering what she'd thought she'd seen last night. A tiny mouse curled in the bottom. She had to have imagined it. That feeling she'd had last night, that something was terribly wrong with her felt even stronger this morning. She'd never imagined things before. She'd never felt like she had last night. Or even this morning.

With a start, she realized that wasn't true. There'd been a time… She shuddered at the memory and looked again at the two aspirin in her hand. Carefully, she set them down on the bedside table.

Heading for the shower, she told herself now that Ethan was safe, the hallucinations would stop. But what about the premonitions? She turned the tap and stood under the hot spray. She hadn't been herself for a while now. She'd made a lot of excuses for her strange behavior and the feeling that she was losing her mind. What if there was more to it? There had to be more to it.

Showered, dressed and with the two aspirin from the bottle in her bathroom medicine cabinet in her jeans pocket, she headed downstairs.

"You're still here," she said as she walked into the kitchen to find Jet making coffee. He started as if he hadn't been expecting to see her yet this morning. "Sorry, didn't mean to startle you."

"I thought I'd make coffee before I left as a thank-you for your hospitality," Jet said, finishing what he was doing before turning to her. He poured her a cup of coffee and handed it to her, then poured one for himself. "So how are you this morning?"

She looked down at the coffee as they took seats at the table. "Great," she lied as she cradled the cup in her hands for the warmth but didn't take a sip. She saw that it was a beautiful Montana summer day outside but she always felt cold in this house, as if there was a draft.

"Ethan suggested a hotel I might like," Jet was saying.

"Yes, I'm sure you will like that one," she agreed when he told her the name. She was anxious for him to leave so she could change the code on the gate at the bottom of the mountain. Maybe it was Hawk's visit. Or maybe it was the realization that she hadn't been herself since walking into this house. But she didn't trust Jet.

"So I take it you've never been down to any of the plants in Mexico City?" She remembered what he'd said about not knowing they had any down there. He'd wanted her to believe that Ethan had been lying. Since Jet had arrived, he'd been undermining his brother.

"No," he said quickly with a shake of his head. "They must be a new acquisition. Ethan doesn't tell me everything, obviously." He grinned. "He didn't tell me about you. I had to hear about your engagement from one of his employees."

"So the two of you aren't close." Which could explain why Ethan wanted Jet to stay at a hotel until he returned. Maybe there was a whole lot more she should know about Jet, she thought as she put down her coffee without touching it.

"Ethan is too competitive to let anyone get too close, especially a younger brother." She heard the bitterness again. "I'm sorry, you don't seem to like the way I make coffee."

"My stomach's bothering me this morning," she said. "It was a nice thought. Last night, were you around when the lights went out?" she asked as casually as she could.

"Why do you ask?"

"I thought you might have heard me scream."

"You screamed?" He seemed amused by that. "Sorry, I suppose you are jumpy in this house. I know I am. I probably didn't hear you because, after waiting for the emergency generator to come on, I went looking for it. Found it on the lower level next to the garage." He looked chastised. "I managed to get it going again only after the electricity came back on."

She studied him. "You know about emergency generators?"

"Only because Ethan was so proud of the one he was installing in this house. Apparently it isn't as grand as he thought. It didn't come on, did it?"

"What is odd is that the elevator was still working, even without the emergency generator coming on," she said.

"It's programmed to come up to the master suite when the power goes off and has its own generator so you can get out of the house quickly if you need to, like in case of fire. Yep, another thing Ethan bragged about during the construction phase. Is it any wonder I wanted to see this place?"

Jet seemed to have all the answers. "Did you manage to get into your brother's phone?" she asked.

He shook his head. "But we don't need to now, do we? Ethan is in Mexico City and will be returning in a few days. So what do you have planned today?" he asked, changing the subject.

"I'm going out to lunch with a friend." She hadn't thought of it until that moment, but she really wanted to see Lillie, among other things. She got to her feet, signaling that it was time for Jet to leave. "By the way, was it your idea or Ethan's for you to move into the hotel?"

Jet laughed. "He thought you'd be more comfortable without me here."

She merely nodded. "Ethan is always worried about my comfort."

His brother laughed as he got to his feet. "Yes, that's our Ethan for you," he said as he started to take their cups over to the sink.

Before he could grab her cup, she covered it with her hand. "I might want that once it cools down more."

He lifted a brow in surprise but left her to take his cup to the sink.

With his back to her, he said, "Let me know when Ethan gets back. I'll move out and I won't bother you further. But I will need to see him when he returns and then I'm out of his hair and yours."

She said nothing, torn between guilt and relief. "I'm sure Ethan just wants what is best for both of us."

Jet laughed as he turned to face her. "You really don't know my brother very well, do you? This is between me and Ethan. I'm sorry you ended up in the middle. I never met my father's expectations. I don't even try to meet Ethan's." He locked on her gaze. "Can I make you something for breakfast before I leave or will you be having an early lunch?"

"An early lunch. But thank you." She picked up her cup, deciding to take her coffee to her room until Jet left. Maybe it was silly. Maybe not. But she couldn't help feeling as if she'd been drugged over the past few days—ever since Jet had shown up.

Also, she was eager to call Lillie and make the lunch date. She just hoped her friend didn't have other plans. She needed to see a friendly face, especially after her encounter with Hawk last night and this unpleasant time with Jet. She'd really hoped he would be gone when she came downstairs.

But first, she stayed in the kitchen as Jet took the elevator. As she watched the dial take him to the parking garage, she realized that he'd already packed his things and loaded them in his sports car before he'd come up to make her coffee.

Maybe it was nothing more than a nice gesture. Maybe there would be no drugs in the coffee. But in that case she had to seriously consider the possibility that she was losing her mind and would need professional help.

Returning upstairs, she reprogrammed the pass code at the gate on a panel she found behind a painting on the bedroom wall. She hadn't known what numbers to use but went with her own birth date. Her reasoning was that Ethan knew it but Jet didn't.

Calling Lillie, she made a date for lunch. She needed to talk to her. The more she thought about it, the more she knew what could be wrong with her. How could she move on with another man, when there was so much still tying her to Hawk Cahill?

She still harbored resentment that she'd thought she'd put behind her. He'd hurt her. She'd hurt him. They'd let each other down.

Until last night, she hadn't realized how upset she still was with him—and vice versa. The antagonism over the past simmered just below the surface, neither of them forgetting—let alone forgiving. Not even the chemistry that had always been between them could overcome the anger.

She'd hoped they could resolve it, but after all these years, it didn't seem likely. What really bonded them wasn't just the disappointment, hurt and anger—but the secret they shared. It was something she hadn't told anyone. Not even Ethan because she felt she would be betraying Hawk. That had to end.

As long as only the two of them knew why they'd broken up, it would keep them tied together for life. Neither of them could move on. It was time to tell and free them both.

Realizing that, she felt better. Even her headache was lessening a little.

WHAT MADE HAWK so cranky and irritable the next day was the fact that he felt like a fool for what he'd done last night. What made it worse was that he knew he would do it again if he thought Drey was in trouble. That was what had him cussing and carrying on as he found a number for the local glass business.

He'd just finished ordering a new window for the Baxter house when he turned to find Cyrus had come into the kitchen. "I thought you were already gone."

His brother shook his head. "I'm afraid to ask what that phone call was about."

"If you're smart, you won't," he said as he stepped behind the breakfast bar to pour himself a cup of coffee.

"Sorry, but it will drive me crazy all day if I don't know why you would be buying a window for your ex at her mansion where she lives with her new husband," Cyrus said with a shrug. "You don't want me driven crazy all day, do you?"

Hawk ground his teeth for a few moments. "I took my horse out yesterday evening. On the way back, I saw the lights go out at the Baxter place. When I heard Drey scream…"

"You rode to the rescue." Cyrus laughed. "At least the husband didn't shoot you."

"He wasn't there. Supposedly his brother was somewhere on the premises, but I didn't run into him. I broke a window to get to Drey."

His brother nodded. "I'm guessing things didn't go well after that."

"She said she'd had a bad dream, and no, she didn't seem to appreciate my heroics."

"Sorry. But you can't change who you are. A woman in distress? Hawk Cahill will ride to the rescue no matter who she is."

"Yep, that's me."

"Is Drey okay?" Cyrus asked, all the humor gone from his tone.

Hawk took his time answering. "I'm not sure." He thought of the state he'd found her in. "I have a bad feeling that she's not."

AFTER DUMPING SOME of her coffee into a container and putting the two aspirin in a plastic sandwich bag, she dropped both into her large shoulder bag.

Pulling out her phone, she hit Lillie's number, anxious to get out of the house. Soon Ethan would be back. But that didn't give her the sense of relief she might have felt a few days ago. She listened to the phone ringing, praying Lillie wasn't too busy to see her.

Lillie answered on the fourth ring, sounding harried.

"Is this a bad time?" Drey asked, her heart dropping.

Her friend laughed. "If you think having baby powder everywhere is a bad time."

"Sounds like you're busy." She hated sounding so disappointed, but she was. Once she'd made up her mind about something, she liked to see it through. Wasn't that how she'd ended up married to Ethan? Or how she'd ruined things with Hawk?

"I'm never too busy for you. What is it?"

"Lunch. I was hoping you could get away for an early one," Drey said. "I need to talk to you."

"One moment." Lillie covered the phone but Drey could still hear her talking to her husband. "Trask said he would love to clean up this mess and take care of TC while you and I escape to a lovely lunch. Not the saloon, though. I'll feel like I should be working."

"I was thinking of the bistro downtown. I could pick you up or—"

"I'll meet you there. Say, eleven thirty?"

"Perfect. And thank Trask for me." As she was leaving to meet Lillie, the repairman from the local glass shop called for the security code to get into the gate down on the county road. She'd gone to school with the man, so Drey had no problem giving it to him. She told him on which floor he could find the broken window, but that she was going to lunch. He assured her he would have it fixed before she returned.

She couldn't wait to get away from the house. It all felt surreal, as if she was escaping the castle to save herself from… That was just it. What did she have to be saved from? She checked to make sure the coffee and pills were in her purse. Yes, what did she have to be afraid of?

Fortunately, she had just enough time before meeting Lillie to stop by the local pharmacy. She found her friend Brittany, the local pharmacist.

"Could we talk for a moment?" she asked, glad that there wasn't a line waiting for prescriptions. In Brittany's office, Drey pulled the two pills from her pocket. "You're going to think I'm crazy. It's okay because I think it's true."

Her friend laughed. "I doubt you're crazy. What are these?" she asked, frowning down at the pills.

"I was hoping you could tell me. I know they look like aspirin…"

Brittany glanced up at her. "But you think they are something else?"

She nodded and pulled the bag from her purse. "I also think there might be something in my coffee."

Her friend said nothing for a moment, but she looked concerned. Brittany had been at her wedding only days ago. "Drey, if you're in some kind of trouble shouldn't you be taking this to the sheriff?"

"I'm not at that point yet. It's just that I haven't been myself the last few days." She shook her head, biting down on her lower lip to hold back a sudden rush of tears. "Maybe I'm losing my mind, but maybe…" She met her friend's gaze. "Maybe someone just wants me to think I am. Will you check the pills and the coffee?"

"Of course. Are you going to be all right in the meantime?"

Drey thought of Jet gone from the house. "I'll be

fine." She felt as if she was at least doing something. All the craziness, the thumb and the mouse and Ethan disappearing on her and Hawk showing up the way he had. She'd been under so much pressure. Maybe that was all it was, she thought as she left the pharmacy.

But seeing Hawk last night had made her realize not only that she had to find out the truth, but also that he was part of the problem. She'd been so upset about living here in Gilt Edge. She wouldn't be able to avoid Hawk, nor he her. They would be running into each other and constantly being reminded of the past, something she hadn't planned on when she'd thought she and Ethan would be living in New York City at least most of the year.

She had to deal with all of it. The present as well as the past. She and Hawk had skirted around it for years. Well, that was going to change. She'd already taken a step to deal with the present. Now she would deal with Hawk and the past. Then Ethan would return and they could begin their married lives together. That thought should have made her feel better.

There were issues that would have to be dealt with between her and Ethan, as well. Especially if her suspicions about his brother were true.

CHAPTER TWELVE

BILLIE DEE COULD tell that Henry thought she was making a mistake.

"If you'd told me you wanted to hire a private investigator, I would have been happy to pay for it," he said. "But are you sure you want to do this? I mean, maybe if you just wait…"

"He might be right," Ashley Jo added. "Not that it's any of my business."

"No, I'd like to hear what you have to say," she told the young woman. The two of them had grown so close, she was almost like a daughter to her.

"It's just that often these things don't turn out like you hope. I'm sure your daughter must be scared. She has no idea what you're like or even if you are that interested in meeting her."

"That's why I have to find her. She has to know that I love her and that I never wanted to give her up."

"Still, she would have had loving parents and might feel she is betraying them by looking for her birth mother," Ashley Jo said.

"I hope she did have loving parents. And I know what you're saying. The thing is, she put her DNA sample in. She does want to find me."

Ashley Jo nodded but didn't look happy.

"Then just give it a little time," Henry suggested. "Let her be the one to make the next move."

She looked to Ashley Jo, who quickly nodded her agreement. "All right, I'll wait for a little longer, but then I'm hiring someone to find her."

Just then the sheriff came in the back door. "I'm meeting Hawk here for lunch," he said after they'd all exchanged greetings.

"I'll show you to a seat," Ashley Jo said.

Billie Dee could hear the two of them as they walked down the hallway to the saloon. "I'm surprised you're against this," she said to Henry.

"The problem with hiring a private investigator is that he will have to start at the beginning. You're opening up a can of worms here, Billie Dee. How can you trust that the father of your child won't find out that you lied to him all those years ago?"

She stared at him, realizing what he said was true. "He can't do anything to me now. Our daughter is raised. He wouldn't do anything."

"But what if he contacted your daughter?"

Billie Dee felt a shudder, remembering how the man had threatened to take her child from her and raise the baby as his own with his wife he'd said he was divorced from. He'd lied to her from the start, and she'd been so young and naive that she had believed him. If she hadn't run away...

"You're right. He must never know that I gave birth to the baby."

Henry hugged her. "You're going to find your

daughter. If nothing comes of the adoption site, then I'll see what I can do."

"I'VE CHANGED MY MIND," Hawk said the moment he joined his brother at a table in the corner of the Stage-coach Saloon.

Flint had debated calling him all morning as his concern for Drey grew. When Hawk had called to say he needed to talk to him, the sheriff had suggested lunch since it was close to that time of the day.

"Changed your mind? Concerning anything I should know about it?" He had a damned good idea.

"I shouldn't have asked you to check up on Ethan Baxter."

Flint sighed. "Mind if I ask why you've changed your mind?"

"How about it's none of my business?"

He nodded. "Except for the fact that you care about Drey."

His brother shook his head. "She's married now. I need to stay out of it."

Ashley Jo came over to take their orders. After they'd both opted for chili and colas, she left and Flint said, "I was going to call you, as it turns out." He met Hawk's gaze and held it. "You had reason to be concerned."

Hawk sat up a little straighter. "What did you find out?" he whispered. The place wasn't full yet, but there were a few regulars at the bar and four women at a table up front.

He hesitated. "In a matter of hours after I made one inquiry, two FBI agents walked into my office."

"What the hell?" Hawk said after Ashley Jo had brought their colas and two large bowls of chili along with tortilla chips, cheese and extra jalapeños.

Keeping his voice down, Flint said, "There's an ongoing investigation into Ethan Baxter's business practices."

His brother let out another curse. "So the guy's a crook. Great."

"I said under investigation. It might turn out to be nothing. But apparently Ethan Baxter has been under investigation. His latest activities—getting married, selling off some property—have heightened their interest in him. Nothing illegal about either, but possibly worrisome to the feds."

"What are you saying?"

"The agents are afraid he got wind of their investigation and is planning to skip the country."

"He hasn't already?" Hawk sounded surprised. "Drey hasn't seen him since the wedding."

Flint shook his head. "The FBI is convinced he's in that house. They're just waiting for him to show his face."

"According to Drey, he's in Mexico City." Hawk took a few bites of his lunch. "Took off on their wedding night without Drey even realizing he'd left, according to my little sister. Drey's a mess. When I saw her last night, she was kind of out of it. I'm even more worried about her."

"What do you mean, out of it?" Flint asked, becoming more concerned. The chili warmed him to his toes. It was just what he needed, he thought, as he took a sip of his cola to cool off his mouth.

"I got the feeling that she was either drunk or had taken something. All I can tell you is that the woman I saw last night wasn't the Drey I've known my whole life. To make matters worse, she's alone in that house with Ethan's younger brother, Jet."

"Jet Baxter?"

"He's under investigation, as well?"

"He works for Baxter Inc. The feds were surprised to hear that he's in town."

"So Lillie had told you." Hawk let out a laugh as he broke a few tortilla chips into his bowl. "She is a worrywart, that one. But in this case, it appears there is reason for concern. I'm worried as hell about Drey. She literally has no idea what she's gotten herself into. What are you going to do?"

"This is a federal case. If they decide to raid the house, I might be asked to help, but otherwise…"

"Raid the house? Drey is in that house with the brother. Maybe Ethan has fled to Mexico City. Drey needs to know what's going on."

"Are you sure she doesn't already know?" He could see that Hawk hadn't considered that. "Wouldn't she know if he was hiding out in the house with her?"

"It's a maze inside. I climbed the balconies to get to Drey last night, but I suspect there are other ways in— and out. I don't think the architecture of that building was only about impressing. I think it was about smoke and mirrors. But if he was in there, why wasn't he the one coming to her rescue?"

Flint sighed. "You had no business climbing balconies at that house. Not only is Drey married, the feds are looking into her, as well."

"No, that's crazy. She couldn't know about this or she wouldn't have married him."

Flint raised a brow. "If Drey is involved—"

"She's not." He finished his chili and pushed his bowl away. "I have to warn her."

"You'll be putting yourself right in the middle of an FBI investigation. The only reason I told you is because you need to stay clear of all of this."

"But what if Drey isn't safe? I've got a bad feeling that she's in trouble."

Flint couldn't help but take his brother's concerns with a grain of salt. Hawk could swear that he no longer loved Drey, but it was clear that he hadn't let go of the woman—at least emotionally.

"I'm afraid you're the one who doesn't know what he's getting into," the sheriff warned him. "If her husband isn't in that house, then he is nearby and probably keeping an eye on his wife."

His brother scoffed. "I'm betting he left Drey holding the bag. I'm more worried about the brother, Jet. I think something is wrong there."

"Hawk, you can't be involved in this for so many reasons."

"I'm already involved. If the feds are watching the house, then they saw me scale the balconies up to her bedroom." He grinned. "Let them think I'm making time with Drey while her husband is out of the picture. I don't care. But I'm not hanging her out to dry like apparently Ethan Baxter has."

Flint swore. Were there any men more stubborn than Cahill men? "You're making a mistake."

"It won't be my first. I'm telling you, she isn't safe there."

"If she isn't safe in that house with the feds watching, then I don't know where she would be safe."

"I have to get back to work. Thanks for lunch."

Flint watched him go and swore. His brother thought Drey didn't have a clue what she was getting involved in? Hawk was walking into more trouble than Flint feared even his brother could handle. If not from the feds, then from a jealous husband once Ethan Baxter returned. But he did wonder where the brother, Jet Baxter, fitted into the picture.

"YOUR SON IS ADORABLE," Drey said as she admired the newest photos on Lillie's phone. They'd both consumed iced tea and summer salads under one of the shaded umbrellas on the patio, while Drey avoided the real reason they were there. Lillie had been telling her about TC and how much she and her husband, Trask, were enjoying their baby.

But Lillie had also mentioned how nice it was to get to sneak away for a while without hauling a diaper bag and a baby everywhere. Drey knew that her friend was trying hard not to ask about Ethan and the marriage.

"There's something I have to tell you," Drey finally said.

Lillie let out a breath. "Finally. I knew it. You've made a mistake. But it's not too late," her friend said quickly as if she'd been anxiously awaiting Drey's confession. "When you invited me to lunch, I knew this was what you wanted to talk about. You can have the marriage annulled and—"

"Lillie, that isn't what I need to tell you. It's about Hawk."

Her friend looked worried. "What has my brother done now?"

"Last night, I realized why Hawk and I have had such a hard time moving on."

"Because you love each other."

Drey ignored that and continued, "One of the things holding Hawk and me back is this secret between us that we've kept all these years. Neither of us has ever told anyone."

Her friend nodded, huge eyed. "I know something bad had to have happened and that it has to be big. Otherwise, the two of you would be together. You love each other. You belong together."

She held up a hand to stop Lillie. "No one knows about this but Hawk and me. That's why we can't have this secret between us anymore."

Her friend nodded. Drey could tell it was a battle for Lillie not to say a word as she impatiently waited.

"Remember that summer before I went back to college alone?"

Lillie nodded again. "The one when you and Hawk broke up."

"All that summer, Hawk had been pushing me to get married. He thought we could go back to college together as a married couple. More than that, he kept talking about wanting us to start a family right away. I loved him more than life itself, but I wasn't ready. I wanted to get my degree. I was young. I had a chance to study a semester abroad—"

"In Spain. I remember. You'd always wanted to see Spain. You went."

"Yes, I went. But the reason Hawk and I broke up wasn't because I went to Spain. Before I left, I realized I was pregnant."

Lillie's eyes widened.

"I was furious with Hawk. I thought he'd done it on purpose. You know I've never been able to take birth control pills without getting ill. Hawk was handling that part of things."

"You can't think he would do that, knowing how much you wanted to study abroad and how much you wanted to wait," she protested.

"I did think it back then. He'd been so insistent and so upset with me for not wanting to settle down with him. He had it all planned, right down to where we would live and what we would do."

"That's Hawk," Lillie said. "Or at least that was the old Hawk." She sounded sad. "He changed after the two of you broke up. It was like he'd given up ever being happy or having the family he'd always wanted." Her voice broke. "But I still can't believe he'd do something like that."

"He swore he didn't, but I didn't believe him," Drey continued after taking a sip of her recently refilled iced tea. "I wasn't ready for a baby, a marriage, especially to a man who I felt had tried to trick me…worse, trap me. Especially with life-changing, awful results."

"But it wouldn't have been that awful, would it have?" Lillie cried. "The two of you would have had a sweet baby to raise."

She shook her head as she met her friend's gaze. "For me, at that moment, it was awful. What I thought Hawk had done. Worse, how I felt not just about him. I felt trapped and angry. I wasn't going to let him tie me down like that."

Lillie shook her head. "You didn't…"

"I didn't. The woman I am now wouldn't have even considered terminating the pregnancy. But I was young and angry. I made the appointment. Hawk found out. I never went through with it. A few weeks later, I lost the baby. There were…problems."

"But if you hadn't lost the baby?" her friend asked.

"I could never have terminated Hawk's and my baby. I know that in my heart. But Hawk—" Her voice broke.

"He doesn't believe you?" Lillie said, tears in her eyes.

"No, he knows I didn't keep the appointment. But that I even thought about it… He's never been able to forgive me."

Lillie dabbed at her eyes with her napkin. "Why are you telling me this now?" she asked in a whisper.

"Because Hawk and I are still angry with each other after all these years. I realized that this secret isn't letting either of us truly move on. I haven't even told Ethan."

Lillie let out a breath as she leaned back in her chair. "You've been carrying this around all these years. You and Hawk both." She looked close to tears again.

Drey reached across the table to take her friend's hand. "I didn't want to burden anyone else with it, but I can't carry it any longer. I'm married now to someone else. It might not be the kind of marriage I once dreamed of, but I'm going to make it work. I'm sorry I called you the other night crying. I had been drinking…" *Was I drugged?* "I wasn't myself."

Lillie squeezed her hand. "You know that I just want you to be happy. But can you be happy without Hawk?"

The question cut deep. "I'm going to try because Hawk and I…" She shrugged, feeling her eyes burn with tears. "Dessert! That's what we need." She picked up the dessert menu. "What do you say to hot fudge?"

After they'd finished lunch, Drey noticed that Hawk had left her a message. She ignored it, turned off her phone again and pulled out her credit card, only to have it declined.

Lillie insisted on paying, assuring her it was probably just a glitch with the credit card company.

CHAPTER THIRTEEN

HAWK CALLED DREY'S cell again but it went straight to voice mail. He hesitated, then left a message. "I need to tell you something." He realized how his message sounded and added, "Please. It's important." It was the second message he'd left.

But an hour later, when she still hadn't called him back, he tried his sister only to learn from her husband that she and Drey had gone to lunch.

"At the Stagecoach Saloon?" he asked as he headed for his pickup.

"I doubt it. Lillie says she feels like she should be working when she eats there," Trask told him.

Hawk slipped behind the wheel of his pickup, considering where else the two might choose to eat and headed to downtown Gilt Edge. The small Western town had only a handful of places to eat lunch so he figured she wouldn't be hard to find.

He spotted his sister's SUV parked just down the street from the local bistro and drove around the block, looking for a place to park. He didn't like the idea of interrupting their lunch, but he really didn't feel this could wait. After parking, he walked back toward the café only to see his sister drive away. He spotted

Drey about to climb into a nondescript white SUV and called to her.

She turned in surprise to see him and waited next to her vehicle as he approached. The sun was in her eyes. She shaded them with her hand, her expression somber. He realized what he had to tell her wasn't going to come as good news. He thought about what his brother had said. He was the last person she wanted to hear this from. He let out a curse, telling himself that she couldn't hate him any more than she already did.

"I don't know if you got my message or not but—"

She cut him off. "I told Lillie."

Hawk stopped inches from her and frowned. "Told Lillie what?"

She sighed and looked down at her boots for a moment. Somehow he'd expected her to dress differently now that she was married to Ethan Baxter. It was good to see her in jeans and a Western shirt. It was good to know that she hadn't changed too much.

"Did you hear me?"

The edge to her voice brought him back. "I guess not."

"I told her why we broke up."

"You what?" He stared at her in disbelief. "After all these years, you just decided to tell Lillie." He swore under his breath as he dragged off his Stetson to rake his hand through his hair. "Why would you do that?"

"I realized something after last night. There is still so much between us." As if she had to tell him that. Didn't she know that he felt it every time he was around her? It was one reason he tried like hell to avoid her. "We're both still angry at each other," she said.

"So what?" *That* was what she thought was between them? Anger was the reason they both couldn't move on? He said as much.

"It bonds us but what really has us shackled together is the secret we've kept from everyone," she said. "It isn't even something you and I have acknowledged. Every time I've brought up the subject—"

"There was nothing to say," Hawk snapped as he shoved his hat back on his head and looked down the street. He couldn't believe they were having this discussion after all these years on the sidewalk in downtown Gilt Edge. "Why the hell would you take it upon yourself to—"

"It's my secret, too. I didn't want anyone to know that I had a weak moment when I was very young and very angry at you."

"I told you I didn't—"

"I know that now. But back then I wanted to blame you for putting me in such an untenable situation."

He ground his teeth. "Marriage to me and my baby was an untenable situation?"

"*Our* baby. And yes, at that age it was. I was heading to Spain. I was continuing my education. I had things I needed to do before I had a child and settled down."

He swore under his breath and looked away. They'd had this conversation too many times already. Why would she air their dirty laundry to his sister? The hot summer sun beat down on him. He felt a little sick to his stomach remembering the day he found out that she'd made the appointment to get rid of their baby. He didn't want to talk about this any more now than he had all those years ago.

"Well, the problem took care of itself, I guess," he said, looking down at his boots.

"I told you, I never went to that appointment. I miscarried, but what I didn't tell you was when I did…" Her voice broke and she looked away for a moment. "I cried my heart out."

At the sound of her pain, he looked up. The distress he saw in her beautiful face tore at his heart. He felt his throat tighten.

"I wanted your baby—just not then, Hawk. But when I miscarried…I couldn't bear the thought that I might never have another of your children. I had lost so much. You and our baby. I will regret losing that baby until the day I die," she said as tears began to course down her cheeks.

He reached out and wiped away one with his thumb. She caught his hand and held it against her cheek for a moment as she tried to stem the flow of tears. He tried to swallow the lump in his throat as she pressed a kiss into the palm of his hand and let go.

"Me, too," he said his voice rough with emotion. "I wanted that child, your child, our child so badly." He looked away. "I had all these dreams for our son or daughter, for us. And when it was gone, and you were gone, too…" He looked away, fighting tears.

"I know."

He pulled himself together and drew out his bandanna and handed it to her.

DREY TOOK THE BANDANNA, wiped her tears and blew her nose.

"You can keep that," Hawk said when she looked around as if she didn't know what to do with it. There was humor in his tone, something she hadn't heard in his voice since before their breakup all those years ago.

"Thanks." She stuffed the bandanna into the side of her shoulder bag and looked out at the mountains that rimmed the town. Hawk's first love was this community, this state, this land. His only true love was her, though, he used to say. "I wish I could go back and change everything."

He cleared his throat. "Me, too."

She met his gaze. What she saw in his gray eyes...

"I'm sorry, Drey. So sorry."

She nodded.

"But you're wrong about one thing. Anger wasn't the only thing between us." He held her gaze. "We both still love each other."

She wanted to argue but couldn't. "I should go."

"There's something I need to tell you." He looked so serious that she felt her heart drop.

"If it's about last night..."

"I'd just as soon forget about last night," he drawled. "Unless that is something else you feel the need everyone should know about."

She shook her head, seeing that he was trying to

lighten the mood. "My window's fixed. All's forgiven. Thank you for rescuing me."

"I wish that's what I'd done," he said. "A long time ago."

She saw the change in him. He seemed to brace himself as if about to give her bad news. She felt the blow even before he said the words. "There's something I need to tell you about your husband. Drey, he's being investigated by the FBI." He looked as if he hadn't meant to blurt it out like that.

She stared at him. "How do you know that?"

"Flint."

"Right." She nodded. She couldn't believe what she was hearing. Her stomach churned. Tears burned her eyes. When she'd first met Ethan, he'd seemed too good to be true. Why would a man like that be interested in a small-town librarian like her?

Of course it *had* been too good to be true. That a man like that could love her. So why? Why had he courted her the way he had? Why marry her if any of this was true? It made no sense.

"Your brother, the sheriff. He just happened to mention it to you?"

Hawk glanced away. "When I heard that your husband was missing, I asked Flint to do some checking into Ethan," Hawk said.

She couldn't believe this. *"You what?"*

"I was worried about you and after last night—"

Drey shook her head, so angry she couldn't speak. Hawk didn't want her, but he couldn't seem to let her go either.

"Damn it, Drey, you needed to know. The FBI is looking for him."

"Well, I'm sure you told your brother that he's in Mexico City."

"He's not in Mexico City. He hasn't left the country. The feds think he's still here in Gilt Edge."

"How do they know that?"

"I suspect they've been watching your house."

Watching her house? She bit her lower lip, fighting back the scream that wanted to scale her throat and burst out. She dug her fingernails into the palms of her hands. But to her surprise, it was a laugh that escaped her lips. "This must give you so much satisfaction."

"Actually," he said, still staring down at his boots. "It breaks my heart."

"You have a heart?" She hadn't meant to be so flippant but all the years of controlling her emotions around him had worn thin. Her life was such a disaster right now she didn't give a damn.

His gaze rose slowly from the sidewalk until those gray eyes burned into her making her own heart thunder in her ears. "You think I wanted to bring you this news? You think I don't want to find that bastard and…" His voice broke, but his gaze remained steady on hers. "You think I don't kick my sorry ass every day for hurting you? Worse, not being able to get past what happened?" He dragged his gaze away.

They stood like that, the past still a barrier between them. If only one of them could break it down and put an end to this.

"I can't change what I did." Her lower lip trembled.

She bit down on it and then, her own voice cracking, said, "You think I haven't wished I could go back and do everything differently?"

"Drey—" He reached for her, but she pulled away.

"I can't do this." She shook her head. "You just had to tell me about Ethan, didn't you? You had to track me down on the street to tell me this?"

He shook his head. "My timing could have been better, yes, but I was afraid if I waited… I didn't do it to hurt you. You have to believe that." His voice broke. "You had to know. If there's a chance the FBI might think you're involved… Drey, surely you see that he isn't the man you thought he was."

"And neither are you," she said, wiping at a tear. She shook her head and turned her back on him as she headed for her SUV.

"Why can't you admit that you made a mistake?" Hawk demanded. "Ethan Baxter? Seriously?"

She bristled as she stopped and slowly turned to look at him again. Trying to still her raging emotions, she closed the distance between them. Across the street, she saw that a woman had stopped to watch them. But she didn't care. It probably wouldn't be long before the whole town was talking.

"Excuse me?" she demanded. "I had to move on. I couldn't keep doing…whatever it was you and I were doing to each other."

Hawk shook his head. "But with Ethan Baxter?"

She took a step toward him, feeling herself getting angrier. "Why not Ethan? You were never going to forgive me."

He looked away. "In time—"

"In time?" she demanded. "Do you realize how long I've been waiting?" She saw something in his gray eyes that made her start. *"Now? Now* you're going to forgive me? *Now* you're going to act like you can't live without me?"

"I didn't say—"

"Exactly. You didn't say anything. You just don't want me to be married to Ethan Baxter. You just want me pining after you for the rest of my life."

"Look, I shouldn't have said anything."

"No, you shouldn't have." Hawk made her angrier than anyone she'd ever known. "You're right, though. I did make a mistake when I thought you and I could talk about the past and maybe free each other from… *this*." She waved an arm through the air.

All her emotions rushed to the surface again. There was no stopping them this time. She broke down and began to sob, her words coming out with both pain and tears as she pleaded, "You can't keep doing this, Hawk. Let me go. Please."

"This isn't about me being jealous. I'm worried about you." He reached for her, but she sidestepped him, jerked open the SUV door and climbed in. As she cranked over the engine, Hawk stepped back.

She pulled out of the parking space and pressed the gas pedal to the floor. *Don't look back. Damn it, don't you dare look back.*

It wasn't until she was a block away that she looked into her rearview mirror. He stood in the middle of the street, his hands in the pockets of his jeans, his head down.

She didn't look back again as she drove away, tears streaming down her face.

COULD YOU HAVE handled that any worse? Hawk mentally kicked himself as he drove back toward the ranch. Cyrus had left a message that he was waiting on more barbed wire. Hawk swung by the store and now the back of his pickup was full of wire and fence posts. He was actually looking forward to another hard hot day stringing fence. After his run-in with Drey he felt as if he deserved it.

But he'd forgotten his gloves at the ranch. He drove down the road only to see his sister Lillie's SUV parked in front of the house. He swore under his breath. He should have known it was only a matter of time before he'd have to face her after what Drey had told her.

After parking, he got out of his truck, telling himself that nothing Lillie could say to him could be worse than what he'd already said to himself. He started toward the house, figuring she'd be waiting for him inside.

But as he passed her SUV, he saw that she was sitting behind the wheel waiting for him. He tapped on the glass, surprised she hadn't gone inside. He braced himself for the dressing-down he was about to get.

It wasn't an angry Lillie who stepped out of the SUV, though. He saw that she'd been crying. With a curse, he realized this was going to be much worse than he'd thought. She rushed to him and threw her arms around his waist as she buried her face in his chest. "I'm so sorry. I had no idea."

He held her, letting her cry it out, fighting his own emotions. For years he'd been trying to put all this behind him. Why did Drey have to tell Lillie? Why bring up the past at all? Did she really think this was going to help things between them?

Lillie pulled back to look up into his face.

"I'd offer you my bandanna but…"

His sister waved off the offer and pulled out a handful of tissues from the pocket of her jean jacket. "Why didn't you tell me?" she demanded after she'd wiped her tears and blown her nose.

"It was something I wanted to forget," he said.

"But you haven't forgotten. Or forgiven Drey."

He groaned. "This is another reason I didn't tell you or anyone else. I don't want to talk about it."

"So you've kept it bottled up all these years."

"Lillie, as you can see, I'm about to take more barbed wire and posts out to Cyrus." He pointed toward his pickup, the back loaded. "I'd say we can talk about this later, but quite frankly, I'd rather not. It's history. Water under the bridge. No going back."

She shook her head. "You are so like all the Cahill men. Stubborn jackasses."

He blinked at her words and couldn't help smiling. "Your point?"

"Drey. Her marriage hasn't been consummated."

Groaning, he said, "I'm not sure that changes

anything. She's married. She's asked me to leave her alone, let her get on with her life."

"And you're going to do it?" Lillie sounded thunderstruck. "Of course that isn't what she wants. Do you know anything at all about women?"

"No, I think I've proved that. I was happy accepting that I would be a bachelor the rest of my life. I believe you're the one who was determined I get married."

His sister shook her head. "Drey still loves you. If you can't see that, well, then, you're just blind."

Hawk pulled off his Stetson and scratched his head. Just minutes ago, he'd told Drey that they both still loved each other. Sometimes love wasn't enough, but he wasn't about to tell Lillie that. "I need to get this barbed—"

"Wire to Cyrus." She practically stomped her feet as the anger he'd expected finally showed itself. "Look at all the years you've wasted. It isn't too late. But if you hesitate, then you will end up a cranky old bachelor and you'll only have yourself to blame for being a lonely, sad old man." With that she stormed off to her SUV.

He watched her go, mumbling under his breath, "There are worse things than being a bachelor, damn it." Like knowing that Drey was in trouble and not being able to do a damned thing about it.

CHAPTER FOURTEEN

DREY CHECKED HERSELF in the SUV mirror after pulling into the pharmacy parking lot. Her eyes were red, her cheeks flushed. That scene back there on the street with Hawk had left her shaken. Ethan was being investigated by the FBI? He wasn't in Mexico City? Apparently the FBI were watching the house because they believed he was holed up inside? It was ridiculous. All of this had to be a mistake.

Why can't you admit that you made a mistake?

Hawk's words echoed in her ears. Hawk. What infuriated her more than anything was the fact that Hawk couldn't wait to tell her the news. She grumbled under her breath as she turned the rearview mirror where she could study her face. She looked as if she'd been crying, but there was little she could do about that.

As she got out of the SUV, she reminded herself that she had worse things to concern herself with. She suspected her husband's brother could have been drugging her the past couple of days. She pushed open the door to the pharmacy and entered the back to find Brittany having lunch. Past her, Drey could see her assistant filling prescription orders.

Brittany swallowed the last of her sandwich, got up

and closed the door to the pharmacy before turning to Drey. If she was surprised to see her tearstained red face, she made no mention of it.

"You had a chance to check the items I left you?" Drey asked.

"I did. The pills are a generic aspirin. The coffee…"

"Was just coffee." Drey nodded, feeling foolish, but a little surprised that Ethan would have the medicine cabinet stocked with generic aspirin. He was such a stickler for only the best brand names of everything.

Brittany seemed to hesitate. "Can you tell me what is going on? I don't mean to pry."

She shook her head. "Just me being silly. I haven't been feeling well…"

"You thought someone was trying to poison you?"

"No, more like drug me. I had some hallucinations. I thought maybe a hallucinogen. Maybe even a heavy-duty sleeping pill. One that might resemble generic aspirin."

"There are some that could resemble generic aspirin. But the ones you gave me were just aspirin." Her friend studied her. "I'm worried about you."

Drey's laugh held no humor. "I've been worried about myself. It was probably simply exhaustion from the wedding and everything. I had a few bad dreams."

"If they persist—"

"I'll go to a doctor," she said and touched her friend's arm. "Thank you. You've relieved my mind." Was that true?

"If you suspect someone might be slipping you something—"

"Obviously, I did, but apparently I was only being paranoid."

"The fact that you even thought it…" Brittany shook her head. "Drey—"

"That person is no longer around," she assured her friend. Jet was gone. Problem solved. It just would have been nice to have proof for her own mental stability. "And, as it turns out, I was wrong."

Brittany looked skeptical. Not half as skeptical as Drey felt.

At the grocery store the same thing happened with the credit card. It was the only one she had since she'd canceled all the ones in her old name. Fortunately, she had enough cash on her to pay for the few things she'd picked up. Had Ethan not paid the bill? He took care of all of the finances for her. Or was there just a glitch, like Lillie had suggested?

She debated going back to the house. Where else would she go? She was married to Ethan. It was her home. But she couldn't help thinking about what Hawk had said. If the FBI really were investigating Ethan's business and they'd found something illegal and were about to close in…

But that wasn't what had her driving toward the house. The FBI thought Ethan was still in the area. They'd been watching the house, Hawk had said. That meant that they thought he was still in there…somewhere.

She punched in the new code at the entrance to the property. The gate slowly swung open. As she drove through, she remembered their wedding night when Ethan had driven through the gate, looked back and cursed. He'd said it was nothing, but she'd seen the car drive slowly past. The FBI? Had they been following them from the church?

In her rearview mirror, she watched the gate close. A dark sedan drove slowly past. She couldn't see the driver before the car disappeared around a curve. Had she been followed? The thought chilled her. Did the FBI think she might be involved? But involved in what?

She shivered as she drove on up the paved road. The locked gate should have made her feel safer along with the chain-link fence that surrounded the property around the house. But it hadn't kept Hawk out the other night, had it? With Jet gone, she told herself she would be fine in the house alone.

But was she alone?

That thought did nothing to alleviate her worry. Was it possible Ethan was somewhere in that house, hiding? The idea was so ludicrous that it made her laugh. Why would he hide? She'd heard about big businesses like his being investigated. Often it came to nothing. Ethan didn't seem like the kind of man who would hide from anyone.

She tried to put it out of her mind. Her talk with Lillie had gone well. It had gone less well with Hawk, but that was to be expected. Well, their secret was out. Other than the fact that Hawk was right. She still loved him.

But it didn't change anything. As she pulled into the parking garage under the house she tried to assure herself that there was nothing keeping her from finding happiness with Ethan.

Unless he really was hiding and the FBI was about to close in.

As much as she disliked the elevator, she didn't want to carry all of her purchases up flights of stairs. After calling the elevator, she began to load what she'd bought into it. At the last minute she realized she didn't have to ride it, she could take the stairs and when the elevator stopped at the kitchen, she would unload the items there and then send the rest on up to the master suite.

Feeling smug at figuring out a way to avoid riding in the elevator, she pushed the button and turned to the stairs. She heard the mechanism begin to hum as she took the first few steps and stopped. Jet had been staying on the staff quarters floor. Out of curiosity, she walked down to make sure he'd taken everything when he'd left.

She checked each of the rooms and found one where the bed looked as if it had been slept in. She stripped it and took the bedding down to the laundry where she got a load going. She felt almost domestic as she took the stairs up to the kitchen. All the way, she couldn't help looking over her shoulder.

Just as she'd planned, the elevator was waiting for her. She quickly unloaded the groceries, telling herself she was fine. Wasn't it possible that the FBI thought Ethan was still around because his phone was still in the area? Or maybe because his car was still parked outside?

She put everything she'd bought away and then sent the elevator up to the master suite before taking the stairs again up the two floors.

As she passed the media and conference rooms level, she glanced in. The only time she'd been in this part of the house was when she and Jet had been searching for Ethan. Now she hesitated. Jet had searched half of each floor. She hadn't been in this area at all.

As she moved deeper into the large living room area, she caught a whiff of a familiar scent. Ethan's aftershave. The realization stopped her cold in the middle of the room.

She took another sniff, telling herself that she'd only imagined it. She found herself listening for him. Did she really expect to hear Ethan moving around in one of the conference rooms? Or maybe on the sundeck?

Still, that feeling of not being alone brushed over her like a spiderweb. She shuddered and willed her feet to move. First the conference rooms. All empty. Then the sundeck. It, too, was empty. No big surprise.

Drey was just starting to turn back toward the elevator when she spotted an ashtray on the small table in the sunroom. Something glittered in the afternoon light from inside the ashtray.

Like a sleepwalker, she moved toward it. She was close when she recognized what lay in the ashtray. Fingers trembling, she carefully picked up the two cuff links. As she did, she turned quickly, as if hearing something behind her.

She listened but heard nothing except her own racing pulse. The scent of Ethan's aftershave seemed stronger in here. She raised the cuff links to her nose and realized why. She could imagine him sitting here after the wedding, removing the cuff links and dropping them into the ashtray next to his chair.

How long had he sat there, knowing his wife was upstairs waiting for him? She frowned. And had he been alone? She looked again at the room and saw that everything was arranged in perfect order—except for one chair. It had been moved out of place. It was angled so it faced the chair she'd imagined Ethan sitting in that night.

Ethan hadn't been alone. But who had sat in the other chair? Not Jet. He hadn't gotten to town yet. So whom had her husband been visiting with down here on their wedding night before he'd come upstairs long enough to lose his phone on their balcony and then disappear?

She started to turn when she spotted something on the tile beside the second chair. Bending down, she recognized it. A toothpick. It had been chewed on—and broken in half—before being dropped to the floor.

CHAPTER FIFTEEN

"ARE YOU STILL talking to me?"

Gigi smiled. She'd just gotten home from the restaurant, taken a shower, poured herself her nightly glass of wine and put her feet up. But AJ and her last call had been on her mind ever since. "Have your ears been burning?"

"You've been talking about me?" AJ asked with a laugh.

"Cursing you to blue blazes." But she laughed.

"I have good news. Billie Dee isn't hiring a private investigator to find you. At least not for a while."

"I suppose that's something."

"Aren't you due for a vacation?" her friend asked. "Montana this time of year is amazing."

"My parents took me to Yellowstone National Park that summer when I was thirteen, remember?"

"Right, but Yellowstone is mostly in Wyoming."

"We drove through part of Montana."

"Okay, I'll drop it." She fell silent.

"So what's she like?" Gigi asked with a sigh. "I know you're dying to tell me." She'd had a hard day at work. When she saw that it was AJ calling she'd considered not taking the call. But she'd missed her friend and just hearing her voice made her feel better. It always had.

"Billie Dee? She's delightful. Everyone up here loves her. The Cahills—that's who we work for, a brother, Darby, and sister, Lillie—have adopted her like she's family." She rushed on, her voice saying more about how much she liked Billie Dee than her words could. "She's always singing. Usually hymns. She does a great rendition of 'The Yellow Rose of Texas,' though."

"Delightful." She curled deeper into her chair by the window and took a sip of her wine. "And you say she can cook?"

"Won that recipe contest. You would love her Texas chili."

Gigi scoffed. "I'd put mine up against hers any day."

"Maybe one day you'll get the chance."

"AJ—"

"I know." Silence filled the line. "How are you doing?"

"Fine. The restaurant is crazy busy. I don't have much time for anything else. How's the bartending gig?"

"I met someone."

She sat up a little. "Really?"

"He's a local rancher."

"A cowboy?" Gigi couldn't help but laugh. "You know we have plenty of those back here in Texas, but I don't remember you ever being interested."

"Cyrus Cahill is…different."

"How so?"

"I don't know." AJ sounded embarrassed.

"You really *do* like him."

"I do, but he hasn't shown much interest."

"The man must be blind and stupid. Maybe you just need to turn on that Somerfield charm," Gigi said.

"He doesn't come into the saloon very often."

She felt for her friend.

"What about you? Anyone interesting come into the restaurant?"

"I'm too busy to notice."

"That's too bad. There are some really cute cowboys up this way."

Gigi laughed. "You and your cowboys." She finished her wine. "I should hit the hay." She chuckled. "If you really like this Cyrus Cahill, go after him."

"Maybe I just need my wingman...wingwoman? Doesn't have the same ring. Remember all the fun we used to have together? You used to say we were an insurmountable team."

"Vaguely. I'm glad you called. Take care, AJ." She disconnected, feeling close to tears. She desperately missed her friend and she couldn't help being curious about this Billie Dee woman whom everyone seemed to love and had allegedly given her birth.

DREY FELT DRAINED after the day she'd had as she climbed the stairs to the master suite. She kept thinking about what she'd found in the sunroom. Proof. But proof of what? That Ethan had been in that room? That he'd taken off his cuff links after the wedding and left them there while he visited with Jet?

Jet. She'd caught him in another lie, she thought as she took the stairs to her room. He'd lied about only showing up the next morning. He'd been in the house the night before. He'd seen his brother. The two of them had been in that sunroom. But why had he lied about it?

She couldn't shake the feeling that he'd known she would be alone when he'd driven up that next day. He'd lied about never being in the house before and yet he'd been in that sunroom with Ethan even before her husband had changed out of his wedding attire.

Drey had the feeling that they'd been arguing. Based on what? Another one of her premonitions? No, she realized. Ethan had taken off his expensive cuff links, dropped them in an ashtray… It was something he would never do. Unless he was upset. He was so meticulous about his clothing, his belongings.

She still held the cuff links in her hand, she realized. Looking down at them, she frowned. Walking over to his side of the bed, she tossed them onto his nightstand, remembering the strong scent of his aftershave. These were the cuff links he'd been wearing at their wedding. But was it possible he hadn't left them there on their wedding night?

If he was still in this house somewhere…

Feeling paranoid, she searched the bedroom the way she had the rest of the house, locking both the balcony door and the double doors to the stairs. But if she was right, someone had a key. How else could she explain locking the doors twice, only to find them standing open later in the night?

This time she was more careful about the way she pushed the chair under the doorknob. If anyone tried to come in, she would at least hear the chair fall.

What if there is a fire? No one will be able to get to you.

No one will know I'm here or even that the house was on fire anyway, she told herself. She had much bigger worries. While Brittany hadn't found anything in the coffee Jet had served or the pills she'd found in her bathroom, she still believed she'd been drugged.

Her head ached and she realized she wasn't going to be able to make sense of it tonight. Outside she could see that darkness now blanketed the mountainside. It appeared to be a lovely evening. She hugged herself. Jet couldn't get back in the gate at the bottom of the mountain. Ethan wasn't in the house.

If that didn't reassure her, she was reminded that Hawk had said the FBI was watching the house. She should feel safe. So why didn't she?

Because she would never feel safe locked in this house. She walked to the balcony, opened the newly fixed door and stepped out, needing the fresh air. The summer night air felt like a caress. She thought of Hawk and wasn't surprised that her yearning for him hadn't lessened. Telling their secret felt like a weight off her shoulders. But it hadn't changed anything.

Turning back to the bedroom, now all she wanted was the oblivion of sleep. She closed the door, locked it and pulled the blinds. She stripped down and put on a pair of the silk pajamas Ethan had bought her and crawled into bed. But her mind wouldn't let her rest. She kept thinking about what Hawk had said. Was she ready to admit she'd made a mistake?

She had so many questions and so few answers. Nothing seemed to make any sense. Sleep. That was all she needed. When the headache persisted, she got up and reached for her purse. Earlier she'd bought aspirin at the grocery store, the brand she'd always used.

Opening the bottle she shook out two, then walked into the bathroom to get a drink of water to wash them down. As she opened the medicine cabinet and put the bottle away, she froze. The bottle that was in the cabinet was the same brand she held in her hand—not the generic kind she'd taken since she'd been here.

Who could have replaced them? Jet? That would mean that he had access to the house. Ethan? She closed the medicine cabinet, determined not to take anything that she hadn't purchased herself. Back in the bedroom, she dropped the aspirin into her purse and sat down on the edge of the bed.

Her eyes felt as if they were filled with sand. She wanted to sit down and cry. Her husband was being investigated by the FBI. Jet said he was in Mexico City. The FBI said he was here in Gilt Edge—probably hidden somewhere in this house. And then there was Hawk.

Why can't you admit you made a mistake?

She fell back, lying there, staring at the ceiling as tears ran down from the corners of her eyes. What was she going to do?

HAWK HADN'T EVEN tried to sleep. When Flint found him, he was about to pour himself a glass of whiskey.

"I'm not sure that is going to help," the sheriff said as he came into the ranch house. "But just in case, pour me one."

He did as his brother asked. Flint took a chair in the living room. Hawk joined him, giving him his drink and taking a chair next to him. "I'd ask what this is about..." He shook his head.

"You told Drey."

Hawk nodded. "I had to."

Flint took a sip of his whiskey and grimaced.

"I heard you'd become a teetotaler," Hawk joked. "This stuff will put hair on your chest."

"I already have hair on mine," his brother said and took another tentative drink. "How'd she take it?"

"Not well. She hadn't known so she definitely isn't involved."

Flint said nothing. He didn't have to. Hawk knew that even Drey pleading her innocence wouldn't help her with the FBI if they believed differently.

"Lillie stopped by my office earlier," the sheriff said.

Hawk let out a rude sound. "That woman just doesn't quit, does she?"

"Not when she loves her brothers. She told me what broke you and Drey up back in college. I'm so sorry, Hawk."

He nodded and took a drink of whiskey and tried to change the subject. "Drey swears that Ethan is in Mexico City."

Flint shook his head. "For whatever reason, the FBI says he's here."

"In that house?" Hawk asked.

"According to them, he never left." His brother finished his whiskey and rose to his feet. "Which is another reason you don't want to go near that place. I got the impression from the FBI agents when they stopped by to ask questions about you that you're now on their radar. I told them that you and Drey are friends. But they're suspicious. I wouldn't be surprised if they were about to make an arrest."

He swore. "Drey is going to be caught right in the middle of it."

"She has been in the middle since she married Ethan Baxter. You can't save her, Hawk. I wouldn't be surprised if the FBI isn't now watching you, as well."

After his brother left, Hawk walked the floor at the ranch house, unable to shake his growing worry for Drey. He felt even more helpless. He'd tried to get her to leave Ethan, leave that house, clear out, but she was determined to see this sham of a marriage through.

He picked up the whiskey bottle but he'd lost his taste for alcohol. All his instincts told him Drey was in more trouble than some FBI investigation. But his hands were tied, he thought, as he looked out into the darkness.

Was his brother right? Were the feds watching him now, too? Hopefully they were watching Drey and would keep her safe.

DREY DIDN'T KNOW what had awakened her. She sat up
with a start. Sun poured in through the balcony windows on another beautiful Montana summer day. She
could see the pines outside the balcony glistening in
the warm golden rays. The door to the balcony stood
open. She frowned. Had she left it open?

It had been such a beautiful evening last night.
She'd had so much on her mind; maybe she had. She
remembered standing on the balcony, looking toward
the Cahill Ranch. The thought made her angry with
herself. Nothing had changed with her and Hawk. Had
she really thought finally telling their secret would
free them both from the past? She refused to rehash
all that in her mind as she breathed in the day.

But her heart was still pounding. She frowned as
she realized what had awakened her. There'd been a
loud noise. Had it been another dream? Whatever it
had been, she heard nothing now. She lay back, listening to a meadowlark outside her window and the
pounding of her pulse. As it began to slow, she was
relieved to realize that she had awakened without any
of that foggy feeling she'd had before. It only strength-
ened her belief that Jet had drugged her.

Drey felt so much better that for a moment she'd
forgotten about the FBI investigation and her argument with Hawk yesterday. She closed her eyes. She
would make a point of talking to Flint about the investigation today. Hawk could have purposely made
it sound worse than it was. Thinking about him made
her ache. He'd said he still loved her. He knew that
she still loved him, too. But did he really think that

was enough to erase the past between them? That all she had to do was walk out of this marriage? And then what?

A shout came from outside, followed by a gunshot.

There was no mistaking the sound. A gunshot. Right outside the house. She realized that must have been what had awakened her as she threw back the covers and rushed to the window. Seeing nothing, she ventured out on the balcony, all the while telling herself it could have been a car backfiring.

She couldn't remember the last time she'd heard a car backfire, but she knew too well the sound of gunshots. Born and raised a Montanan, she had learned to fire a gun at a young age and had gone hunting with her father and, later, friends for years.

Out on the balcony, she glanced around, wondering if it had been kids taking target practice somewhere nearby. But the shot had seemed so loud, so close. At first she saw nothing in the bright summer day. The breeze stirred the pine boughs nearby and sent ripples across the surface of the pond.

Suddenly she saw Jet. He staggered onto the pond dock. He was holding his hands over his stomach. The pale blue shirt she'd first seen him in appeared to be dark with... Was that blood? She heard another shot and let out a cry as she saw his body jerk an instant before he fell face-first into the water and lay unmoving.

FLINT HAD TAKEN the emergency call from Drey, praying it had nothing to do with his brother.

"Someone shot Jet," she cried. "I heard gunshots. I saw him fall into the pond."

"Did you see who fired the shots?"

She let out a sob. "No."

"Where are you?"

"I'm upstairs in my bedroom. I saw the whole thing from the balcony."

"Okay, listen to me." He could hear how upset she was. "I need you to lock your door and stay right where you are. Don't go out on the balcony again. The shooter could still be out there. Do you understand?" He heard her sudden intake of breath. Clearly she hadn't thought that she might be in danger.

"I understand," she said. He could hear her closing doors and locking them.

"When you last saw Jet, was he moving?"

"No. He was just lying facedown in the water."

"Okay, will you be able to let us in at the gate in about five minutes?"

"Yes."

"Promise me that you'll stay where you are and not open the door for anyone but me. I'm on my way." He got off the phone as quickly as he could.

Jet Baxter shot to death out by the pond? What the hell?

He pulled out the card Federal Agent Mike Taylor had left him. If the FBI were watching the house like they'd led Flint to believe... He quickly called the number and waited. The moment Taylor answered he told him who he was and what had happened according to

Mrs. Baxter. All the time, he was wondering if they knew more about this than he did.

But if anything, the agent sounded surprised. Maybe they weren't watching the Baxter house as closely as the agent had indicated they were.

"Handle it like you would any shooting," Taylor told him, sounding upset.

The moment he hung up, he told the dispatcher to radio two of his deputies to meet him at the gate into the Baxter property. Then he called his undersheriff, Mark Ramirez.

DREY STOOD IN her bedroom, hugging herself for a long moment after she hung up from talking to the sheriff. She hadn't even considered that the shooter might still be outside and that she might be in danger. She'd been so shocked to hear the gunshot and look out in time to see Jet wounded and being hit by another shot before he fell into the pond, that she hadn't even thought she might be in danger herself.

She wanted desperately to go back out on the balcony. He was dead, wasn't he? What if he was still alive? What if— She told herself she had to do what the sheriff had told her. Whoever shot Jet could still be out there. Or worse, could be trying to break into the house right now.

Nervously, she glanced toward the balcony. Look how easily Hawk had been able to get to her. The way Ethan had designed the house, the balconies were like stairs that at least one man had been able to scale.

Realizing that she was still wearing silk pj's, she

hurriedly dressed, all the time listening for the sound of sirens. Who had killed Jet? What had he been doing on the property? She hadn't seen his vehicle. He didn't know the new pass code at the gate. So what had he been doing here? Her mind whirled as she remembered that someone had switched the aspirin in her medicine cabinet.

She'd been so sure that Jet had drugged her. But what if it hadn't been him? What if—

She couldn't bear the thought that Ethan was anywhere but Mexico City—just as he had told Jet. But then Jet could have been lying about even talking to Ethan. She certainly wouldn't have put it past him.

Either way, the FBI was wrong. Ethan wasn't hiding out here. If he was in the house, wouldn't she know it? She'd searched the entire place.

Pacing, she couldn't sit still. Where was the sheriff? *Shouldn't he be here by now?* It felt as if the horror of it was just starting to sink in. Jet. Shot. Dead? If so he'd been killed right outside her window. Who had shot him in cold blood like that? Was the killer still around? Was he in the house?

When the intercom buzzed, she jumped and rushed to it to allow the sheriff's department to enter. She waited until Flint was at the front door before she ran down the stairs. She threw open the door. He quickly stepped in. She'd known Hawk's brother her whole life. He was like family.

"Where is the body?" Flint asked, not family right now. The county sheriff doing his job.

"In the pond. I heard a gunshot. It woke me up.

Then I heard a second one and looked out…" She shuddered and the words poured out of her. "That's when I saw Jet. I could tell something was wrong. He was staggering down the dock, holding both hands over his stomach. I could see his blue shirt was dark with what looked like blood. Then there was another shot. He jerked and fell face-first into the water at the edge of the dock. That's when I called you."

"Okay, I want you to stay right here, all right?" She nodded. "Have you seen or heard anyone else around the house since you called?"

"No. Nothing until you came to the gate."

"I'll be back. Meanwhile, Deputy Harper is going to stay with you," the sheriff said. "Where's the kitchen?"

"Up two floors."

"Maybe you could make some coffee for the two of you?"

She knew the sheriff was suggesting busywork to keep her mind off what was happening outside. But she was thankful for it.

"One more thing," Flint said. "Do you own a gun?"

Drey started at the question. "A .45 handgun. It was my father's."

"Do you have it here in the house?" he asked.

She felt her stomach turn. "It's upstairs." She'd seen it in a drawer where whoever had moved her belongings from her apartment had put it. "Do you want to see it?"

Flint shook his head. "Not now." He turned and, opening the door, let the deputy in. She nodded at

Harp since she'd also known him since she was a girl growing up here. It was one of the joys of living in a small town.

As the sheriff left, she glanced toward the pond, but she hadn't been able to see anything but another deputy headed toward the dock.

"Did I hear Flint say something about coffee?" Harp asked.

"I have some sweet rolls, too," she said, her mind on Flint's question about her gun. He couldn't think that she had anything to do with Jet's being shot, could he? She reminded herself that as sheriff, these were the kinds of questions he had to ask everyone involved. But she wasn't involved. She'd been in her bedroom when Jet was shot.

She led Harp up the stairs, tuning him out as he commented on the house with each level they passed. Fear had her heart pounding again. In the kitchen, she put the coffee on, pulled out the sweet rolls along with plates and silverware. She couldn't help thinking about how she'd suspected Jet of drugging her. How else could she explain the thumb in the disposal, the mouse in her sparkling water and the feeling that she was losing her mind? But now someone had killed him here on the property? Nothing made any sense.

"I need to get something from my bedroom," she said to Harp. He looked wary. "It's just right upstairs. I won't be a minute. Help yourself to coffee and rolls." She left before he could argue since she knew the sheriff had probably told him not to let her out of his sight.

In her bedroom, she headed straight for the walk-in

closet. She began to open drawers, trying to remember where she'd seen her gun. She'd thought it had been right on top, in the first drawer. She checked all of the bureau drawers before she frantically searched the rest of the closet.

A shiver sprinted up her spine. She shuddered, fear making her scalp tighten.

Her gun was gone.

CHAPTER SIXTEEN

FLINT STOOD ON the dock looking down into the dark water for a long moment before he headed for the house. Harper let him in and escorted him toward the kitchen and dining room level. The house was everything he'd heard it was. Was Ethan Baxter hiding somewhere inside it?

Or was the FBI wrong and Baxter was thousands of miles away from here, sitting in a bar drinking a rum and cola and laughing his ass off?

His skin crawling as he climbed each level of the house, Flint had a bad feeling that Baxter was much closer to home. Which meant Hawk was right. Drey was in trouble.

She was standing at the kitchen counter holding a steaming mug of coffee in her hands as if needing the warmth. She looked even paler than she had earlier.

"Mind if I have a cup of that?" Flint asked as he joined her. He watched her hands trembling as she poured him a mug full.

"There are sweet rolls," she said, her voice breaking. "Jet?" she asked as if unable to hold back. "Is he dead?"

Flint glanced toward his deputy, who had just

picked up what he knew must be at least his third sweet roll. "Harp, would you go help outside?"

The deputy looked from him to Drey and back again. He then considered the sweet roll in his hand. He'd taken only one large bite out of it.

"You can take that with you."

Harp nodded quickly and left. Flint waited until he heard the deputy exit the house before he turned to Drey. "We didn't find a body."

All the color drained from her face, making her look as if she might faint. "What?"

"I need you to tell me again what you saw."

She was shaking her head, her brown eyes wide and filled with terror. "His body had to be there. He was shot. He was holding his stomach. The blood. I saw him get shot again. He fell into the water. He wasn't moving. He…" She looked up, tears welling.

"Drey?" She was visibly trembling. "I think you'd better sit down."

She didn't argue as he helped her to a chair at the huge table. She hugged her coffee mug to her.

"Is it possible he wasn't so badly wounded that he could have gotten out of the water?" he asked as he took a chair facing her.

She shook her head. "No." But then she seemed to change her mind. "I don't know. I suppose…" She met his gaze. "Flint, I saw him get shot. I'd heard two shots before that. He was bleeding, holding his stomach…"

"Drey, there was no blood on the dock. If he'd been bleeding… If he'd been shot what you believe to be a third time, there should have been blood. Lots of blood on the dock."

She stared at him, wide-eyed. "What are you saying?"

"There is no sign of a murder on the dock or anywhere around it. Jet Baxter has a red sports car registered to him. Is that what he was driving the last time you saw him?"

She nodded.

"It doesn't appear to be on the property, but we're still looking. Do you have any reason to believe he was here this morning? Did you let him in the gate?"

"No, I changed the code. He wouldn't…" She faltered. "He wouldn't know how to get in." She put down her coffee mug and covered her face for a moment. "I don't understand. I saw him." When she looked up at him again, tears welled in her eyes. She hurriedly wiped at them.

Flint's cell phone rang. He checked it, glad to see it was the call he'd been expecting. "Yes?" he said into the phone. "I see." His gaze returned to Drey as he hung up. "That was Undersheriff Mark Ramirez. I sent him into town to check the hotel where Jet has been staying. He talked to Jet. He's fine, Drey. He swears he wasn't anywhere near your property this morning. In fact, there was a woman with him who confirmed that he hadn't been anywhere since last night."

She looked shell-shocked. "He's lying. Whoever is with him…" She suddenly buried her face in her hands again. "I saw it. I didn't dream it. He was shot. He fell into the pond…"

"Drey, I don't like you being here alone," Flint said. "Maybe you could stay with Lillie for a while until your husband returns."

DREY COULDN'T BELIEVE THIS. She wasn't going crazy. She'd seen it. She'd heard the gunshots. She hadn't imagined or dreamed any of it.

She wiped her face. She'd felt so much better this morning. Her head had been clear. She'd been wide-awake. What was going on?

"Jet has been lying since the day he showed up here. I don't know how he did it this morning. But I know what I saw." She pushed back her chair but didn't rise. "I'm not going anywhere." Was that what Jet wanted? To get her out of the house?

"I know Lillie would love to have you stay there," Flint was saying.

She managed a smile. "I know I'm welcome there, but this is my home now. I'm sorry that I involved you in this."

"Drey—"

"I don't know what Jet is up to, but I'm going to find out."

That didn't make the sheriff look any happier.

"Is there anyone I can call for you? Maybe your local doctor. He could prescribe something if you aren't sleeping well or—"

She let out a bitter laugh. "All I have done is sleep." Flint thought she was losing her mind. But maybe that was Jet's plan. The drugging. The thumb. The mouse in the water bottle. And now making her think that she'd witnessed a murder.

"I thought you might want to talk to someone."

"I'm going to be fine," she told him as she got to her feet, although a little unsteadily. "I just hate that I got you out here this morning for nothing."

He rose slowly. She could tell he didn't like leaving her alone here. But she wasn't alone, right? Ethan was somewhere hidden in this house. Or in Mexico City. And there was the FBI out there somewhere. But if that was the case, wouldn't they have seen what she saw at the pond?

"Before you go," she said, realizing there was something she needed to know. "Hawk mentioned that Ethan is being investigated by the FBI. If that's true, wouldn't Ethan know it? Wouldn't he have told me?"

The sheriff looked at the floor for a moment. "As a matter of course, law enforcement agencies don't notify you when you are being investigated for criminal activity."

Her stomach dropped. Criminal activity? "So it's true? What happens now?"

Flint shook his head. "The feds may not act for months while they're getting evidence together to make an arrest. Or they may not be able to get enough evidence and drop it."

She shook her head. "I'm just supposed to wait to see what happens, then."

"I know it doesn't seem...fair. But they don't inform you of what's going on or they risk the possibility that the suspect will attempt to interfere with witnesses or other evidence. Often the person under investigation, though, either suspects or someone tells him."

"You think Ethan knows, and that's why he's not here right now."

Flint didn't answer. "You might want to hire a criminal defense lawyer."

"*Me?* But they're not investigating me." She felt her eyes widen. "You mean because Ethan and I are now married?"

He nodded. "I'm sorry, Drey."

"How long would an investigation like this have been going on?" she asked, fear making her voice tight.

"I don't know. I suspect for some time now." He met her gaze again.

"That doesn't mean that Ethan knew about it, right?"

"Right." It didn't mean that Ethan had known about it when they'd met eight months ago.

"Drey—"

"I'm fine," she said and tried to give him a reassuring smile. Ethan had known he was being investigated. But for how long? Maybe he really had gone to Mexico City on business. Or maybe he'd made a run for it and had left her holding the bag—just as Hawk had suspected.

Or maybe the FBI was right and Ethan was hiding somewhere in this house.

She picked up her mug and took a sip of coffee. It instantly curdled in her stomach.

What was she going to do now? She had no idea.

AFTER THE SHERIFF LEFT, Drey went back to her bed-room. She tore the closet apart looking for the gun and then searched the entire bedroom, including Ethan's walk-in closet and bathroom.

The gun wasn't there. But it had been. Which meant Jet must have taken it. Or Ethan. Or whoever had fired those shots this morning. Whoever had wanted her to think she was losing her mind. What was more, they now had the sheriff thinking the same thing.

For a moment she stood in the middle of the master suite, breathing hard. She knew what she'd heard, what she'd seen. She wasn't sure how Jet had done it, but she wasn't losing her mind. She stood trembling from fear, weak from tearing the bedroom apart looking for the gun. Now what?

It kept coming back to Ethan. She couldn't bear the thought that he really was hiding in this house in some secret space—like the one that held the bar in their bedroom. That was so ridiculous. She and Jet had searched it. Right. Jet. He'd searched his half of each level. He'd lied about so much. Why would she trust him to not have lied about that?

Drey began the search, taking each floor until she reached the staff quarters and the parking garage. No Ethan. But she'd found an extensive wine cellar and storage areas she hadn't known about on the garage level—and made a few discoveries that surprised her. She'd found all their unopened wedding gifts stacked in one of the areas. When, she wondered, though, had Ethan planned to open them? Or did he ever?

Not that she felt like opening them. Right now, her

marriage felt like a sham. Until she heard from him…
If she ever did.

As she searched, it felt as if the house was watching her digging for its secrets and was silently amused that she hadn't found them. If anything, she hated the house more. Hated the massive cold, sterile rooms as well as the echo of her footfalls. But she hadn't found any secret passages or rooms. That didn't mean that they didn't exist, though, she told herself. Still, she couldn't imagine a man like Ethan holed up somewhere in a secret room in this house for any length of time.

Ultimately, as her search concluded, she'd found no sign of Ethan.

But like the gun, he'd been here.

Tired and sweaty, she made her way back up the stairs and had just reached the kitchen when the intercom at the gate buzzed, making her jump. She tried to settle her racing pulse as she stepped to the control panel on the wall, telling herself it had better not be Jet.

"Yes?" she asked into the intercom.

"Delivery, madam."

Madam? "Can you just leave it in the large container next to the mailbox?"

"No can do. Need a signature on this one."

She stepped to the balcony, leaning out for a better view of the road. Catching sight of a familiar delivery vehicle, she went back to the intercom. "Come on up."

After opening the gate, Drey hurried downstairs to the front door, reaching it only moments before the deliveryman roared up. She hugged herself as she watched the driver leap out with a clipboard and package about a foot square and a good eight inches deep.

All his attention was on the house as he held out the clipboard and attached pen for her to sign. "This is some house."

"My husband designed it." She signed.

"Huh." He said as he handed her the package.

The weight surprised her. For its size, the box was quite heavy. She'd expected it to be addressed to Ethan, but she saw that it was to Dierdre Baxter. Her first package in her married name. She couldn't read the return address. It appeared to be smudged. Something from Ethan?

She wanted to ask the driver if he knew where the package had originated because there was no return address, but he'd already bounded back into his truck and was quickly gone.

Drey watched him tear down the road. The sun was low in the sky. She felt as if she'd lost another day. Soon the sun would dip behind the mountains to the west, the air would cool and she would be facing another night alone here.

For a moment she almost weakened and called Lillie to ask if she could stay there. Sheer stubbornness wouldn't let her do that. Jet was trying to either make her believe she was crazy—or run her out of this house. She told herself that Ethan would be back in a few days. She would tell him about the FBI investigation—if he didn't already know. He would reassure her that it was nothing.

She shivered, though, as she took the box inside

the house. It was heavy and she was tired enough that she put it into the elevator. For a moment, she considered riding up. After the day she'd had, the thought of climbing all the stairs again felt almost overwhelming.

But she couldn't chance that the electricity might go off again and this time the backup generator for it might not work. She'd be trapped in that small space for who knew how long. She couldn't imagine anything worse. No one would know. It could be days, even longer, before someone found her.

She hit the kitchen level button. The elevator closed and began to climb. She did the same thing, reaching the kitchen level just moments before the elevator. As the door opened, she pulled out the box and carried it over to the table. She left it to make herself a cup of tea. She hadn't eaten all day. No wonder she felt so tired. Spotting a leftover sweet roll, she devoured it even before the water had boiled for her tea.

Drey felt a little better. When the teakettle whistled, she made her tea and then took a knife from the block by the sink and walked back to the table and her package.

It took a few minutes to cut through all the tape, all the time making her even more curious what someone had sent her. Another wedding gift? She was grateful for a diversion from her thoughts for the moment.

Could it be from Ethan? She realized how much she needed to hear from him and be reassured. *Let him really be in Mexico City on business*. But even as she thought it and wished he really would be coming back so she didn't have to face all this alone, she feared it wasn't going to happen.

Jet knew his brother was gone. Was that why he'd been trying to get her out of this house? Why else would he want her to think she was losing her mind? But what was in the house that he wanted that badly?

She cut the tape on the package, taking her time. She couldn't help but think about all their wedding gifts downstairs in the storage area. She had wondered what had happened to them. It bothered her that she had no interest in opening any of the packages. Worse, she couldn't shake the feeling that they would never be opened.

Never had she felt so down. She'd been so sure that Jet had been drugging her. How else could she explain the way she'd been feeling? But what if there was more going on with her? Normally she woke up each morning delighted to see the sun and ready to face the day. But that was back when she had a job to go to, something to do that brought joy to her life. Ethan didn't want her to work. But if he was going to be gone all the time…

With the tape cut, she put the knife aside, peeled back the two flaps and stepped back with a gasp. *What in the world?*

The box was filled with hundred-dollar bills. Stacks of bound hundreds. Dozens of them. She stared at the bills in horror. Where had it come from? Who had sent it? Ethan? Some business associate? She looked on the top for a note, but saw nothing but money.

She was afraid to touch it, feeling as if even opening the box had somehow incriminated her. Whoever had mailed it had sent it to her personally. It had to be Ethan. Why would he send this much money by a deliveryman?

Because he's being investigated and he's trying to hide this money.

Or… She had another thought, this one even more disturbing. Or it was intended to incriminate her, to draw her into whatever mess Ethan was in, to make it look as if she was involved and had been since the beginning.

She pushed the box away, wondering what to do with it. Hide the money? Burn it? Burn at least the box that it came in? Whatever this was about, she didn't want anything to do with it. What kind of business was her husband involved in? Worse, was this an attempt to make it look as if she was a part of it?

CHAPTER SEVENTEEN

BLESSEDLY HAWK HAD spent the day stringing barbed wire so he didn't hear about all the sheriff's patrol cars that had been called to Mountain Crest until this evening when he returned home. He hurried inside and called his brother.

"What's going on?" he demanded the moment Flint answered.

"Dinner."

"I heard you and several deputies were at Drey's today." He could hear his brother chewing. "I'm sorry if I interrupted your dinner. Tell Maggie hello. But I need to know. Has something happened?"

"Drey's okay. Let me finish dinner and I'll stop over," his brother said and disconnected.

Mind racing, Hawk walked the floor, waiting for Flint to arrive. He desperately wanted to call Drey and ask her, but common sense told him to wait until he talked to his brother. He and Drey hadn't left things well. She'd pleaded with him to leave her alone.

He knew he should. She was married. Then again, it wasn't much of a marriage since, as far as he knew, it hadn't even been consummated. Not that that was the point. Unless he had something more to offer Drey than concern...

With relief, he heard his brother drive up. He raked a hand through his hair and waited. "Well?" he said the moment Flint walked through the door.

"Yes, I would love a beer, since you're offering," his brother said and pulled up a stool at the breakfast bar.

Hawk went to the refrigerator, opened it and pulled out a bottle of beer. "Can you twist off the top? Or would you like me to?" he said as he handed it to his brother.

The sheriff didn't seem to appreciate his sarcasm. Hawk took a bottle of beer for himself, irritably twisted off the cap and threw it into the sink. "Are you going to tell me?" he demanded without taking a drink.

"It was a false alarm," Flint said and took a long swallow of his beer.

"A false alarm. What does that mean?"

His brother put down his bottle carefully before meeting his gaze. "Look, let me say I'm worried about Drey, too. Okay? She called this morning to report that she'd seen Jet Baxter killed on the pond dock outside her balcony window. She'd heard three shots. She saw him take the last one and fall into the pond."

Hawk let out a surprised curse. "Was he dead?"

"When we got there we couldn't find a body or any sign of a murder."

He stared at his brother. "What are you saying? That she made it up? Imagined the whole thing?"

"We contacted Jet at his hotel. He had come straight

from bed—and not alone. There was a woman with him. He swore that he hadn't left his room all morning and the woman backed up his story. The hotel valet said Jet's car was right where it had been last night and hadn't been moved."

Hawk came around the end of the breakfast bar, pulled out a stool and sat. "I don't understand."

"Neither do I," Flint said. "Seems there are two options. Jet somehow staged it, used the woman in his bed as an alibi, had someone take him to the Baxter property so he didn't have to use his own car. Seems pretty elaborate and to what end?"

"And the second option?" Hawk asked, knowing he wasn't going to like it.

"That Drey imagined the whole thing."

Hawk scoffed. "You know her. She isn't one to take flights of fancy." Even as he said it, he remembered what she'd been like the night he'd broken the window to get to her.

"You said you thought she was out of it the night you saw her." Flint toyed with the label on his beer bottle for a moment. "Jet told us that it isn't the first time she's…imagined something that never happened. He blames whatever prescription drug she's taking."

"Drugs? Drey?" He couldn't believe this. "There is no way. Not Drey."

His brother said nothing for a moment as he took another drink of his beer. "He said he saw her take them but didn't get a look at the prescription bottle. But he said they really seemed to knock her out and leave her…confused when she was awake. He said that they apparently gave her nightmares."

Hawk thought of the woman he'd found in that huge master bedroom the other night. She'd been screaming, terrified, looking around the room as if she expected to find… That was just it, he had no idea. He'd thought it was just a bad dream—like she'd said. But he had to admit that night she was nothing like the Drey he'd known and loved.

"If he's telling the truth, which I doubt, then she's in trouble and needs help."

"Not from you, Hawk." Flint finished his beer and rose to leave. "She's not your responsibility anymore. You need to back off, especially with the feds watching her."

"Wait a minute. If the feds are really watching the house, then they would have seen Jet—"

"Give me some credit. Don't you think I thought of that? I called the agent in charge right away hoping I could verify what Drey thought she'd seen."

"And?"

"The agent watching the house had been called away on a possible lead on Ethan Baxter's whereabouts."

"*A possible lead?* Let me guess. This lead, was it an anonymous call? It was, wasn't it? How perfect."

Flint shook his head. "Sometimes, my brother, if it looks like a duck, quacks like a duck, it is just a duck. Isn't the simpler explanation that Drey is on drugs and imagined the whole thing?"

"Or someone is setting her up." And now she was in that house alone.

"I can only guess what you're thinking of doing right now," the sheriff said as he headed for the door. "Don't do it. If she wanted your help, she would ask for it."

Not likely, he thought, as his brother left. So what was he going to do? He couldn't just stand back and let... Hell, let what happen? Drey self-destruct? Even if he believed for a moment that Drey was on drugs...

Hawk swore, hating that Flint was right. He couldn't go storming up to that house again. It wasn't the feds he was worried about. It was Drey. She'd begged him to leave her alone. But how could he do that? He loved her, and to hell with the past, he was going to get her back.

That thought was an ice-filled bucket of water poured over his head.

IT WAS STILL dark out when Drey woke, disoriented. Her mouth felt dry as ash. She tried to swallow. Since the sparkling-water dream, she'd gone to water from the tap.

Now, barely opening her eyes, she reached for her glass and started to take a sip. Through her veiled gaze, she saw the container of prescription pills and automatically reached for it, suddenly aching for that wonderful calm that she knew would be coming once she'd downed them.

Still half-asleep, she popped the cap and shook two pills into her hand. But as she started to lift them to her mouth and chase them down with the water, she froze.

Breath coming fast now, she carefully put the glass on the nightstand and reached over and snapped on the lamp. The sudden bright glare instead of the moonlight coming through the windows made her blink.

She stared down at the pills in her hand. So familiar. The memory of their effect even more familiar and enticing. How easy it would be to lift them to her lips again. To swallow them with the rest of her water. To lie back and wait for the wonderful oblivion.

Her chest ached with a need so strong… Swinging her legs over the side of the bed, she got up and hurried to the bathroom. She felt confused, scared and, worse, tempted.

She dropped the two pills into the toilet, flushed and watched them disappear. But there were still more back by her bed. A container full of them. It would have been so easy to take them to make herself feel better.

Turning, she walked slowly back to the bedroom, picked up her phone and hesitated as she looked at the clock. Three twenty in the morning. She couldn't call Lillie and wake up not only her and Trask, but also the baby. There was no one she could call. Not with this.

A whimper escaped her lips as she realized there was only one person. When Hawk answered, she said, "You told me that if I ever needed—"

He'd sounded as if he'd been sound asleep when he answered, but now was wide-awake. "What is it, Drey?"

She almost hung up. She really was losing her

mind. Worse, she was in serious trouble. And even if Hawk took satisfaction in this, she needed his help.

"I'm scared. I need help."

"I'll be right there," he said.

"You'll need the code for the gate." She rattled it off before he disconnected.

A short time later she let him in the front door. She'd turned on all the lights as she'd gone from the master suite down the levels to wait for him.

As she did, she thought she saw a dark figure move at the edge of the pines. But when she looked again, it was gone as if she'd only imagined it.

THE MOMENT HAWK saw her looking disheveled and scared, he drew Drey to him, holding her tightly. She hadn't bothered to dress after her call to him. She wore a robe over what appeared to be pajamas. She was sobbing hysterically and shaking like a leaf in a gale. He'd never seen her like this. He wanted to demand to know what was wrong, but he held his tongue, giving her time.

The fact that she'd called him asking for help told him that she was desperate. He'd been terrified and still was. What kind of trouble was she in? He was half-afraid of what she was going to tell him for fear Flint was right and he didn't know this Drey at all.

He didn't say anything until she quit sobbing and trembling. "Coffee?" he asked as she stepped from his arms.

She nodded and he followed her up to the kitchen level. He watched her put on a pot of coffee, seeing how nervous she was. Was she regretting calling him? It wasn't until she'd poured them both a cup that she seemed to have gained the control he'd always known she possessed.

Drey wasn't the kind of woman who was easily rattled. She was the one who didn't fall apart in a crisis. Look how well she had taken everything that had happened to them. She'd gone on to Spain and finished her degree as if putting what he'd never been able to get over behind her without a second thought.

Or at least that's what he'd believed she'd done. He'd been shocked when she'd told him how hard she'd taken the miscarriage. He'd always thought that she'd been happy about it. He wanted to kick himself for thinking the worst of her.

As he studied her now, he wondered how different things might have been if he'd known that like him, she hadn't gotten over them easily, had suffered over what had happened to them...

"Talk to me," he said as she handed him his coffee cup and the two of them took seats at the table. "I know you wouldn't have called me and asked for my help in the middle of the night if something wasn't horribly wrong. I've known you all my life." *And a good portion of it intimately.* But he'd never seen her in such a state as when she'd opened the door. "Drey, what's going on?"

She looked up, her lower lip trembling, but couldn't seem to speak. The sight of her like this made his heart race. What kind of trouble was she in?

"You're scared," he said. "I can see that. The thing

is, you don't scare easily. You're strong. Let me help you."

She shook her head and took a breath that came out on a sob, but she didn't break down again. "I'm either going crazy or someone wants me to think I am. I woke up and found these on my bedside table," she said as she reached into the pocket of her robe and pulled out a prescription drug container.

Oh shit, he thought as she handed it to him. Was it possible Jet was telling the truth?

He glanced at the label before his gaze shot back up to her. "Have you been taking these?"

"No. At least not for years."

Hawk knew that couldn't be true because there was a recent date on the label along with her name. "Drey, these are a powerful antianxiety medication. Why would you have ever been taking them?"

Her fingers trembled as she hugged the hot cup of coffee to her. She seemed to be getting up her courage. "After I lost the baby," she looked away as if ashamed. "I couldn't eat or sleep. I went to a doctor who prescribed them. Once I started taking them, I..."

He couldn't believe this. "You got hooked. Was this in Spain?"

"Right before. I lost the baby two weeks before I left for Spain and school."

Hawk rubbed a hand over his face. When he looked at her again it was with true concern. "But you got off them?"

She nodded quickly. "I went to a doctor in Spain but he refused to give them to me. A friend got me some, but I only took a few of them. I knew I had to stop. I did. Cold turkey. It was horrible."

"So where did these pills come from?"

Drey met his gaze. "That's just it, I have no idea. I swear I didn't buy them, but…"

"Your name is on them. It appears they were re-filled recently," he said. "Is it possible you just don't remember getting them? You said you've been under a lot of stress."

She shook her head adamantly. "I wouldn't have purchased them. I know how dangerous they are. I don't want to go back there, believe me."

"Drey, this drug has side effects—extreme tired-ness, problems with awareness and impaired thoughts and judgments. The other night I thought you were drunk, but now I'm wondering if you weren't on these pills."

"I think I've drugged me, but I swear, I didn't pur-posely take them."

"What about your husband? Did he know that you—"

"No, I never told Ethan. I never told anyone."

"*Someone* knew. If you didn't refill this prescrip-tion, then someone did under your name, left them beside your bed, knowing you were once addicted to them."

"Or I did it and don't remember." She began to cry again. "It would explain everything that's been hap-pening to me. The hallucinations…"

"When you found these next to your bed, did you take any of them?"

"No. But I started to. It was like muscle memory. I saw them, shook out two and almost swallowed them. But I didn't. I dumped the two down the toilet."

"But you didn't dump the rest of them," he said.

She nodded. "I wanted to take them so badly, to not feel… I was so scared that I called you."

The implication was clear. He was the last person she had wanted to call because he was one of the reasons she'd gotten addicted to them before—and still was. But also she'd said she didn't want to feel. He realized that what his sister had told him must be true. Drey wasn't just scared, she was so unhappy she'd almost taken drugs to relieve the pain.

"Is this all the drugs in the house?"

DREY HADN'T EVEN considered that. Had she been taking them without her even being consciously aware that she was back on the pills? "I don't know."

"Why don't we start there?" Hawk said, getting to his feet. "In the meantime…" He opened the container and dumped the pills into his palm.

She watched him count them, amazed that her body still wanted them and the release they offered. Right now, given everything that had been going on in her life, it would have been so easy to get back on them. She hugged herself at the thought and then finished her coffee.

"More than two are missing. Are you sure you haven't taken any of these?" he asked.

"I don't know. You're going to think I'm…" She met his gaze. "I think Jet was drugging me."

"He moved out, right?"

She nodded. "But right before you arrived, I thought I saw someone in the trees near the house. When I looked again… Hawk, I don't know what's real and what's not. I don't trust myself. But if I haven't been drugged, then how do I explain what has been happening to me."

"What *has* been happening?" he asked as he put the pills back into the container and pocketed it.

"Shouldn't we dump those down the drain?"

"They might be evidence at some point because I don't think you're crazy. I think someone is trying to manipulate you. You said strange things have been happening?"

She told him about the thumb in the disposal and the tiny dead mouse in her water bottle. "That's why I was screaming the night you climbed the balconies and broke my window to get to me. I swear there was a mouse in the bottle, but when the lights came back on…"

"So the night I broke in here, it wasn't a bad dream."

"I've been under a lot of strain but—"

"Drey, that's what I'm trying to tell you. I have no idea about the thumb. But I saw the bottle with the tiny mouse in the bottom of it." He nodded at her shocked expression. "It was down on the ground under the balconies, as if someone had tossed it down there from up here."

She hugged herself. "So I didn't imagine it. You saw it? It was real."

He nodded. "Probably as real as you seeing Jet dead in the pond. Let's see if he left you any other pills around."

HAWK HAD SEEN little of the house the night he'd climbed the balconies to get to the screaming Drey. Now he looked around and couldn't shake the feeling that they were being watched. Maybe it was all the glass. He felt as if he was in a fishbowl.

But the large windows that covered the entire front of the house were treated with something that made it impossible to see inside from outside. Inside, there was a great view of the mountains, but a person had to step out onto one of the balconies on either side of each level. From the balcony, he could see the valley without the tinted glass of all the windows.

"You think there are more pills hidden in places that I'm apt to find them so I'll be tempted to take them."

"I do, but I suspect there's a lot more going on in this house. Let's start at the top and work our way down." He followed her up to the master suite, stepped out onto the balcony closest to the pond and looked down. "This is where you saw Jet get shot?" He turned when she didn't answer to see her nod and hug herself.

"It was horrible," she said in a whisper. Her gaze rose to his. "Afterward, I had this terrible thought. I went into the closet where I'd seen my gun in one of the drawers after Ethan had had my personal items brought up here."

He took a wild guess. "The gun was gone."

She nodded and swallowed. "Why is this happening to me? Why would someone want me to think I'm going crazy?"

Hawk shook his head. "I don't know, Drey. But damned if we aren't going to find out." He stepped back inside and moved to the nightstand he knew was hers. She always slept on the right side of the bed.

"Drey, have you looked in this drawer?"

"Oh, the money."

He turned to look at her. "'Oh, the money'?" he asked in shock. "Drey, there must be thousands of dollars in that drawer."

She nodded. "It was delivered today. The package was addressed to me. I didn't know what to do with it."

"So you put it in your bedside table?"

She looked close to tears. "I thought about burning it or throwing it out. Hawk…"

"I know." He could see that all of this was taking its toll on her. Add in the pills… "It's going to be all right," he said, stepping to her. But he had no way of knowing if that was true. Someone had sent her thousands of dollars. To incriminate her? To make it appear she was involved in whatever her husband was being investigated for? Or had Ethan had it sent because he was planning to make a run for it and maybe take Drey with him?

Hawk didn't know what to do with the money either, so he simply closed the drawer. The damage was already done; she'd opened the box. "Let's see if there are more pills hidden around here." Right now, that was his biggest concern.

They searched the bedroom, found another container of pills in the back of a drawer. Some of them were missing.

He shook his head. "We're going to search this place from top to bottom. I can't leave you, knowing how afraid you are of finding more of them."

"I won't take them."

But they both knew that in the state she'd been in lately, she might. All his instincts told him that Drey was in trouble. But then she'd been in trouble all those years ago. He just didn't want to fail her again.

"I trust you, Drey. I don't trust whoever is determined to get you back on the drugs."

Hawk thought about the bottle of pills and Drey's confession. He hadn't believed that she'd miscarried their baby. He'd said he believed it, but in his heart, he hadn't. It was why he hadn't been able to forgive her.

But now, knowing about the pills, about how badly she'd suffered after the miscarriage…he felt like the heel he was. "I'm so sorry," he said, reaching for her hand. He'd thought she might pull away, but instead, she closed her eyes. Tears seeped out.

They covered the rest of the house but found no more pill containers.

In the kitchen again, Drey poured them both another cup of coffee. The sun had come up on another day. He had fence to string. By now Cyrus would be wondering what had happened to him. He was surprised his brother hadn't called.

"I don't like you staying here," he said.

"It's my home now. Jet is locked out. Ethan should be back soon."

He doubted Ethan would be coming back—if he'd even left the country, which the feds were sure he hadn't.

"Are you going to be all right now?" he asked Drey, hating to leave her alone especially in this house after what she'd told him. He hadn't been there for her all those years ago. He'd been struggling with his own loss, his own pain, his own anger. He didn't want to be that man anymore.

"I'll be fine." She still looked scared, but he got the feeling it wasn't of Jet or Ethan or even this house. It was the two of them being this close. So she felt it, too. They'd once been as close as any two people could be. They'd shared an intimacy that he hadn't known since. It was hard not to remember how good they'd been together when they were this near each other. It was why he'd kept her at arm's length for so long.

He looked down at the huge diamond on her ring finger as she nervously turned it. She covered it with her hand before looking into his eyes.

"I know," he said. "You're married."

She looked away. "I shouldn't have called you last night—"

"I told you to call me if you needed me. You needed me."

She nodded. "But I put you in a terrible position, I'm sorry."

He shook his head. "I'm a big boy. You just worry about yourself." He grimaced. "That came out wrong."

"Ethan would understand why I had to call you."

"Would he?" He could see that it was a lie. Ethan was the kind of man who would be jealous. "You know you can always call me."

She nodded, no doubt wondering if that was true. "Thank you for your help."

He started to turn when he spotted something they'd missed. "Drey, is that your purse?" He pointed to where the strap of her bag was looped over a chair back.

She glanced at it, then at him. "You think I have more pills in there?"

He said nothing. Didn't have to.

She stepped to her purse, picked it up and unceremoniously dumped the contents on the table. The bottle of pills fell out, rolled toward Hawk. She let out a cry, her eyes wide with a growing horror. "Oh, Hawk."

He caught the bottle of pills and read the label. Again they were in Drey's name. He checked to see how many were missing.

"No," she said, shaking her head. "I'm telling you—those weren't in my purse just yesterday when I had lunch with your sister. I know because when my credit card didn't work..." She looked up at him. "I swear to you I didn't take any of those."

"I believe you, all right? But that's not to say that someone didn't put these pills in your drinks or your food..." She stood hugging herself, looking more afraid than when he'd gotten here. "Are you sure you don't want me to stay? I'm assuming there are guest rooms."

"No. My husband could come home at any time."

"Right, your husband."

"Take the pills with you, please. If I find anymore, I'll flush them. I promise. I feel better now. Really."

"Drey, if you didn't refill the prescription..."

"I know what you're saying. If no one knew about my former addiction to these particular pills, then how could they have planted them on my nightstand, in my drawer and in my purse?"

He pocketed the third pill container. "*Someone* knew. You must have told someone or... Wait, didn't you say a friend in Spain got you more?"

"Yes, but I haven't seen Lena in years. She dropped out of college shortly after that. I have no idea what happened to her. Maybe it is just a coincidence that the pills are the same kind as the ones I was addicted to."

"Maybe." Hawk didn't believe that for a moment.

DREY CHANGED INTO jeans and a T-shirt before joining Hawk on the next level down. She felt stronger. Calling Hawk had been hard, but it had been the right thing to do. He'd taken the news about her former addiction well. It was such a relief having him here. Before they'd been lovers, they'd been friends. Their issues aside, she knew she could trust him.

And she'd been so afraid that she would weaken

and take the pills. If she'd been the one to refill the prescription—

That was what really terrified her. How could she not remember something like that unless she'd already been on the drugs?

She shook her head, telling herself she hadn't taken them since Spain. But that didn't explain how the containers had ended up on her nightstand and in her bathroom and purse. It wasn't just that, she realized. There'd been times over the past six months that she'd felt...out of it.

Ethan had always insisted she lie down for a while. He would make her a nice glass of warm milk. Often when she woke up, though, she felt...confused. Just thinking about it made her sick to her stomach. She refused to believe that Ethan had been drugging her, so who did that leave? Just her.

She shuddered as she remembered the last time she was under so much stress. She'd gotten hooked on these very pills.

Drey found Hawk in one of the conference rooms on the next floor. "Did you find any more pills?" she asked, worried. Jet might have hidden them throughout the house. If it was Jet behind this... That was what she wanted to believe, but Jet Baxter had no way of knowing about her addiction.

"No more pills," Hawk said, sounding distracted. He motioned for her to follow him out on the balcony. Once out there, he closed the door behind them and turned her so they weren't facing the house.

The day was bright and sunny. Just the thought of

spending another day in this house followed by another night terrified her. If Hawk was right, whoever
had left those drugs would make sure she got more.

"I think someone is watching you."

"The FBI." She couldn't understand why they were
standing out here and why he was acting so strangely.

"We need to disable the camera in one of the
rooms."

"Camera?" she said.

"I spotted it under the sconce on the wall in one of
the guest rooms," he said. "Don't say anything when
we go back in. Don't look for the cameras. Just act
natural and play along."

Cameras? She'd forgotten how to act natural, but
she nodded as they reentered the house. And play
along? He'd said someone was watching them. On
cameras, inside the house?

Once inside, he took her hand and led her to one of
the guest rooms. The moment they entered, he pulled
her to him as if he was going to kiss her. But instead
he swept her into his arms, spun her around, her feet
hitting the sconce. It shattered.

As he put her down, she couldn't help feeling disoriented. He walked over to the sconce and then nodded. "The camera's busted," he whispered. "They
shouldn't be able to see us."

For a moment she thought he would kiss her. Or really carry her over to the bed. The thought made her
pulse leap. Being here in this bedroom with him…

But Hawk had other things on his mind. He moved

to the guest room closet. "I noticed that the guest room next door is smaller than this one."

She watched him step into the closet. She followed, intrigued and yet a little disappointed. For a few moments there, she had forgotten she was married. Being with Hawk felt so natural... And Ethan... She had no idea where he was or if he was ever coming back.

All the times she'd looked through this house she hadn't noticed the discrepancy in the room size. But Hawk had. He quickly moved to the back of the closet. Removing a stack of down comforters, pillows and sheets from the shelves at the end, he let out a triumphant sound and stepped back as a door opened.

Drey stared in shock. Past the door, several rows of monitors glowed in the small room. "Is that—"

"Surveillance equipment. I suspect you've been watched from the moment you walked into this house."

CHAPTER EIGHTEEN

DREY STARED AT the monitors. There were at least a dozen of them, all screening various rooms in the house, as well as around the place. "I knew someone was watching. I could feel it. This house, it's been watching me the whole time," she said with a curse.

"Not just the house," Hawk said. "But whoever has been monitoring this system from some remote location." He sat down at one of the monitoring stations. "If I'm right, there should be video of the pond. Do you know how to work any of this?"

She shook her head as she saw a clear view of the pond and the forest beyond it on one of the camera screens. "So if I really did see Jet—"

"The camera would have captured it." Hawk got up. "We need to get someone who knows how to work all the electronics. My brother Cyrus has a knack for this sort of thing. He set up the surveillance at the ranch when we had someone stealing our hay." He looked at her. "Are you all right?"

Drey felt as if she would never be all right again. "You think Ethan has been spying on me."

Hawk didn't need to deny it. She could see the answer in his face. It was Ethan's house, so of course he knew about the cameras and the surveillance equipment. If Hawk was right and Ethan hadn't left, then he'd been watching her this whole time?

The thought gave her the creeps. She shuddered and hugged herself, feeling anger make her eyes burn with tears. Why would he do such a thing? She felt a chill race up her spine as she thought of how jealous he'd been of Hawk. He'd made her wish she'd never told him about her first and only love.

Was it possible Ethan had set up his whole disappearing act to see if she would turn to Hawk? The thought turned her blood to ice because that's exactly what she had done. When she was in trouble, Hawk had shown up and now...

If Hawk was right, she didn't think she could ever forgive Ethan.

"It could be anyone. Anyone with a smartphone or a computer," he said.

"Ethan doesn't have his phone." That gave her only a little comfort.

Hawk said nothing.

"It's not Ethan," she said with more conviction than she felt. "It's got to be Jet. But why watch me? Unless..." She met Hawk's gaze. "He really is trying to drive me crazy, isn't he?"

"Someone is," Hawk agreed as he stepped to her to put an arm around her shoulders and draw her to him. She felt stiff in his arms as she stared at the monitors, wondering if someone was watching them at this moment. Ethan? Jet?

"Come on, it's going to be daylight soon," Hawk

said. "We'll get Cyrus to take a look at these. Hopefully we can find out what's going on."

GIGI GOT THE call from the fire department just before daylight. She was half-groggy when she answered the phone, but instantly came awake when she heard the word *fire*. "My restaurant?"

"One of the apartments upstairs, but I'm afraid you're going to have both smoke and water damage," the officer calling on behalf of the fire chief told her.

"I'll be right there." She started to get up, but his next words stopped her.

"We're not letting anyone back into the building at this time. We're just notifying property owners right now whose space has been affected."

Gigi threw herself back onto the bed. "Thank you for letting me know. When is the soonest I can see the damage?"

"Not until after the investigation and we're sure the structure is safe to enter."

She groaned inwardly as she disconnected. Smoke and water damage. Depending on how bad it was, it could take weeks, if not months, to get reopened.

Unable to sleep any longer, she got dressed and made the calls to her employees. "I'll let you know as soon as I know how bad it is and what it will take before we can reopen." She heard it in their voices. They would have to look for other jobs if the remodel took months. She couldn't even think about her head chef. She'd had to pay him a bonus just to get him to come to work for her.

Her losses just kept mounting up. She sat for a moment, wishing she could call her parents. Her mother would be sympathetic. Her father would be practical. Both would offer money she would turn down. From the beginning she'd wanted to do this on her own. But she'd never been more on her own than she was right now.

She started to call AJ but it was an hour earlier in Montana. Assuming her friend had worked last night, she would still be in bed asleep. Gigi held the phone in her hand, debating what to do next. It was too early to call her insurance company. She could drive downtown and see what she could from the street. Or wait until the fire department called back, but that might not be for several days.

Looking down at her phone, Gigi knew even before she touched the screen what she was going to do. It only took a minute to book a flight to Montana. Getting to Gilt Edge wasn't easy, though. She would have to fly into Billings, the largest city in the state, rent a car and drive northwest.

She called up a map, surprised to see how few roads there were in a state the size of Montana. "Great." Was she really going to do this? Why not? Even after the fire department got back to her, her insurance company would have to estimate the damage. She could leave a key to the restaurant with a friend. She'd be back before any work could begin on the interior.

Booking a rental car, she told herself she was going to Montana but that didn't mean she had any intentions of meeting her birth mother.

WAITING FOR CYRUS, Hawk thought about calling his brother Flint. Wasn't it time to bring the sheriff in? But what did they really know? It wasn't illegal to spy on your own house—or the wife in it. Nor did they have proof yet that Jet had done anything. Hawk was just hoping Cyrus would be able to help them find the evidence they needed.

The gate buzzer made him jump when it went off. He and Drey had been in the kitchen, both of them lost in their own thoughts. She still seemed out of it and he suspected she'd ingested some of the missing pills from the container unknowingly. Who knew what in this house might have been doctored since Jet had been staying here—and possibly Ethan had been here, as well.

Drey opened the gate for Cyrus. As Hawk watched her, he had to fight a growing need in him to comfort her. But he knew that they were both vulnerable right now, especially Drey. Earlier in the guest bedroom, he couldn't help remembering their lovemaking. They were good together, always had been. Had she remembered how they'd been together?

As she turned toward him, he saw her toying with her wedding ring. It appeared to be too tight.

"I'll run down and let Cyrus in," he said, not wanting to read too much into the gesture. Every time he'd mentioned Ethan, she'd taken up for her husband. Which made him respect her even more. He was just going to hate seeing her heart broken, though, when this was over. All his instincts told him there could be no happy ending for Drey and Ethan Baxter.

Then again, maybe that was just wishful thinking on his part. He felt guilty for the thought as he trotted down the stairs to the front door. He wanted Drey to be happy. Even with someone else. Just not Ethan Baxter, he told himself.

"Your call sounded urgent," Cyrus said.

"When you see what we found, you'll see why." He let his brother up through the house. Cyrus lagged behind, rubbernecking as he took it all in.

"This place is wild. Not to my liking, but still pretty impressive. How does Drey like it?"

Hawk shot him an are-you-kidding look as they neared the kitchen where Drey was waiting on them.

"What're you doing here anyway?" Cyrus whispered as they entered the huge commercial kitchen and massive dining room.

"Long story," Hawk whispered over his shoulder before turning to Drey. She looked nervous and still scared. He could understand why. She had two Cahill men in Ethan's house. Hawk had to wonder what would happen if the man suddenly returned. But at the same time, he didn't believe any of them would be seeing Ethan Baxter again. He'd put his money on Ethan having skipped the country with the FBI hot on his trail. A man like that would have funds stashed in banks all over the world. No, they'd seen the last of Ethan Baxter.

After a quick greeting, they led Cyrus down a floor to the guest bedroom with the secret entry into the surveillance room. His brother let out an oath and, rubbing his hands, stepped in as if entering a toy shop.

"This is impressive," Cyrus said, taking in all the gadgets.

"I'm assuming that some of the video might be saved for a few days or at least twenty-four hours?" Hawk asked.

"Possibly. What are you looking for?"

"The video from yesterday morning about what time? From the camera on the pond and dock."

"Ten thirty in the morning," Drey said.

Cyrus sat down at the computer in the room and typed on the keyboard for a few minutes before looking up at the computer screen. "That video screen was turned off for some reason that day."

"We know the reason," Hawk said. "That proves that someone has been remotely accessing this equipment, just as I suspected," Hawk said. "Can you call up the kitchen? What day was the disposal incident?" he asked Drey.

"That would have been my first day here." She had to think for a moment before she gave him the date of the day after her wedding.

"Can you call up the kitchen video? Time?"

"About eleven in the morning," she said and moved closer to the screen to watch.

It took a few minutes for Cyrus to find the video from that date and time. The screen flickered and suddenly Jet appeared, his back to the sink.

"You want audio?" Cyrus asked.

"Not yet," Drey said, mesmerized as she watched

herself come on-screen and Jet move away. "He went to make himself another drink."

The bird's-eye video continued with her standing at the sink. She watched herself look around for the disposal switch as Jet bent over the glassware at the bar.

Jet appeared next to her again. "Audio now," she said.

Cyrus tapped the keyboard. There was that horrible grinding sound before Jet flipped off the disposal. They all watched him feel around in the drain for a moment before—coming out with what looked exactly like a man's thumb.

Both Hawk and Cyrus swore. "Is that real?" Cyrus asked. They listened to the discussion she and Jet had, then watched Jet put the thumb into a plastic bag and place it in the freezer.

"I didn't imagine any of it," Drey said as if talking to herself. "I knew it. He lied. He's lied about all of it."

"I don't think we need to look at the video from the night I broke into your bedroom," Hawk said. "I saw the mouse in the bottom of the water bottle that had been thrown from your balcony."

"What the hell has been going on here?" Cyrus asked.

"Someone wants Drey to believe she's unstable."

"Why?" Cyrus asked with a frown.

"We don't know yet," Hawk said. "One more video. This one would have been from two nights ago—if whoever is watching hasn't already wiped it clean."

Cyrus called it up. "Which room?"

"My bedroom," Drey said beside him as if she knew exactly what he was looking for.

The room came up on the screen. "The infrared camera is a nice touch," Cyrus commented. They could see the room and Drey sleeping in the bed as clearly as if it were daylight.

"Can you zoom in on her bedside table?" Hawk asked.

He did. The bedside table held nothing but a lamp and a water bottle that was still half-full. The video kept playing. Hawk could feel Drey next to him, her tension palpable. He reached over and took her hand, squeezing it. If he was right, someone had left those drugs for her.

There was nothing to watch on the screen except for an occasional movement from under the covers on the bed. Then, off to the left, a dark figure came into view. Back to the camera, the figure moved toward Drey's bedside table.

Hawk held his breath as a man dressed in all black, including the hoodie he wore, took something out of his pocket and placed it on the table. The container of pills. Drey moved on the bed. The figure froze, then stood over her for a long moment, before turning to leave. As he headed back in the direction of the surveillance equipment, he kept his head down until almost the last minute.

The camera caught him before he stepped out of view and was gone.

Drey let out a cry. For just a moment, Jet looked

so much like his brother that it was clear that she'd thought it was Ethan.

"Who was that?" Cyrus asked.

"Jet Baxter, Ethan's brother," she said, her voice breaking.

CHAPTER NINETEEN

HAWK PULLED DREY to him. She stepped into his arms, burying her face in his broad chest. She was feeling so many conflicting emotions. She needed his strength right now and wasn't up to fighting it. And yet she wasn't free, wouldn't be until Ethan returned, until she could get control of her life again.

Jet. Of course it was him.

Not Ethan. Hawk had been so sure that Ethan was behind it. Even the FBI didn't believe he was in Mexico City.

"Any way to make a copy of that video?" Hawk asked his brother.

"I can email it to your phone."

Drey felt numb. For that second, she'd thought it was Ethan. What still made her sick to her stomach was that she wouldn't have been surprised if it had been him. He'd left her on their wedding night and she hadn't talked to him since. All she had was Jet's word—for what that was worth—that Ethan had called from Mexico City.

Drawing back from Hawk's strong arms, she tried to pull herself together. She wasn't going crazy. It was just as Hawk had suspected. She hadn't trusted

Jet and for good reason, as it turned out. But why? It made no sense.

"I don't understand what Jet hopes to gain," she said, hating that her voice sounded so small.

Hawk shook his head. "I don't know. But I'm going to find him and when I do…" He turned to his brother. "Is there any way to disable this entire system?"

Cyrus raised a brow. "I suppose you could just pull the plug on everything in this room. But if you're right and someone is watching all this from another location…"

"He'll come see what is wrong," Hawk finished.

Cyrus made a not-sure-that's-a-good-idea face.

"We have to flush him out," Hawk said.

"Don't you think you should get Flint involved before we start flushing out anyone?" his brother asked.

"Before I go to Flint, I want to do a little investigating on my own. So far Jet hasn't done anything that Flint could arrest him for. Ethan Baxter is being investigated by the FBI. Supposedly the feds are watching the house. Probably looking for Ethan. But now they know that you and I have been here."

"I'm not worried about the feds. But I am worried about what you're planning to do," Cyrus said.

"Nothing right now." Hawk looked to Drey. "Right now, we all need to get out of here and go somewhere and talk. For all we know, this room is also being monitored. It could have a camera just like the rest of the house. They are so well hidden that no one would know they were being spied on. Drey?"

She nodded, still looking a little shell-shocked by everything.

"This remote location," Hawk said as a thought struck him. "He could be in this house, right?"

Cyrus raised a brow. "You mean hiding out somewhere in some hidden part of this place?"

Hawk saw Drey shudder and hug herself. "We can talk about it at the house."

"I better take my own car," she said.

Well, not hers exactly, he thought.

Cyrus checked his phone and said he had an appointment with a neighboring rancher he was going to be late for. Also, they had a local beef growers association meeting after that, one Hawk had forgotten about. "I was headed there when I got your call. Big brother will have to chew me out some other time."

"I guess I'll see you back at the house later tonight," Hawk said, making it clear that he wasn't leaving Drey alone—especially for the beef growers meeting.

"Fine," Cyrus said. "But if something comes up and you need me…"

"We'll holler. And for now, let's keep all this under our hats."

His brother agreed. "Seriously, after what we saw on that video… Just be careful."

GIGI THOUGHT ABOUT calling AJ to let her know she was coming to Montana. But she wasn't sure she was going through with meeting her birth mother.

Once in the rental car, she headed out of town with a map of Montana and Gilt Edge marked in red. She'd forgotten how beautiful the country was. Mountains lush with pines, creeks running crystal clear through tall green grasses, an endless blue sky dotted with puffy snow-white clouds.

She rolled down her window, taking in the scents. It surprised her how quickly all the tension left her body. While she'd told herself there was nothing she could do about the restaurant for days, the amount of work ahead had been on her mind constantly.

She smiled to herself thinking what AJ would say. "I told you so. You needed this." That much at least was true. But she wasn't sure she needed to see Billie Dee.

She thought about the first time she'd laid eyes on Ashley Jo Somerfield.

The memory made her smile. They'd both been eleven and sent off to boarding school. AJ, she suspected, for disciplinary reasons. Gigi, because that was what every young Buchanan woman had done for years.

That she and AJ just happened to be roommates could have been only fate—at least according to her friend.

But still Gigi would never forget the moment she walked into her dormitory room and saw the girl. Skinny, barefoot, wearing cutoff jeans and a tank top, her dark hair pulled back in a ponytail, she looked like a waif.

Gigi had stopped short in the doorway, thinking this couldn't be her roommate. The girl had turned then.

She hardly noticed the scabbed nose or the curse the girl let out. Instead she saw the big blue eyes and a face that was so much like her own that they could have been twins.

AJ had broken into a huge grin. "Tell me this wasn't meant to be," she'd said.

Gigi could laugh about it now. The two of them—it seemed at first—couldn't be more different. AJ, so laid-back and yet so ready for anything. Gigi, uptight, serious and cautious. It was like they'd brought out the best in each other and toned down the worst.

Gigi knew she wouldn't own a restaurant now if it wasn't for her friend. And AJ wouldn't be a high-priced attorney turned bartender.

She laughed. It felt good. She sped up a little, anxious to see her friend.

HAWK FOLLOWED DREY in his pickup to the ranch. She still looked shaken. He couldn't imagine what a shock it had been for her to see her husband's brother leaving the drugs by her bed. He wanted to go find the bastard, but he feared what he'd do to him. He had no desire to end up behind bars in his brother's jail.

"How are you doing?" he asked as he took a seat across from her in the ranch's large living room.

She let out a laugh. "How do you think? You were right. Somehow Jet knew, but how could he have known about my drug problem in college?"

"You're sure the only person who knew was the roommate you had in Spain? Because someone connected to Ethan had to have known about the drugs you were hooked on all those years ago," Hawk argued. "Did you tell Lillie?"

"No, I couldn't tell her the reason for our breakup, so we had drifted apart at that point."

"But there must have been someone you confided in? Or at least someone who knew about the drugs other than your roommate in Spain."

"Lena. Lena Franklin. She knew, but she left school shortly after she got me the last bottle of tablets that I took. She met a boy our first semester in Spain and dropped out of school. I haven't even thought of her in years."

"Was she the only one?"

Drey nodded. "Right after that, I threw the pills away. I never took them again. But Hawk, you think Lena has something to do with this? That's crazy."

"Someone told Jet. It's too much of a coincidence that he just happened to leave you the very pills you were addicted to all those years ago. You're sure there is no way Ethan could have known."

She shook her head. "What would Ethan have to gain by drugging me?"

That was a question Hawk couldn't answer. "What does Jet have to gain? How did you and Ethan meet?" He could see that the question took her by surprise.

"What are you insinuating?"

"It was just a question." But of course it wasn't.

"He came into the library one day looking for a book," she said.

"And you just happened to be working."

"Hawk, what are you saying? That you think he *targeted* me?"

"What was the book?"

She seemed to think for a minute. "It was an architecture book. We didn't have it. He told me about the house he was building and we got to talking."

"He expected a small library like the one in Gilt Edge to have this architecture book?"

She mugged a face at him. "He's not involved in this."

But Hawk had heard her gasp when the figure on the monitor had turned toward the camera. For just a second, she thought it was her husband. That meant it had been a possibility in her mind. "So he asked you out, right?"

"You don't think a man might like me just for me? Does he have to have had an ulterior motive?"

He didn't dare touch that, but he could tell she'd already asked herself the same question.

"Again, what would have been his point in targeting me?" she demanded.

"Lillie told me it was a whirlwind romance. That he swept you off your feet. Short engagement, don't you think?"

He could see that he was upsetting her. That hadn't been his purpose and he said as much. "I'm just trying to figure out who knew about the drugs and why your husband's brother is clearly trying to harm you."

JET WANTED HER to think that she was crazy. Drey knew what Hawk was saying. That was what made it all so hard. Jet had nothing to gain by getting her sent to the loony bin. But Ethan, now that they were married… Except what did he have to gain? He was the one with all the money, not her.

Even if he feared he'd made a mistake by marrying her, he didn't have to go to these extremes to get rid of her. No, it made no sense.

The pills. That was a mystery. It made her doubt herself. Except that she'd never told anyone. She was too ashamed. She swallowed, hating that she had to remember that awful time in her life. It was something she'd hoped no one would ever find out about. It had been the lowest point in her life and she'd found out that she wasn't as strong as she'd always believed she was. She still felt shame over it and disappointment in herself.

"No one knew but Lena Franklin. At least that was her name back then. I suppose she could have told someone." Drey hadn't thought about Lena in years. Her name probably wasn't even *Franklin* anymore, given how serious she was about that boy she met. He was American. She tried to remember his name.

"She knew about your drug use," Hawk said. "You said she actually bought you the drugs."

"Just that once before she left college."

"So she would know that you were addicted to the antianxiety medication."

"But I quit. I didn't even take more than a couple of the pills she got me."

"Did she know that?"

Drey shook her head. "She had left by then and we didn't keep in touch. In retrospect, her leaving helped me quit. I had no one to get me more so I knew I had to stop and not wait until I used up the bottle she'd gotten me."

"So she supported your dependency."

She hated to admit it. "She could see that I was hurting. It wasn't like Lena encouraged me."

Hawk raised a brow. "But you weren't such good friends that you kept in touch after that."

She shook her head. "That's why I can't imagine she could be involved."

He pulled out his cell phone. "*Lena? Franklin*, right?"

"Right. I have no idea how we can find her, let alone that she has anything to do with—"

"I think I found her."

Drey stared at him in disbelief. How was that possible out of all the Lena Franklins in the world? Especially if Lena had married in the interim. And yet she heard something in Hawk's voice. Her heart pounded as she watched him look up from his phone. Drey didn't know what to say. "You're sure it's the same—"

"Lena Franklin."

"I just remembered. Brett Coldwell. That's the one she left college for. As I recall, he was from Houston. I thought they would have been married by now."

"A lot of women keep their maiden names."

"There have to be thousands of Lena Franklins."

Hawk nodded. "But not that many who are employed by Baxter Inc."

CHAPTER TWENTY

DREY WAS TOO stunned to speak for a few moments. She had convinced herself that Lena couldn't possibly be involved in this. But she continued to be surprised. And yet, she still didn't want to believe it.

Lena worked for Ethan's company? "It can't be the same woman I knew."

Hawk handed her his phone. "Here is her employee profile."

She looked down at the screen. Even as she made the photo of the attractive woman larger, she told herself that there had to be a mistake.

For a full minute, she studied the dark-haired woman in the photo. Lena looked good, much better than she had that semester in Spain. She had dressed like a bohemian back then. Now, though, she wore what was obviously an expensive suit. Her once-long hair was cut into a perfect bob. Diamonds glittered at her ears.

"She seems to have done well for herself," Drey said, handing back the phone and trying to make sense of this. She couldn't keep denying the connection between her past—and Ethan Baxter. Even she couldn't buy that this was just some crazy coincidence.

But did she really believe that she'd been "targeted"? That Ethan had come after her? How could she explain any of this otherwise? She felt sick to her stomach. "So Ethan targeted me."

"I'm sorry, but it certainly looks that way," Hawk said as he took his phone back.

"Why, though?"

He shook his head. "That's what we need to find out. We know Jet's behind the crazy things that have happened at the house."

"But we don't know how Ethan is involved."

"Lena Franklin works for him."

"She works for his company. The same company Jet works for," she pointed out. Drey didn't know why she kept defending Ethan. Because he was her husband, because she felt she owed him at least a little loyalty, because he could be innocent in all this. Not that he hadn't proved to be a questionable husband, all things considered. Worse, if she was being totally honest with herself, she'd married him while in love with another man.

"We'll try to give him the benefit of the doubt—until he shows his face."

She nodded. Unfortunately, she thought Hawk was probably right. What man left his wife on their wedding night without a note or even a call? She couldn't trust that anything Jet had told her was true. Ethan might not have even called from Mexico City. He could be anywhere. Even still in Gilt Edge, if the FBI was right. The big question was why hadn't he called his wife?

She wasn't so naive that she hadn't considered that Lena and Ethan might have a relationship. But if so, where did she fit into all this? Ethan was the one who'd pushed the marriage. What did he have to gain? It had to be more than him setting her up to take the fall if the FBI closed in, didn't it?

Her heart ached at what a fool she'd been. Of course she'd questioned why Ethan Baxter had come into the library and almost instantly taken a liking to her. It had all happened so quickly. Too quickly.

If he'd targeted her... Even if Lena had told him about her...

You're building a mountain retreat in Montana. I used to know someone from Gilt Edge, Montana. Dierdre Hunter.

Unless Lena had kept track of her, she wouldn't even know that Drey was the local librarian. But Lena might have remembered that Drey was from Gilt Edge, Montana. And in a town the size of Gilt Edge, Drey wasn't hard to find. She hadn't married, so that would have helped with a general internet search. Just months ago, she'd been promoted to head librarian. But it wasn't like that kind of news went viral.

With a start, she thought of the local write-up in the newspaper. It had been accompanied by a photo of her. That had come out only a week before she'd met Ethan.

Coincidence? If Lena had mentioned her to Ethan... But when would Lena have told him about the pills she used to take? She couldn't imagine how that part of the conversation would have come up.

The girl was a junkie back when I knew her, but I heard she cleaned up her act.

Ethan wouldn't be interested in a woman who'd relied on antianxiety medication for months after losing her baby. Or maybe that was exactly what he was looking for.

"Drey, I just checked. Lena is on vacation. Montana or Mexico City?"

She shook her head. This wasn't happening. "I still don't understand what's going on."

"But at least we know that there is nothing wrong with your mind." He gave her a reassuring smile, but right now little could reassure her.

She got to her feet and moved to the window to look out on the Montana summer day. This was her favorite time of year. She couldn't help but think of her life before Ethan. Yes, she still had ached for Hawk, but she'd been happy without him—or at least as happy as she could be on her own. Had she really thought someone would come along and sweep her off her feet? No, wasn't that why Ethan had such an easy time of it?

"I feel like such a fool." She crossed her arms, fighting tears, as Hawk rose and came up behind her. She could feel his warm breath at her neck, but he didn't touch her, as if he was afraid to. For fear she would shatter like an expensive crystal vase?

"No," Hawk said quietly. "You're not the fool. Ethan Baxter is. His company's in trouble. All I can figure is that he was looking for a scapegoat. If he had any idea what he was giving up…"

She heard the catch in his throat and knew he was no longer talking about Ethan. Turning, she looked into the familiar gray eyes fringed with dark lashes. His own pain was so visible that she forgot her own.

"Damn it, Drey, I've never stopped loving you."

She nodded, knowing it was true as she stepped into his arms. He held her tightly. She could hear his heart thumping loudly under the strong muscles of his chest. He still loved her. At that moment, it was all that mattered.

Drawing back, she looked into his gray eyes. She wanted him to kiss her like nothing she'd ever wanted before. His gaze locked with hers and he slowly lowered his mouth to hers. She closed her eyes as his lips gently brushed over hers. A moan of pure relief and release escaped her lips.

Hawk dragged her to him, his demanding mouth taking hers. She wrapped her arms around his neck, wanting nothing between them. Her breasts crushed against his chest. She yearned for even their clothing to be gone. She wanted this, needed this, and from his ardent kiss, Hawk did, too.

She tore open the snaps on his Western shirt, desperately needing to feel her palms against the warm, taut flesh of his chest. Pulling back from the kiss, she lowered her mouth to his neck, then made her way down only a few inches, before he drew her up.

"Drey?"

She shook her head no. She didn't want to think, let alone talk. Slowly she pulled her T-shirt over her head. She heard Hawk groan. He reached for the strap

of her bra and slipped off one side and then the other.
Her nipples peaked hard against the lace of her bra in
anticipation of his touch.

His gaze locking with hers, he slowly pulled down
the bra to expose her breasts. She saw desire burning
in his eyes as he dropped his mouth to one nipple, then
the other. He tugged hard, making her arch against
him with a moan of desire and need.

She reached for his belt buckle and froze at the
sound of a vehicle.

Hawk swore. "It can't be Cyrus." *But it could be
just about anyone else.*

Drey pulled her bra up and reached for her T-shirt,
disappointment making her weak. She felt as if she'd
been dropped into a freezing mountain lake. What
had she been thinking? She hadn't. She'd just wanted
Hawk, needed him.

Behind her, she heard Hawk curse again as he re-
buttoned his shirt.

"It's a neighbor. I forgot he was stopping by to
borrow our log splitter. I'll take care of this and be
right back."

DREY TRIED TO pull herself together. She'd been so
close to making love with Hawk. Her pulse was still
pounding, her body aching, her center on fire with
need for the man she loved.

She felt a wave of shame. She was *married*. Her
face flamed with the realization of what she'd almost
done. Fortunately she hadn't. She'd wanted him,
needed him, yearned for him. Because she was still

in love with him, but she wasn't free. Not to mention that sleeping with Hawk wouldn't solve anything. It would only make everything worse.

Once Ethan came back… But she knew it wouldn't be over until she figured out who was behind this—and why.

Drey picked up her purse and keys. She couldn't keep falling into Hawk's arms. She'd needed him last night when she'd found the pills and she would be grateful for his help. She wasn't losing her mind. But she felt as if she'd come close when she'd seen those pills. When she'd almost taken them.

Now she knew the truth. Jet had left them beside her bed. Jet must have found out about her addiction from Lena Franklin, who now worked for Baxter Inc. What more did she need to know?

She was out the door and almost to Ethan's SUV when she heard Hawk call her name. She slowly turned to face him, hating the reminder of how close they'd come to making love. Yet, at the same time, just the thought of being in his arms…

"Drey?" He caught up with her.

She stopped, holding up both hands as if to ward him off. "I can't."

He stopped a few yards from her. "I know. My fault. You're right. You're…married."

She nodded and swallowed the lump that had formed in her throat. "I—"

"You don't have to say anything." He looked down at his boots for a moment, before his gaze rose and locked with hers. She felt that slow, hot heat begin at her center and grow outward. "I won't lie to you. I want you. I—"

She couldn't bear this. After all these years of being estranged and now… "I have to go." She stepped to the SUV and opened the door.

"Please, don't go back to that house," he said, his voice sounded strangled.

"I'm not." With that, she climbed into the vehicle, started the engine and left without looking back. Her heart felt as if it was breaking. She'd desperately wanted to know what he was going to say, but at the same time, she couldn't bear it. Not now. Maybe not ever. When Ethan came back—

Drey realized that might not happen. Didn't Hawk believe that Ethan was up to his neck in all this? That Ethan had targeted her for some strange reason and now wanted her to believe she was losing her mind. She had to find out the truth.

She drove into town and parked a block away from the hotel where Jet was staying. Jet had left the pills next to her bed. She'd seen it with her own eyes. She shuddered, remembering that she'd been watched the entire time she was in that house. But watched by whom?

Now that the shock had worn off, Drey realized she was furious. There was no longer making excuses for why she didn't trust Jet. Nor could she keep pretending that she hadn't been targeted. But by Ethan? Or Jet? Whichever, it had been Jet who'd left her the pills. She was mad and wanted to get the bastard.

She called the hotel. By now he could have checked

out. Her mind was whirling. No wonder she had a headache. No wonder she thought she'd been drugged. This morning when she'd awakened to see the bottle of pills, she'd reached for them instinctively.

Of course she had—because she was being systematically drugged. If she hadn't called Hawk—

The front desk answered. She asked for Jet Baxter's room.

"One moment," the desk clerk said.

Drey waited, her mind racing. Lena worked for Baxter Inc. But that still didn't mean that anything was going on with Ethan and Lena.

It could have happened just like she thought. All of it innocuous. Lena mentioning that she knew someone from Montana when she heard Ethan was building a house here. Drey's name could have come up. Ethan could have seen the newspaper article about her promotion. He would have said hello when he stopped by the library and one thing could have led to another.

The phone in Jet's room rang.

She thought of the drugs and felt her scenario punched full of holes. Lena wouldn't have mentioned the drugs. Not unless there had been more than one conversation. Not unless Lena and Ethan were closer than that.

The phone continued to ring. Maybe he'd gone somewhere. She didn't see Jet's red sports car, but then, he probably had the valet take it to the hotel's underground parking area.

"Hello?"

It startled her. She'd been about to hang up, con-

vinced he wasn't in his room. But she'd been expecting Jet to answer. Instead, it was a woman's voice.
"Hello?"

CHAPTER TWENTY-ONE

BILLIE DEE LOOKED up from the pot of Texas gumbo she had going on the stove as Ashley Jo came in for her shift. She'd been singing an old gospel song when the young woman came down the stairs from her apartment into the kitchen.

"Don't stop singing on my accord," Ashley Jo said. "I love that song." She moved to the stove. "Oh, Billie Dee, you're killing me," she joked as she took a whiff.

"Can I fix you a bowl?"

"Maybe later. I saw a car drive up. I have to take care of the customers first."

Henry came in the back door and Ashley Jo took off to open the front door and turn on the lights, as it was almost eleven, when the saloon opened for business.

Billie Dee stepped to Henry for her hug and kiss. She still lived in the small house she rented in town, while he still lived on the ranch with his two sons. The sons, both grown, had taken over the ranching part.

Henry shook his head. No news about her daughter. She tried not to show how much it hurt. Her daughter had put her DNA in. She'd wanted to find out who her mother was—but had done nothing since.

"These things take time," Henry said, as he always did.

Billie Dee was tired of hearing that. "She's changed her mind," she said as she turned back to her gumbo. Cooking was the one thing that had always given her peace, but not even that helped now.

"Billie Dee, I'll wait as long as it takes," he said behind her.

She nodded, fighting tears. "I want to marry you, you know I do."

"I do," he said, putting his arms around her. "But you want your daughter at the wedding. I told you. I'll wait."

"But can I?" She turned to look at his handsome face. He was the most patient man she'd ever known, the kindest, the most generous. "I feel awful making you wait. Making us both wait."

He chuckled and shook his head. "It isn't as if we're not together in every other way."

She smiled up at him through her tears. He wiped one away with his thumb. "I love you so much."

"I love you." He kissed her. It felt like a promise, one she planned to take him up on.

From inside the saloon, Billie Dee heard Ashley Jo let out a startled cry, then the sound of happy laughter. She wondered what that was about.

GIGI THREW HER arms around her best friend, laughing at AJ's surprise at finding her standing in the Stagecoach Saloon. "Come on, you knew I'd have to come up here."

"I didn't. I know how stubborn you can be." She pulled back to look at Gigi. "I've missed you so much. I was afraid when I told you what I'd done, you'd never talk to me again."

"So is she here?" Gigi whispered and looked down the hallway.

"She is. Can't you smell the gumbo cooking?"

Gigi laughed. "I couldn't believe it when I came through the front door. I'm not sure I'm ready to meet her."

"Whatever you want, I'm just glad you're here."

"That gumbo smells so good," Gigi said, looking down the hallway to the kitchen again.

"I can get you a bowl. Or you can come back to the kitchen. We don't have to tell Billie Dee yet—if that's what you want."

Gigi hesitated, but only for a moment. The smell of the gumbo was like a lasso dragging her toward the kitchen. Her curiosity tugged at her.

"Maybe I'll just meet her, one cook to another." She realized she was trembling. She'd wondered about the woman who'd given her birth and given her up.

Her mother had assured her that her birth mother had wanted her. But Gigi figured all adoptive mothers said that. According to AJ, it was true that she'd been loved. That her mother hadn't wanted to give her up. She'd said Billie Dee had been forced to give her up. But forced by whom?

"Not today. I want to get a motel and freshen up. Maybe we could talk later?"

AJ looked disappointed for a moment but quickly

hid it. "Absolutely. We have a lot of catching up." She hugged her tightly. "I'm so glad you came to Montana. You won't be sorry."

Gigi hoped she was right.

DREY HUNG UP at the sound of the woman's sleepy voice, recalling that Jet had an alibi for the other morning. According to the sheriff, he'd been with a woman who swore Jet had been with her the whole time. Apparently he was still with her. Or was this a new one?

Settling in to wait, she told herself that Jet and his friend couldn't spend all their time in the hotel. Within thirty minutes she realized that she should have brought something to drink and eat. Her first mistake. Also, she was going to have to use the bathroom at some point. Maybe this hadn't been the best idea.

But as she was doubting herself, she saw Jet come out the front door of the hotel. He stopped on the front steps and looked around.

Drey quickly slid down to hide behind the steering wheel. She didn't think he would notice the SUV because there were so many like it around town.

He stood for a moment, then turned back to the doors he'd just exited. She realized that he was waiting for someone. Her heart began to pound. He couldn't be waiting for Ethan, she told herself. But she knew that it wouldn't have surprised her that much if Ethan had come through those doors—especially if the two of them were in this together.

Drey watched as Jet waited, clearly getting impatient. The doors began to open. Jet stepped to them, grabbed one of the handles and swung it wide, but it wasn't Ethan who stepped out.

The woman was tall, slim and redheaded. She wore jeans, a blouse and sandals. Gold twinkled at her wrist, her throat, her earlobes. She smiled broadly as she took Jet's hand and the two walked to his sports car.

Drey's heart was in her throat. The red hair had thrown her for a moment, but the smile... She would never forget that smile or the fact that Lena loved gold jewelry. She'd borrowed one of Drey's bracelets, a gift from Hawk, and hadn't returned it before she'd dropped out of the university.

Jet and Lena, she thought with a curse as she sat up and watched the two wait for the valet to get their car. What did surprise her was the midsize rental-looking car that was brought around. Not Jet's sports car.

Lena took the keys from the valet and gave him a big smile along with what must have been a handsome tip before sliding behind the wheel. Jet went around to climb into the passenger seat, but she could tell he didn't like it.

Meanwhile, Lena had her window down and appeared to be asking for directions. She patted the valet's hand before she pulled out, making the tires chirp. Drey thought about following them, but it would be next to impossible in a town this size not to be spotted.

Also, it appeared they were leaving the city limits as Lena turned onto the highway headed out of town. They hadn't taken any luggage so she knew they would be back.

She sat for a moment before she started her car. Hawk didn't want her going back to the house. But now she knew. Jet and Lena. She no longer had to wonder how Jet had known about the drugs Drey had been addicted to. One mystery solved, she thought.

But what were they after? They thought she was taking the drugs. She didn't feel as worried about staying in the house. Wouldn't they be surprised when they realized she was onto them?

GIGI HAD A restless night after AJ left. They'd talked until the wee hours. This morning, she knew what she had to do. She had to at least see her birth mother. She'd come all this way. She couldn't pretend it had been only to see AJ, although it was wonderful being around her friend.

"I thought I'd stop by the saloon again," she'd told AJ over the phone.

"You picked a great day. Billie Dee is making her Texas chili. Come to the back entrance because we don't open for a few hours."

Driving over, she couldn't help being nervous. She was finally going to lay eyes on the woman who shared her genes. While her adoptive parents had been everything she could have asked for, she had still yearned for someone who looked like her.

When people in the family talked about getting traits from various grandparents, she had wondered about her own biological family and what traits she might have gotten from them. She'd always thought she would never know.

After parking, she climbed out of the car. Someone was singing. She remembered what AJ had told her as she stopped to listen. It had to be Billie Dee. She had a wonderful voice. The song was an old one, the kind her nanny used to sing to her.

Gigi tried to swallow around the lump in her throat. She hesitated for a moment, not sure she could do this. But the music seemed to pull her. Following the sound, she walked to the back door of the saloon. As she pushed the door open, she instantly became lured by the wonderful kitchen scents.

Just inside the door, she stopped. Standing at the stove was a large woman singing and stirring a huge pot of what smelled like chili. Billie Dee? The woman was just winding up her song.

Out of the corner of her eye, Gigi saw an older, handsome cowboy sitting at the small table off to the side. He seemed startled to see her.

AJ came noisily down the stairs, all grins. Gigi had a moment where she wanted to turn and run.

"Billie Dee?" her friend said, grabbing Gigi's hand as if she'd seen her need to escape. "I want you to meet a friend of mine."

Billie Dee turned from the stove, Gigi locked eyes with the woman. Blue eyes—eyes the same color and shape as her own. The cook froze, those blue eyes widened. The large spoon in her hand dropped to the floor at her feet. She opened her mouth as if to speak, but before she could, she fainted.

CHAPTER TWENTY-TWO

DREY SAW THE next morning that she had six calls from
Hawk and four voice mail messages. She listened to
the first and last message. She texted him to say she
was fine, then showered, dressed and headed back
to the hotel where Jet and Lena were staying. She'd
seen Lena talking to the valet and was curious what
she'd asked him.

Parking down the street, she saw that the same
valet was on duty who'd been there yesterday evening. She reached for her door handle as her cell phone
rang. It was Hawk. She pushed Disregard and stepped
into the street. He wouldn't like what she was doing,
but she had to take her life back and she felt as if this
was a start. Her phone went off again. This time it
was a text.

I can see you.

She stared at the text startled for a moment until
she saw it was from Hawk. She looked up and spotted his pickup parked down the block.

What r u doing here?

Obviously the same thing you are.

Drey looked down the street in his direction.

I think we should have coffee in the café since we're both here.

She started to pass. Then—

I have a plan.

She did love a man with a plan especially since right now she didn't have one.

Drey texted back. I love a plan.

She crossed the street and caught the valet before he could park one of the guests' cars. "That woman, the redhead, who you got her car for yesterday evening. Was she by any chance asking for directions?"

He was a little younger than Drey and quite cute up close. He didn't seem surprised by the question. "Wanted to know if there were places to eat in any of the towns around here."

"Are there?"

He laughed. "Not much for miles. But I told them about the cafés in Grass Range. You looking for a good place to eat?"

"Right now I'm going to have a coffee at the hotel restaurant, but you seem to be the person to ask when I get ready for my next meal."

He smiled at that and gave her a wink. "I'll steer you in the right direction."

"I bet you would." She looked up to find Hawk watching the exchange. He didn't look happy.

BILLIE DEE BLINKED as she came to. For a moment she thought she was seeing double. She looked from Gigi to Ashley Jo and back again. She saw Henry looking worried behind them. "How did I—"

"I carried you upstairs. You're in Ashley Jo's apartment over the saloon," Henry said. "I was afraid you might have hit your head on the stove."

She tried to sit up on the couch where she lay.

"Easy," he said, quickly moving to her.

Henry was right. She felt light-headed as she sat up.

Billie Dee stared at the young woman with Ashley Jo, feeling faint again.

"Why don't we all sit down?" Henry suggested.

She watched Ashley Jo and the other woman take a chair in front of the couch. Ashley Jo glanced at her friend. The young woman, who was the spitting image of Ashley Jo, nodded slowly.

"Billie Dee, I'm so sorry. I wasn't sure how to spring this on you," Ashley Jo said.

"What is going on?" Billie Dee asked.

"Where do I start?" Ashley Jo said.

Her friend groaned. "AJ—"

"This isn't easy for me either, Gigi."

"Maybe you could introduce us to your friend," Henry suggested.

"This is Georgia 'Gigi' Buchanan. We met in boarding school. We were roommates. The first time we saw each other, we were shocked how much we looked alike. We even almost share the same birth-day. What are the chances of that? On top of that we are so much alike."

"AJ," Gigi said again, "we're nothing alike."

Ashley Jo laughed at that. "We're like sisters. Don't let her kid you."

"AJ…" Gigi prodded.

Billie Dee couldn't take her eyes off the young woman.

"I'm getting to it. Gigi lost her parents last year. It's been really hard on her and I wanted to do something nice for her. I knew she was adopted—"

At the word *adopted*, Billie Dee felt herself start.

"I decided to find her birth mother for her." She rushed on. "Even though she swore she wasn't inter-ested. I thought if I found the woman, I could get to know her and see if she was someone my best friend in the world would want to meet."

Billie Dee felt her eyes widen, then tear over. "Ash-ley Jo? What did you do?"

"I was the one who sent in Gigi's DNA sample. I was the one who tracked you down. Once I got to know you, I had to tell Gigi. The two of you have so much in common."

She felt her heart swell to near bursting. "Are you telling me…"

"Gigi is your daughter."

Billie Dee began to cry. "I never thought I'd ever get to meet you. But the moment I saw you…"

"You have to understand," Gigi said, clearly fight-ing her own emotions. "I had two wonderful parents."

"I knew that would be the case. I made sure of it," Billie Dee said. "I was told they were amazing people."

"I just can't understand how you could have ever given up your child," Gigi said.

"AJ, why don't we leave these two alone to talk?" Henry said. "Is it okay for me to call you AJ?"

"All my friends do," Ashley Jo said.

Gigi waited until they left. "I have to know why you gave me up. I'm assuming you were young."

Billie Dee nodded. "Young and in love. Unfortunately, I was also naive." She patted the couch next to her. "Won't you come sit by me?"

Gigi hesitated but only for a moment.

"I fell in love with an older man who I thought was separated from his wife. He lied about that. I didn't find out until I realized I was pregnant…" She swallowed. "He told me that his wife couldn't have children and that he was going to take my child and raise it as their own. He said that if I fought him, he would have me put away somewhere. This man was very powerful and used to getting his own way. I never doubted that he could do what he said."

"This was my biological father?"

"He still is a very powerful man. He's not evil. He's just used to getting his own way."

Gigi sighed. "So how did you…"

"I went to my church pastor and asked for help. Fortunately, he knew someone. I had a doctor certify that I'd miscarried the baby and another friend who got me out of town. I knew that I couldn't keep you, as much as I wanted to. I had friends who told me your father didn't believe I'd miscarried and was looking for me. When I gave birth, my pastor had a couple waiting to adopt you. He assured me that they would be the kind of parents I would want for my daughter."

"They were," Gigi said. "You're not going to tell me who my father is, are you?"

Billie Dee shook her head. "No good could come of it. You have to know, I was heartbroken giving you up. I loved you so much. I've thought about you every day since and prayed that one day..." She had to stop; she was so choked up with tears. Wiping her eyes, she said, "I'm so glad Ashley Jo tracked me down. You look like I did at your age."

"I have to be truthful with you. I don't know what I want from you—if anything," Gigi said.

"It's all right. I'd love to know all about you. But I won't push. Just getting to see you, tell you that I loved you and wanted you, that's more than I could hope for."

Ashley Jo appeared in the doorway with a bowl of chili. "Gigi, you have got to try this."

"THAT VALET WAS flirting with you," Hawk said as he opened the front door of the hotel for her and followed her in.

"You think?"

He hated that he sounded jealous. Hell, he was. "Let's talk in the café."

Hawk led her to a booth in the restaurant where they would be able to see the lobby. After what had almost happened yesterday, he still felt shaken. That he'd cared about Drey all these years, had never been able to get her out of his mind, had been one thing.

Being thrown together with her like this... She looked so beautiful. His heart ached at the thought that he might not ever get to kiss her again. He found himself wishing he'd done what his sister had suggested and ridden into Drey's wedding on his horse and carried her off. But he hadn't. And he feared he would always regret it.

Now all he could do was try to keep her safe until... Until what? He ground his teeth at the thought of Ethan Baxter. Drey was married and he'd let it happen because of his stupid stubbornness and pride. He mentally kicked himself because now he had no idea how to get her back. Ethan Baxter wasn't the only hurdle.

"So we both had the same idea it seems about spying on Jet," Drey said after they'd ordered.

"Great minds. Drey, we're going to have to talk about what happened yesterday."

She shook her head. "It was just a moment of weakness."

"Was that all it was? It sure didn't feel like—"

"Hawk, can we please not talk about it?"

"All right. For now. But we will talk about it once this is over. You have to know how I feel and how sorry I am for everything."

She looked away for a moment as their coffees were served. "I don't think I've ever been in this restaurant before," she said after the waitress left them alone again.

Hawk took a sip of his coffee, telling himself this wasn't the time. But the memory of her in his arms was killing him. He'd screwed up in the past. He was determined that if there was any way to get this woman back...

"I was here yesterday evening. I saw Jet leave—with a woman," Drey said, turning the conversation to the reason they were both there. "It was Lena Franklin."

"So she is involved," he said with a curse.

"They left to go to Grass Range. They didn't take Jet's sports car. Apparently Lena has a rental."

Hawk had been watching the lobby and now touched her arm and motioned in that direction. "There's Jet with a redhead. Is that Lena?"

Drey nodded.

The two of them were leaving. He watched Lena give the valet her ticket as the two waited. A few moments later, the couple stepped outside as a car pulled up and the valet driver hopped out.

"I wonder where they're going," Drey said.

"I'm more curious how long they will be gone."

She shot him a look. "Are we breaking into their room?"

He smiled over at her. "I *would* like to know if they're sharing the same room."

"What I want to know is what they hope to achieve."

Hawk took a sip of his coffee. What he wanted to know was how her husband fitted into all this—if he did. He knew he wanted to think the worst of Baxter.

Of course there was always the alternative. That the man wasn't a crook—that he'd met Drey, fallen for her and married her. That Ethan had realized just how special she was. Any man with a brain would want her. She was smart and pretty and fun and—

Was it possible the man really was away on business—no matter what the FBI thought? And that he knew nothing about what was going on at the house with Drey and Jet? And Jet was simply taking advantage of his brother's absence by trying to get rid of Drey?

"I just had a thought. Jet isn't trying to get rid of you. If he was, he could have. What if he is just trying to get you out of that house? What if there is something in there that he needs?"

Drey nodded. "That's what I've been thinking, as well. Things have gotten moved around. Like the drawers in the kitchen. The contents had been moved to other drawers. I thought he'd done it just to mess with my mind. But if he'd been looking for something…"

Hawk smiled over at her. "See, we really are a team." He saw someone he knew across the room. "Wait here a minute, okay?"

DOWN IN THE KITCHEN, Gigi took a bite of the chili. "This your own recipe?" she asked as she stepped over to the stove. It was nothing short of amazing.

Billie Dee looked embarrassed. "It was my mother's but I tinkered with it a little. Do you like it?"

"It makes me want to lick the bowl," Gigi said honestly.

"Gigi has her own restaurant in Houston," AJ said.

"You like to cook?" Billie Dee sounded surprised but happy to hear that.

"I tinker a little," she said. "I'm picking up a spice I'm not used to in chili."

"Watch her, she'll steal your recipe," AJ joked.

"She can have it, if she wants it," the cook said. "It's nutmeg, just a touch."

Gigi nodded, tasting it now. "Interesting." She finished her bowl and put it and the spoon in the sink. "I should get going."

"Going?" AJ asked in surprise.

"I need to check in on my restaurant. There was a fire," she told Billie Dee.

"Don't go back to the motel. Stay with me upstairs," her friend said, just as she had yesterday. "There's plenty of room. It will be just like in the dorms at boarding school."

"You're also welcome at my house," Billie Dee said. "I have a couple of guest rooms. I understand if you prefer a motel."

She felt as if all of this had happened too quickly. She needed some space. Some time alone to think. "I appreciate the offers, but I really do have to take care of some business and I could use some time alone." She looked to Billie Dee. "I see you're engaged," she said, having noticed the large rock on her ring finger.

"You met him. Henry Larson. He's a local retired rancher," the cook said.

"With two really handsome sons," AJ added.

"One's a little young for you, but the other..." She grinned.

"You and your cowboys," Gigi said with a shake of her head before turning back to Billie Dee. "Maybe I'll see you tomorrow." To AJ, she said, "You, I will definitely see tomorrow."

DREY WATCHED HAWK leave the table. She'd hardly touched her coffee. She'd seen the change in Hawk. He was no longer holding her at arm's length. He was no longer angry and upset with her. But what had caused it? She suspected it was her marriage. Had he really thought she wouldn't go through with it?

Her marriage. That thought almost made her laugh. So far it hadn't been much. And now with Hawk acting the way he was...

She had enough to think about without worrying about Hawk's change of attitude. Seeing Jet and Lena together still blew her mind. It always amazed her what a small world it was. Where did Ethan fit into this puzzle? Wasn't it still possible that he had nothing to do with any of this?

As the days went on, though, she was having a hard time believing he was in Mexico City on business. She saw Hawk talking to a woman behind the check-in counter. To her surprise, she witnessed the woman pass Hawk something. A key card?

"Ready?" Hawk said when he returned. He was grinning and looking like the cat who ate the canary.

She quickly slid out of her seat as he tossed money

onto the table for a tip and let him lead her out of the café.

"Is that what I think it is?" she whispered, motioning to the key card in his hand.

He smiled. "Come on. Let's do some sleuthing."

Once inside the elevator, he pushed the button for the sixth floor. The elevator door closed. Neither of them spoke until the door opened again.

"Five hundred twenty," Hawk said, and they started down the hall.

She followed him and stood keeping an eye out while he used the card to get them into the room. The moment the door opened, he swiftly pulled her in.

"We don't want them to know we've been here," he warned in a whisper.

"You think this is the first hotel room I've ever searched?" she asked with a grin. "I'll start over here." She made her way to the open suitcase lying on the large king-size bed. She went through Jet's carry-on suitcase quickly and found nothing of interest.

Turning, she saw Hawk come out of the bathroom. "I found two more bottles of the same antianxiety medication, only these were prescribed to Jet by two different doctors."

Drey groaned. "So he isn't finished with me."

Hawk shook his head. "I thought about dumping them down the drain, but I'm not sure we want him to know just yet that we're onto him."

He stepped over to the small desk and opened the laptop lying there. She watched but saw that it was password protected. When he looked up, their gazes met.

"He has to be the one monitoring the house," she said.

Hawk didn't comment but turned to the other items on the desk. "I wonder why this is out," he said, pointing to several bottles of glues. Looking about the room, he said, "Lena's suitcase isn't here."

She checked the closet. "You're right." Was it possible they weren't sharing the same room? They'd looked pretty chummy when they'd left the hotel both times.

Hawk stepped to the adjoining room door. They both fell silent as he tried the knob. It swung open. "They have connecting rooms," he said as he stepped in and she followed. In this room, the king-size bed had definitely been slept in.

She headed right for Lena's suitcase. This one took longer because the woman didn't travel light.

"Anything?" he asked next to her.

"Nothing." She was feeling disappointed as they wandered back into Jet's room when she heard someone at the door. Someone slipped in a key card.

Hawk grabbed her hand and quickly pulled her toward Lena's room. They started toward the door to leave the room. Hawk was no doubt thinking the same thing Drey was. Once Jet and Lena entered his room, they would slip out of hers and into the hallway to make their great escape.

But at the door, they could hear voices still out in the hallway.

"I don't care," Lena was saying, sounding annoyed. "I'm already sick of this town. What was Ethan thinking, building here?"

"Some people think this is paradise," Jet said. "My key's not working. Try yours."

"Some people don't know their—"

Realizing what was happening, Drey and Hawk looked at each other wide-eyed and scrambled away from the door as a key card was put into Lena's lock just feet away.

Back in Jet's room, Drey could hear Jet still trying to get his key card to work. Hawk pulled her into the closet between some of Jet's clothes and closed the door as they heard Jet's door start to open. Hawk pulled her close at the sound of footfalls only feet away. She leaned against him, trying to catch her breath.

In the light leaking in under the closet door, she saw someone approach the closet and held her breath. Hawk held her more tightly, but the shadow disappeared as she heard Lena call Jet into her room.

"Just get what you need and let's go," Jet complained. "I can't believe after I had to wait on you, that you still weren't ready."

"I didn't realize how cold it is here. It's supposed to be *summer*. If you hadn't rushed me earlier..." Drey could hear Lena digging in her closet. A hanger pinged against another empty one. "Oh, this is much better. You like?"

"It's a fine jacket. Come on, I'm starving. I hope we can find a decent breakfast somewhere around here."

Drey listened to what sounded like the door closing. The voices died off. She slowly let out the breath she'd been holding, but Hawk still held her as if he didn't want to let go of her. She closed her eyes for a moment and leaned against his strong, solid body. She didn't want to leave his arms either. *This is where I belong*, she thought. *This is where I've always belonged.*

CHAPTER TWENTY-THREE

HAWK BREATHED IN Drey's sweet scent as he held her. He could smell the shampoo she used to wash her hair that morning. It was the same kind she'd used when they were together. The scent alone ignited that old passion in him for her.

"That was close," she whispered, her voice cracking.

"Too close." Being in the small space near Drey brought back a rush of memories of the two of them. She hadn't tried to open the closet door and step out. Instead, she leaned against him as if captivated also by this innocent moment of intimacy between them. He'd been tempted to dip his head and nuzzle her neck. To place a kiss in that hollow spot on the side of her throat. To press her even tighter against him.

But he didn't want to break the spell. He'd always wanted this woman. There'd never been another who made him feel like this. He felt his desire quicken and knew she had, too. Still, she didn't reach to open the closet door for another few moments.

"I think they're gone," she said, her voice filled with emotion.

"I think you're right." With a sigh, he reached past

her and opened the closet door so they could step out. "Let me check the hall." He moved to the door, opened it a crack and looked out. The hallway was empty. "Let's take the stairs."

But once in the stairwell, they both froze at the sound of a familiar voice.

He turned and pressed one finger to his lips, not that it was necessary. He could see that Drey had heard it, as well.

"Do we have to run?" It was Lena's whine. One of the footfalls stopped, followed shortly by the other. "Why not take a perfectly good elevator?"

"I wasn't waiting for the damned elevator again. What is your problem now?" Jet demanded, his voice sounding farther down the staircase.

"I turned my ankle."

"You have to be kidding." He let out a loud sigh. "How bad is it? I'm going to need you to be able to walk."

"I turned my ankle, that's all. I just need to rest it for a moment. I'm not going to hold up your great plan."

"I'm not the only one whose head is on the chopping block. So keep that in mind." It sounded as if Jet was climbing the stairs to go back to where he'd apparently left her. Hawk could hear him talking more quietly to Lena. "How's your ankle? Here, let me rub it."

Lena giggled. "That's not my ankle and you know it. We could go back to the room. Order room service and spend the rest of the day in bed."

"I'm sick of hiding out in the room," Jet said. "This

is almost over. We're almost home free. Until then…
Can you put weight on your ankle?"

"It hurts but I'll manage." Lena made a rude noise
but the sound of the footfalls began to diminish again.
Hawk heard a door open below them and then silence.

"You can't go back to the house," he said to Drey as
he walked her to the SUV. They'd both said nothing
in the hotel. "You heard them. They aren't finished
with you."

"We already knew that they weren't finished. But
if I move out, we'll never know what this is about." Jet
knew where Ethan was. If he'd lied about him being
in Mexico City, then he had to be confident that Ethan
wouldn't call her himself with another story. But was
Ethan working with them? Or were they taking advantage of big brother being gone—just as she'd suspected?

"Drey, this could get dangerous. Look at the
lengths they've already gone to."

"What would you have me do?" she asked, feeling despondent. Sleuthing with Hawk had been fun.
For a while it had been like old times. She'd forgotten the danger she was in. She'd also forgotten for a
while earlier that she was married.

But she reminded herself that it didn't mean that
things were different between them. Yes, they were
attracted to each other. How they could possibly put
the past behind them and find each other again, she
had no idea. It didn't seem possible after the years
they'd stubbornly resisted each other.

Not to mention, she *was* married. It was a fact. Even if Jet and Ethan were in this together, Ethan would be returning at some point. She had to believe that so she could right this wrong. She had made a mistake. She couldn't stay in this marriage—and not just because she was still in love with Hawk.

"I have to stay in the house. Ethan—"

"Seriously? You're going to keep waiting for him to show up?" Hawk shook his head, pulled off his Stetson and raked an irritated hand through his hair. "So you're sticking by your man? Even though he deserted you on your wedding night? Even though he hasn't called or tried to contact you for days and you have only his lying brother's word that he's in Mexico?"

It would have been so easy to fall into Hawk's arms and let him soothe away the hurt of Ethan's sudden departure on their wedding night. Hawk made her feel wanted and needed.

She had worried that she was making a mistake when she'd married Ethan, but she'd gone through with it. She'd made vows to him. If he turned out to be a criminal or even the jerk his brother kept telling her he was, she would deal with Ethan and her marriage then.

Wasn't it bad enough that she already felt that she'd betrayed him because she hadn't loved him as much as she had Hawk—still did love Hawk? Yes, her marriage was a mistake in hindsight. But she had to draw the line at adultery. Maybe it was old-fashioned, but she wasn't raised that way. She said as much to Hawk. "What would you have me do?"

Hawk sighed. "You're right and I love you for being the way you are. But it's killing me not being able to touch you the way I want to. Damn it, can you at least admit that you made a mistake?"

"Can you?" She met his gaze and held it.

"I made a huge mistake letting you go. I've regretted it every day since then. I let my own stupid stubbornness keep me from coming after you all those years ago. Worse, for not knocking down this wall that's been between us on the day you returned to Gilt Edge. Instead, I stood back and let you marry the wrong man."

"Just like that, you can forget about the past?"

"No, not just like that. This has been a long time coming. Only my mule-headedness has stood in the way. Every time I saw you, it tore me up inside. But taking that first step to get you back seemed impossible…" He locked eyes with her. "Then I heard you scream the other night. I didn't give a damn about the past. I just had to get to you to make sure you were all right."

He reached out and brushed his knuckles over her cheek. "I'm going to fight for you, Drey," he said, his voice rough with emotion. "You belong with me. So if you're telling me you want to stay in this marriage—"

"I'm not saying that. But you have to understand. I gave up everything for this marriage, including any chance I might have had with you. So no, I can't bail before I talk to Ethan."

"While you're waiting, though, you have his crazy brother-in-law and your old friend from college wanting to harm you."

"As for Jet and Lena, I'll deal with them."

He swore. "If you're determined to stay in that house, you won't deal with them alone. I'll camp outside until your husband shows up. Then he can explain to me why he left you alone, knowing how much trouble he was in."

His cell phone rang. He answered it. "It's Flint. He wants to see us both. He'll meet us at the ranch."

THE SHERIFF COULD see that he'd walked into something the moment he stepped through the door of the ranch house. The sexual tension between Drey and Hawk was almost palpable. Drey immediately excused herself to go to the restroom. The moment she disappeared up the stairs, he turned to his brother, "What's going on, Hawk? I just got a call from one of the FBI agents."

"You might want to sit down." Hawk explained about Drey's call in the wee hours of the morning, the pills, the search that ended in the surveillance room and what Cyrus had been able to find on the videos.

"The camera on the pond that would have showed Jet Baxter being shot had been turned off that day. Someone has been watching Drey since day one—and fooling with her," Hawk finished.

Flint had known when he walked in that he wasn't going to like this. "I knew you'd been at the Baxter house. Now you've gotten Cyrus involved, as well? The FBI is ready to haul you in—and your brother, too, now."

"Take a look at this. Jet Baxter was in that house.

We saw it on the video. He's trying to get Drey back on drugs."

"Back on drugs? Drey was on drugs?" Flint said as he took Hawk's phone.

"It was a long time ago and under extenuating circumstances," Hawk said.

"Isn't it always?" He heard her coming back but didn't look up as he watched the video. "It's Jet, the brother." Flint frowned. "Why would he do any of this?"

"That's what we don't know," Hawk said and looked up as Drey came down the stairs.

Flint would have to be blind not to see the look that passed between them. He swore under his breath. What was going on between these two? All these years of pushing each other away and *now* they decide they're still in love? He wanted to kick his brother's ass. Drey was legally married, whatever her husband was up to.

"Drey," Flint said as she stepped to where she'd put down her purse and car keys.

"Flint was just saying that the FBI isn't happy that Cyrus and I were at your house," Hawk said to her.

"At this point, you and Drey have become suspects in their investigation," the sheriff said. "I believe they've frozen all of Ethan's accounts."

Drey looked up in surprise. "My credit card Ethan gave me isn't working."

"You won't be able to access your joint bank account either," he said.

She shook her head, looking close to tears. "Luckily, I don't have to worry. Someone sent me a box full of hundred-dollar bills."

Flint didn't like the sound of this. "I would suggest you not spend any of those."

"I don't plan to. I still have some money of my own, fortunately."

"Baxter hasn't skipped the country yet according to the feds, right?" Hawk said. "I was thinking that there might be a way to draw him out. If we shut off his surveillance room, he'll come to see what's going on."

Flint shook his head. "You have to stay out of this."

"I have to go," Drey said as she picked up her purse and keys and started to leave.

"Wait, I don't want you going back to that house," Hawk said as he got up to follow her to the door.

Flint could hear them whispering, clearly arguing.

It wasn't until Drey left that Flint turned to his brother. "What's going on, Hawk?"

"She's going back to that house. She won't listen to reason."

"Reason? I keep having to remind you that she married Ethan Baxter and at this point, we don't know that he's guilty of anything."

"What about the FBI investigation?" Hawk demanded.

"I have no idea why they are investigating him or if he's personally responsible," Flint pointed out. "They haven't made an arrest even though they led me to believe it was pending."

"But we do know that his brother is trying to gaslight her," his brother said angrily as he began to pace in front of the fireplace. "Who knows what he and his girlfriend are going to do next?"

"So far they haven't done anything that I can prove and arrest them for," he said.

"*So far.* That's just it. Drey is in danger. And you expect me to sit back and do nothing?"

Flint shook his head. "The FBI is watching the house. Drey knows what she's up against. I suspect she's safer right now than with you."

"What?"

"You ready to put the past behind you now?" Flint demanded. "That's right, Lillie told me your secret. So all is suddenly forgiven?" He swore. "Damn it, Hawk, you break that woman's heart again and so help me..."

ETHAN'S HOUSE WAS the last place Drey wanted to go.

Hawk had put up an argument, but ultimately, she felt she had little choice. If she had any hope of finding out what was going on, she had to stay, especially since she had the feeling that Jet wanted her out of that house.

What she had to her advantage was that Jet didn't know she wasn't back on the drugs. Once the FBI moved on Ethan... And she had no doubt now that they would. But when? Within days—or hours? They'd frozen Ethan's assets. Fortunately, she'd held back some money of her own.

Ethan had been insistent that they have a traditional marriage. It had appealed to her after all of these years of being on her own. Also it was what her parents had had. No separate checking accounts. Ethan would handle the money, she would run the house. At that time, she'd thought the house would be a penthouse in New York City. She'd welcomed the change.

Yes, she thought looking back as she drove toward Mountain Crest, Ethan had promised her exactly what she wanted, almost as if he'd already known.

Lena, she thought with a curse. They'd shared their hopes and dreams, so of course Lena would know what a small-town, conservative girl Drey was—the drugs aside. Did she need any more proof that she'd been targeted? She was exactly what Ethan had been looking for.

She slowed as she pulled up to the gate to the property. A chill ran up her spine as she put in the pass code. The gate yawned open and she drove through, telling herself she could do this. If Ethan was somewhere watching her through the surveillance equipment in the house, then he knew what Jet was doing. He condoned it, maybe even was in on the plan.

So why didn't she believe that? Maybe she had been targeted in some way. And even though Ethan wasn't the love of her life, she didn't believe he was that cruel. Unless all this had been a test to see if she would reach out to her former lover, Hawk Cahill.

In that case, she'd failed miserably again.

So what would happen now? she wondered as she pulled up in front of the house. The lights came on— just as they were programmed to do. She had to hand it to Ethan, he really had built himself a very technologically advanced house. No wonder he was so proud of it.

She got out, not looking up at all that glass because this time she knew she was being watched. Being watched by the house, Ethan, Jet and Lena, and maybe the FBI, as well. Ethan's car was still parked where he'd left it on their wedding night, the keys still in it.

It struck her as odd that he'd left it there after opening the house for her that night. Ethan prided himself on taking care of his possessions. He would have put it in the underground garage beneath the house. He definitely would have put it away if he'd left for Mexico and hadn't planned to come back soon.

She supposed he could have been called away just as Jet had said. The helicopter could have picked him up and taken him to the airport where he flew to Mexico City. It was possible. Wasn't that why she hadn't packed up and left? Because she had to believe he would be back and then...

She didn't want to think that far ahead. First she had to survive another day.

As she entered the house, she tried not to look for the cameras watching her. Act normal. Right. She no longer knew what normal was.

All she could think about was being at Hawk's ranch. If the neighbor hadn't shown up when he did... She shook her head, telling herself it had given her time to come to her senses. This was not the way she wanted to start again with Hawk—if that was even possible. If there was a chance they could find their way back together, she didn't want it beginning with an affair.

Drey brushed the painful thoughts away and

steeled herself for staying in this house until… Until she knew why Ethan had married her, why he'd left her on their wedding night, why his brother was trying to destroy her, she couldn't think about the future, especially one with Hawk.

She spent the day keeping busy, figuring Jet and Lena wouldn't make their move until that night. In the kitchen she made herself a cup of hot tea. She'd been tempted to look in the freezer, wondering if the thumb was back. Then, taking her tea, she wandered up to the master suite, going through the motions, all the time, knowing that Jet and Lena were watching her. Maybe Ethan, too. Watching her and waiting for her to do what?

CHAPTER TWENTY-FOUR

BILLIE DEE WAS surprised but delighted when the kitchen door opened the next morning and her daughter stuck her head in.

"I heard you always have a pot of coffee going?" Gigi said.

"You know it. Come on in. How do you take yours?"

"Black and strong," the young woman said. She took the chair at the table Billie Dee offered her.

Carrying over two cups, she joined Gigi. Her heart was pounding. After yesterday she feared she might never see her again.

"You have to understand," Gigi said after they'd talked about the weather, Montana and AJ. "All this has happened so fast." She stopped to take a sip of her coffee as if needing time to say what she came for.

"I do understand. You had to be shocked when Ashley Jo—AJ—told you," Billie Dee said. "I know how shocked I was when I saw you, when I opened my eyes…" Her voice broke. She, too, took a sip of her coffee, telling herself to let the young woman talk.

"In a way, I feel as if this is disloyal to my parents and yet at the same time, I know they would be happy that AJ found you." She looked away for a moment. "They would want me to have all the family I could."

"Gigi, I don't expect anything from you. I mean that. We don't know each other. I'm a stranger—"

"That's just it. I feel...something," she said, looking up to lock eyes with her birth mother. "I know it's crazy. Not according to AJ, of course. But it feels so odd, this...connection I feel."

Billie Dee held her breath. "I feel the same way."

"I have to get back to Houston," Gigi said after another sip of her coffee. "The fire inspector says I can get back into my restaurant and work can start on gutting the part that was so badly damaged."

"I know you can't stay." Billie Dee pulled out a piece of paper from her pocket. "I wrote down my phone number and address. I wasn't sure I'd see you again, but I thought if I did..." She laid it on the table between them. "You don't have to use either of them."

Gigi pulled the sheet of paper to her. There was a pen on the window ledge. She took it, tore off a piece of the paper and wrote down her phone number and address. She passed it over to Billie Dee.

"Just give me a call sometime," Gigi said.

"You can take all the time you need."

The young woman hesitated. "AJ told me that you've been waiting to get married until you found your daughter."

"That AJ, what are we going to do with her?"

Gigi smiled. "Let me know when the wedding is going to be. I'd like to come."

Tears welled in her eyes. She reached across the table and took her daughter's hand in hers. "Thank you."

DREY WOKE TO a text from Hawk, surprised that she'd slept fairly well and that nothing had awakened her in the night.

Are you okay?

Quiet, uneventful night. So yes.

Good. I was worried. I still don't like you being there alone.

But I'm not alone remember?

When this is over...I want another chance.

You sure about that?

Positive. I love you.

We'll talk then.

Her heart was beating a little faster as she held the phone to her chest. Was it possible for her and Hawk to find their way back to each other?

She couldn't think about that now. She started to put her phone away but had an idea. The one thing she remembered about Lena was how she loved her coffee shop coffee first thing in the morning. She called the hotel, described the valet and a few moments later, Bobby, the valet, came on the line.

"We met yesterday. You were going to tell me about someplace to get a good meal in the area."

He chuckled. "Auburn hair, cute as a button? Oh, you bet I remember you," he said with a laugh. "You ready for that meal?"

"Actually, there's something else I need." She told him. "I will definitely make it worth your while. And yes, I mean with cash."

He laughed. "You're on."

Thirty minutes later, her cell phone rang.

"She just left, headed up the street toward the coffee shop. It's where she's gone every day since she's been staying here."

DREY FOUND LENA sitting at one of the outdoor tables, drinking her coffee and staring at her phone. She walked over to the table. It took a few moments for Lena to look up.

"Drey." Lena quickly tried to hide her surprise. She looked around as if trying to determine whether Drey had come alone and then seemed to relax.

"I thought we should have a talk. Mind if I sit down or are you expecting Jet?"

"No, I'm alone, but I suspect you knew that before you approached me," her former friend said. Up close, Lena wasn't half as put together as her Baxter Inc. photo had made her appear.

"You and Jet. How exactly did that happen?"

Lena leaned back in her chair and gave her a look filled with attitude. "Actually, I met Ethan first."

"I see."

"Hmm, I doubt you do. We were married."

She hadn't expected that. Then again Jet had kept calling Drey his brother's new bride as if there had been an old one. "I thought you were in love with Brett Coldwell?"

"He was a passing phase. I met Ethan and Brett was history."

"So it was love at first sight." She thought of the way Ethan had swept her off her feet. She suspected it was the way he operated his business—and his love life.

Lena smiled. "You could say that."

"But now you're with his brother."

Lena looked away. "The marriage didn't work out."

"Another woman?" Drey asked, half-afraid of what she would say.

Instead Lena laughed. "You? Not hardly. I was young. He had his work. He never had time for me. I wanted more. He divorced me like I was one of his companies that wasn't meeting his expectations." Her words reeked of bitterness.

"But you're still at Baxter Inc."

"I got the job at Baxter Inc. as part of my settlement and I met Jet."

"And the rest is history." Drey nodded. "This explains a lot. So you both have an ax to grind when it comes to Ethan. So where do I fit into all this?"

Lena met her gaze. "I don't know what you mean."

"Sure you do. How was it that Ethan just happened to come into the library where I worked here in Gilt Edge?"

"I might have mentioned I knew someone who used to live in Gilt Edge when I heard that Ethan was building his monument to himself."

Drey had to smile. Wasn't that the way she thought it might have gone down? "Playing matchmaker?"

"Not hardly. No one could have been more shocked when Jet told me that Ethan was engaged—to you— and then so quickly married. It was like déjà vu. Ethan and another merger at the snap of his fingers. So how are you enjoying being married to him?" She chuckled. "Something tells me he never mentioned his first wife to you."

"I'd rather talk about what you and Jet are doing."

"Vacationing here in Montana? You have a problem with that?"

"I have a problem with the two of you trying to make me think I'm crazy. So, what is it you want?"

The woman's face remained expressionless.

"Maybe what I should be asking is where does Ethan fit into all this?"

"You'll have to ask him that when you see him."

"Did you know he's being investigated by the FBI? Oh, I see you did. Why do I get the feeling that I won't be seeing Ethan?"

Lena's smile was filled with venom. "It could be the pills you're taking."

"Sorry, but I quit those right after you moved out at college."

"My mistake. I thought I heard you were back on them." Lena picked up her coffee, pushed back her chair and rose. "I'd stay but I think this conversation has run its course. Whatever problems you're having, they have nothing to do with me."

"Really? You might want to tell Jet that I have him on video leaving those pills beside my bed." She had caught the woman flat-footed. She hadn't missed Lena's surprised expression. She hadn't known about the videos? Did that mean she didn't know about the surveillance room? "I have other videos as well, of his…tricks. I've turned them over to the sheriff. So whatever else you have planned… I'm onto you. And so is the sheriff and the FBI."

AFTER A RESTLESS night with little sleep, Hawk had awakened with only one thought: Drey. He'd texted and was now relieved that she'd had an uneventful night. But he couldn't shake the one question he'd awakened with.

Why was the FBI so convinced that Ethan Baxter was still in that house hiding somewhere? Of course they would be tracking any use of his passport and now they'd frozen his credit cards and accounts.

Which meant he wasn't going anywhere unless he'd planned ahead for this particular problem. Hawk thought of the money that had been sent to Drey and told himself Ethan had believed he had more time before the FBI moved in. He wouldn't use that much money simply to involve Drey in his mess.

Having seen the house, Hawk didn't believe there

was a room where the man could be hiding. It would have to be large enough for the man's ego. Which meant, if it existed, Ethan Baxter could be very close by. It made sense, given that his car was still parked in front of the house, the last place Drey had seen him was in the house and the FBI was watching the house and hadn't seen him come out.

The thought gave him the creeps that Ethan was in there with Drey and had been watching them all this time. Then again, the whole place and the man who built it did. It was so sterile and cold. The house he and Drey had planned to build when they got married was an old farmhouse style with a wide front porch and lots of bedrooms for all the children they were going to have.

He told himself that it wasn't too late. Damned if he wouldn't get her back. He hated to think of the lost years, but he wouldn't let any more time go by than he had to, he told himself.

Showered and dressed, he headed for his pickup. He didn't know why he hadn't thought of this before. Of course there would be a secret room in that house. A panic room. A man like Ethan Baxter would have one, Hawk was sure of it. But where was it? Maybe a whole secret area where a person could hide out and not be detected.

Harvey Construction had an office uptown in one of the old bank buildings. The business specialized in more modern design and had built several of the newer buildings downtown in the past five years. So it was no surprise that the Baxter house was one of the first ones they'd taken on when they'd opened their doors.

Damon Harvey sat behind a huge desk in a large open room. Several other employees from architects to drafters and construction workers were busy in other parts of the first-floor office.

Hawk had met the six-four blond, blue-eyed Viking-looking Damon only once. But when he walked in the door, Damon remembered him.

"Hawk Cahill," the man said, rising from his desk to come around and shake his hand. "What brings you off the ranch?"

"I was hoping you could help me," he said. "But it is kind of a private matter."

"No problem." Damon asked the others to step out for a coffee break and lock the door behind them. "So what can I do for you?" he asked as he motioned Hawk into a chair in front of his desk before taking his own.

"Baxter house. You built it, right?"

"We worked with Ethan Baxter on it."

Something in the man's tone told Hawk that it hadn't been easy working with Ethan. "I need to know if you put in any kind of secret room, possibly underground."

Damon raised an eyebrow.

"I only ask because I'm afraid a friend of mine is in trouble. It's a long story… I wouldn't ask if it wasn't very important."

The owner leaned back in his chair as if giving it some thought. "You can't ask Baxter?"

He shook his head. "No."

"What about his wife?"

"Between you and me? She is living in the house alone right now and has had some...strange, frightening things happening. I suspect there is a way for a person to come in and out of that house without being noticed."

Damon chewed his lip for a moment. "We did most of the work on the house, but Ethan had already brought in a crew out of California for the bunker."

"Bunker?"

"Used to call them bomb shelters."

"How is it accessed?"

"Now *that* I don't know. Baxter saw to all of that along with the one carpenter he made sign a non-disclosure agreement about its location and operation."

Hawk let out a curse. "How many people know about this bomb shelter?"

"Only the California crew who put it in and my carpenter who constructed the secret access panel, but he moved to Florida last year. Baxter didn't want anyone else on the job to know about it. He was that way about most every part of the house. I can give you the carpenter's name, but I doubt he'll talk to you for fear of Baxter retaliating. I only know about it because my carpenter hated working for the man and kind of feared him. So much so much that he quit on me and left the state. He was a damned good carpenter. I was sorry as hell to see him go."

"Wouldn't the plans have to be on file in the building department in order to get permits?" Hawk asked.

But the man was already shaking his head. "It's county. So this was outside of that."

"So we aren't talking one of those old 1950s' bomb shelters," Hawk said. "We could be talking—"

"A billionaire bunker."

"What is that?"

"You ever meet Ethan Baxter?" the man said. "Only the best for him."

CHAPTER TWENTY-FIVE

DREY SWUNG BY the hotel to pay Bobby for his help later that afternoon. She'd spent the day trying to keep busy by running errands all over town and having a late lunch with Lillie.

"Not sure what your interest is," Bobby said after she slipped him a twenty, "but I overheard her and her...boyfriend...saying they would be checking out tomorrow."

So whatever they had planned was going down today, Drey thought. "Thanks for your help. You have my number if there is anything else you think I might be interested in."

"Like dinner?"

"Probably not."

He grinned. "All a guy can do is try, right?"

It was late afternoon when she finally put together somewhat of a plan. She climbed into the SUV and put in a call to the sheriff, then Hawk and asked them to meet her at their ranch.

"Whatever Jet and Lena have planned, it's going down tonight," Drey said when they had all gathered. She quickly filled them in on what she'd learned from Lena—and the valet at the hotel.

"Now that they know you're onto them, you definitely can't go back to that house," Hawk said.

"How else am I going to find out what they're after?" Drey argued.

"I don't like it either." Flint spoke up.

"Well, if you go back there, I'm going with you," Hawk said.

"You know that won't work if Jet and Lena are the ones watching the monitors."

"Or Ethan," he said. "I've been doing some investigating, as well." He told them what he'd found out at the contractor's office. "I think Ethan is hiding out in the bomb shelter. It's perfect since he went to a lot of trouble so that no one knew about it. Possibly not even the FBI knows about it."

"What are you suggesting?" Flint asked.

"Find the entrance to the bomb shelter and you'll find Ethan Baxter."

The sheriff shook his head. "Even if he is hiding out there, he has every right. It's his house. But that's not why you want to bust him, is it?"

Hawk looked at Drey. "No. If Baxter is hiding in his bomb shelter, then his wife needs to know about it. She needs to know that he's been watching her all this time on surveillance equipment."

Flint raised an eyebrow. "Let's just think about what he's seen so far, if that is the case."

Drey held up a hand. "Ethan can't be the one monitoring the surveillance system. It's got to be Jet. We saw his laptop when we searched his room."

Hawk didn't look convinced. "We need to know one way or the other."

"You're talking about tearing up his house to find the entrance to his bomb shelter," Flint said. "I repeat, so far the man hasn't done anything illegal. But the two of you are treading damn close. Start damaging that house and you're looking at jail time, not to mention Ethan Baxter suing you into next week."

"If we shut down the surveillance equipment," Hawk was saying, "he'll show his face."

"Or know that you are onto him and run," the sheriff said.

"Run? Not if the only way out of that bomb shelter is through that house and we're waiting for him," Hawk shot back.

"And what about Jet and Lena?" Drey asked. "At this point, they are more of a threat than Ethan."

"We don't know that Ethan isn't in cahoots with the two of them," Hawk reminded her.

"Both of you seem to have forgotten about the FBI," Flint said.

She sighed and turned to Flint. "I want to talk to the FBI. I want to help them put Ethan behind bars if that's where he belongs." Both Flint and Hawk looked as if they were about to argue. "We have to end this before Jet and Lena do. Maybe it was a mistake telling Lena that I found the surveillance equipment. I told her that I'd turned copies over to the sheriff and FBI."

"There wasn't anything on the videos that we could have used anyway," Hawk said.

"But don't you see, now that Jet knows, if he's the

one who's been monitoring the house, he will erase all of the videos," she said. "It will prove that he's the one behind all this. And since so far, he hasn't done anything illegal..."

"What bothers me is what Jet is after," the sheriff said. "He knows you're onto him. So why not run? After you called, I checked. He's still registered at the hotel—and so is Lena Franklin. Whatever he's after in that house must be something he needs desperately." He looked at Drey. "Desperate people can kill."

"It could be the money, I suppose," she said.

"That's why she isn't doing this alone," Hawk said. "Don't worry. I'll wait until it's dark and sneak into the house. Jet won't know I'm there because when you get back to the house, Drey, I want you to pull the plug on the surveillance equipment. Jet will have to go in blind."

"What about the FBI?" Flint asked.

"I guess we'll find out if they're watching the house," Hawk said, making his brother cuss under his breath.

"No," Drey said. "Let me talk to the FBI. It's the only way."

"I KNOW DIERDRE HUNTER," Flint was saying into the phone with the FBI agent. "She was part of our family growing up. She was dating my brother Hawk all through high school and college. I'm convinced that she knows nothing about Ethan Baxter's business. However, since she married him and moved into that house a few days ago, someone has been trying to gaslight her. His brother, Jet—or Ethan himself, if as you believe, he's still in that house. But Drey hasn't seen him since their wedding night. He never came up to bed."

She watched the sheriff listen to whatever the agent was saying to him, only occasionally nodding or saying "Okay."

"Yes, she can go to my sister's house…Yes," Flint said, looking over at her. "I can give you my word she won't leave town…Yes, you have her full cooperation, as well as mine and my department's." He disconnected and looked over at them.

"The FBI is going to raid the house first thing in the morning. I told the agent that you would go stay with Lillie," Flint said to Drey and then looked at his brother. "They don't want either of you around when they make the bust."

"But Ethan's not there," Drey said. "All they are going to find is an empty house. And I can assure you, Ethan isn't the type to hide out in some bomb shelter all this time."

The sheriff shrugged. "Then that's all they'll find. But we'll know for sure that Ethan isn't in there. After that, they'll want to talk to you, Drey. I told them you would cooperate and that you would be at Lillie's. Don't make a liar out of me."

"So I can't even go by the house to pick up a few of my things?" she asked.

"No, and if you try to contact Ethan to warn him—"

"You know me better than that, Flint."

"But you can see how any phone call could be misconstrued—"

"Of course. I'll go straight to Lillie's, I won't talk to anyone but her and Trask and TC, the baby. I promise."

"I know," the sheriff said. "That's why I stuck my neck out for you."

"So you're going to be part of the raid?" Hawk asked.

Flint nodded. "Just as backup."

"Does this mean it will all be over?" Drey asked.

"If Ethan is anywhere in the house or on the property, he will be arrested, if that's what you mean," the sheriff said.

"And if not?" Hawk asked.

"A warrant has been issued for his arrest so I would imagine they will continue to look for him."

Drey groaned. "And if they don't find him?"

"They might find evidence or a lead where he might be," Flint said. "Maybe they will get lucky and tie this all up quickly."

That didn't sound very hopeful, she thought. "What about Jet and Lena?"

The sheriff shook his head. "If they do come to the house for whatever reason, at least you won't be there."

"But what if they find whatever they're after?" she asked.

"We don't know what their game is," Flint said. "But it's nothing for you to worry about. With luck, they'll get caught up in the raid tomorrow and we'll finally get some answers."

Drey nodded and looked at the time. "I should call Lillie and let her know I'm on my way."

"I checked with her earlier," Flint said. "She's expecting you."

Drey saw the two brothers exchange a look. It appeared the sheriff was doing his best to keep her and Hawk away from each other until this was over. She could have told him it wasn't necessary—at least until... Until what? If the FBI was right and Ethan was in that house...

Then there really wouldn't be anything to say to him, would there? He would have deceived her. He and his brother would have put her through hell for whatever purpose. And she might never know why. But at least it would be over for her and the marriage.

And if he wasn't in the house? How much longer could she live in limbo? How much longer could she go without admitting that the marriage was a mistake and doing something about it?

She felt emotionally drained and realized she couldn't make any decisions tonight. After tomorrow, she would know something. Until then... She couldn't wait to get to Lillie's. Seeing her friend always picked her up. And seeing their beautiful little son both helped and hurt.

She looked to Hawk, feeling the need to say something.

"I'll come by Lillie's first thing in the morning if it's all right," he said before she could speak. "I know I don't want to be alone and who knows how long before we hear something." Obviously he'd also felt the need to say something to her.

"That sounds good."

"I'll let you know as soon as I can what happens tomorrow. I know one of the agents will be talking to Drey no matter how it goes down," Flint said.

"If they don't find Ethan, then we'll get you a good lawyer," Hawk said.

"I don't have money for a lawyer."

"Don't worry about that," Flint said before Hawk could. "We won't let you get railroaded by all this."

She smiled at him. "Thank you. Thank you for everything." Turning to Hawk, she said, "I don't know what I would have done without you."

IT WAS DARK by the time she walked to the SUV parked in the ranch yard. Over by the barn, a farm light cast a golden circle of light. Still, she felt jumpy. Was this really going to end? Tomorrow, if they found Ethan...

Her cell phone rang, making her jump. As she opened the SUV's door, she checked it. Lillie. Smiling, she took the call as she climbed in.

"I'm just leaving the ranch now."

"I was just checking," Lillie said. "I have your room all made up."

She climbed behind the wheel. "I hope you didn't go to any trouble."

"You mean like finding some rom-com movies for us to watch along with a big bowl of popcorn?" Lillie asked with a laugh.

"I'm on my way." She disconnected and reached for the key in the ignition. It wasn't there!

The realization hit her at the same moment she felt the barrel end of the gun press against the side of her neck. Her gaze shot up to the rearview mirror as Lena's face appeared in it from her hiding place in the back.

"Don't do anything stupid or I will kill you," Lena said.

"The sheriff and his brother are right inside the house," Drey said, thinking all she had to do was lay on the horn or—

"Jet is also in the house. One wrong move from you and he kills them both. Trust me, he has nothing to lose and neither do I." She jabbed the barrel of the pistol harder into Drey's neck. "Now, here is what we are going to do. I'm going to give you the key. You are going to start the car and drive away. Once Jet hears us leave, he will meet us up the road without harming either the sheriff or your old boyfriend, Hawk."

She knew about Hawk? Her shock must have shown in her face because Lena said, "You think I don't remember you talking about him ad nauseam back in college?" Lena laughed. "Seriously, he is everything you said he was from what I can see. So if you don't want to get him killed…" She held out the keys.

Drey took them carefully. Her fingers trembled, though, as she slipped the key into the ignition. Her mind was racing. She wanted desperately to slam on the horn or drive the SUV into the side of the barn.

The last thing she wanted to do was leave with this woman, let alone pick up Jet down the road.

"Why don't you tell me what is really going on?" she asked as the SUV engine turned over and she cranked the wheel to drive out of the ranch yard.

"We're going back to the house. Hand me your phone. Your friend is going to have to eat that popcorn alone."

Drey saw no choice. She handed her phone back as she drove slowly down the ranch road. If Lena was telling the truth, then Jet was still in the house, still capable of hurting two people she loved. She watched the road ahead, but also Lena as she texted Lillie, then pocketed the phone.

"Why do you need me back at the house?" she asked.

Lena didn't answer. "Slow down up here. Jet should be crossing that pasture anytime now."

As dark as it was, she was still able to see a figure coming from toward the back of the house. Lena had been telling the truth. So if Jet had really been in the house... Had he heard about the raid by the FBI in the morning?

"Why don't you tell me what's going on?" she said as she opened her window.

"You'll find out soon enough. Stop right here."

She braked and looked out her open window. She could see Jet coming across the pasture. Past him the lights of the house glowed from behind the curtains. If anyone happened to be looking out the back door they would see her stopped on the road and be concerned. But she doubted anyone was. Flint would be leaving soon, though. She looked for his headlights behind them but all she saw was darkness.

The passenger-side door opened and she turned to see Jet climb in. "Any trouble?" he asked Lena.

"Nothing I couldn't handle." She sounded as pleased with herself as Jet looked.

"One problem," Drey said. "The sheriff will be coming down this road in a few minutes."

"We won't be here," Jet said. "Get the car moving."

She had a bad feeling that if she drove them back to the house on the mountain, her premonition would come true. She would die in that house.

"You hear me?" Jet snapped.

"I hear you." As she started to shift the vehicle into gear, she reached past the shifter, grabbed the keys and started to hurl them out into the darkness.

Jet was faster than she expected. He caught hold of her arm as she made the throw. The keys didn't make it all the way into the tall grass of the pasture. She heard them hit an instant before Jet cursed. "Bitch!" Then he backhanded her.

Her head snapped back. Lena grabbed a handful of her hair and pressed the barrel of the gun against her cheek. She felt it smack into her teeth and tasted blood.

The passenger-side door banged open as Jet jumped out. "Did you see where they went?" he demanded of Lena.

"Not far. Straight-out."

Drey held out hope that he wouldn't be able to

find them, but unfortunately it didn't take long. She heard the driver's-side door open, felt him release her seat belt.

"Get over," Jet said, giving her a shove.

Lena let go of her hair, but not quickly enough. It yanked her head back as Jet shoved her over into the other seat. She banged her knee on the center console and her head on the side window as Jet reached across her and slammed the passenger-side door and locked it.

"Put your seat belt on," he ordered as he inserted the key and got the engine going.

He must have seen what she was thinking. Her hand started to go to the door handle...

"Don't make me hit you again," he warned.

She fumbled the seat belt on, checking the side mirror, hoping to see headlights. But she saw nothing. Flint must still be at the house talking to Hawk. Her knee hurt and so did her head. Her lip and mouth were bleeding. But she had a bad feeling that whatever these two had planned for her was much worse.

"She tries anything else, shoot her," Jet ordered. "I'm already tired of dickin' around with her."

"She asked why she had to go back to the house with us," Lena said.

"Well, our plans have had to change, thanks to you," he said. "If you'd just taken the pills like a good girl..."

"But you had to call your hunky cowboy boyfriend, didn't you?" Lena said. "I just wish Ethan had been here to see the two of you together. He would have lost his mind. You probably don't know this, but Ethan goes crazy with jealousy when he thinks any man has anything he wants."

"You've made some bad decisions right from the start, including marrying my brother," Jet said with a grin. "I wouldn't suggest you make any more."

She'd been trying to put all the pieces together as she drove. While she couldn't see the whole picture, at least a couple of things had become evident to her.

"You drugged me on my wedding night," Drey said and realized it could have begun even earlier than that. At the reception? She realized he could have been one of the serving crew and she wouldn't have noticed. She'd been so…off balance her whole wedding day, fighting the nagging thought that she'd made a terrible mistake.

"No," she said, remembering how weird she'd felt on the way to the house that night. "You drugged me at the reception."

Jet laughed. "Not me. That would have been your loving husband. He told me he put something in your water glass at the reception and insisted you drink it because he knew you wouldn't even take a sip of your champagne. He said not to worry about you. You'd be out until late the next day. Apparently it wasn't the first time he'd used the pills on you." He lifted an eyebrow at Drey's shock.

"So why did he marry me?" Clearly it hadn't been out of love.

"He needed a witness when he faked his death," Jet said as if she was incredibly slow-witted.

Faked his death? That was all she'd been? A witness? Another device for Ethan Baxter to get what he wanted. She said as much.

"Don't take it so hard," Jet said. "He said he wished there was some way to take you with him when he disappeared. He was fond of you and actually felt bad about leaving you to deal with the FBI."

Drey shook her head. Fond of her? And she'd been feeling guilty about not loving him the way she felt she should have? She'd told herself that she'd loved him, but being around Hawk, she knew that wasn't true. She'd been flattered by his attention, swept up in the fairy tale, but at their wedding all her instincts had told her to run.

If only she had.

"Where is Ethan now?" she asked.

"Oh, you'll be seeing him real soon," Jet said with a laugh. He glanced in the rearview mirror and grinned at Lena. "We'll all be seeing Ethan and then the fun can begin."

CHAPTER TWENTY-SIX

"You might as well have a drink and settle in for the night," Flint said after Drey drove away.

"What? Are you my babysitter?" Hawk couldn't see himself settling in, not tonight, not knowing what was going down in the morning. "I just want this to be over."

"Then what?"

Hawk looked over at his brother. "Then Drey will be safe. Look, I know what you're getting at. I love Drey."

"That's not news."

He sighed. "I want a second chance with her."

"Why now?"

He groaned and raked a hand through his hair. "What are you asking?"

"Did it take her getting married for you to realize that you want her?"

"What if it did? I know it sounds stupid, but maybe I thought we would get back together somehow. But when she told me she was getting married…"

"You could have tried to stop her."

He shook his head. "I thought about it. But she was marrying a wealthy businessman." He shrugged.

"I couldn't compete with that. I wished her the best. What else could I do?"

"So what's changed?"

He stepped to the fireplace and rested his arm on the mantel. "He doesn't deserve her." He shrugged again. "When I realized Drey was in trouble, nothing else mattered but making sure she was all right."

"Not the past?"

Hawk shook his head. "Drey and I have talked. In the past all we did was fight. Things have come out that have changed things. That's why I just want this to be over. Once the truth comes out about Ethan Baxter…he'll be history."

"He might not be guilty in all this. Then what?"

"He's guilty enough and I suspect more will come out tomorrow. She can divorce him."

"If she wants to after tomorrow. Don't get ahead of yourself, little brother," Flint said and got to his feet. "Whatever we find out tomorrow, Drey is going to need time."

Hawk nodded, although the thought made him anxious. They'd already lost so much time. "Let's just see how it all goes down tomorrow. If Ethan Baxter is in that house…" He shook his head.

"I need to get home," Flint said and started toward the door. "You going to be all right?"

"I am, knowing that Drey should be at Lillie's by now."

"Try to get some sleep and don't leave this house."

"No problem," he said sarcastically. He looked at his watch. *Cyrus should be back soon*, he thought.

He thought about waiting up for him, but maybe he would try to get some sleep. It was that or get drunk.

But first he had to call Drey.

AT THE GATE, Jet demanded the code. Drey gave it to him, knowing from the look on his face that he would get it from her one way or another anyway.

As they drove in, she looked around for the FBI. Not that they would be out in the open but right now she needed some sign that they were still watching. That they had a clue about what was going on. Not that she expected them to do anything until morning. They were after Ethan—not Jet.

"Looking for the FBI?" Jet asked, amusement in his tone. "Wastin' your time. They're only interested in Ethan."

The house came into view and this time the premonition felt too real. But if she was going to die here, she had to know why.

"What do you want from me?" she asked, hating that her voice broke.

He seemed surprised by the question. "Just a little help with a problem we have. You'll see." He glanced in the rearview mirror at Lena. He gave her a satisfied look as if now everything was finally working out.

She couldn't understand why they were taking her back to the house. Before, with the pills, it was as if they hadn't wanted her around. Now they needed her? That didn't make sense. Her heart pounded harder. She couldn't imagine how she would be able to get away from these two. Her only hope was finding out as much as she could.

"Ethan didn't call you from Mexico City, did he?" Drey said.

Jet laughed. "Seriously? You really believed that?"

"She still wants to believe that he's her prince come to save her from her doldrums in life," Lena said and scoffed.

"You said we were going to see him soon," Drey reminded him.

"True enough. So he couldn't be in Mexico City, now, could he?" He pulled into the underground garage, parked and used Ethan's phone to close the door. She recognized it and wondered how he'd gotten into it. Maybe Ethan had a backup pass code that Jet had figured out. Or—

The lights went out, pitching them into darkness for a few moments until the lights came on.

He chuckled as he pocketed the phone. "Ethan really thought of everything, didn't he? Too bad his system still has a glitch in it." He turned to Drey. "Get out."

Drey started to, thinking this might be her chance to make a run for it. But even as she thought it, she knew she couldn't outrun a bullet—or Jet for that matter.

Not that she was given a chance to run. Lena jumped out of the SUV and grabbed hold of the back of her jacket. She still had the gun pointed at her. Jet came around the vehicle and grabbed Drey's arm.

"Come on. Let's get this done. Keep the gun on her just in case she does something stupid."

They all three moved to the elevator. Once inside the small glassed-in box, Jet hit the button she noticed for the floor with the conference and guest rooms. That was where Ethan was meeting them?

Drey felt sick to her stomach in the small space with the two of them. Jet still had a tight grip on her arm. In the reflection of the three of them in the glass-sided elevator, she could see that Lena kept the gun trained on her. Why were they so afraid she might get away?

"What are we doing?" she asked. Jet had Ethan's phone. He could operate all of the house with it. Why did he need her?

"We ran into a couple of small problems," Jet said. "Ethan lied to me about where he planned to put a few things. Like the safe. It took me forever to find it," he said with a curse. "Ethan did one hell of a job hiding it."

"That's what you've been looking for," she said. The elevator stopped. Jet dragged her off, Lena following in their wake as he led her into one of the conference rooms.

"Ethan and all his hidden rooms," he said under his breath. "What kills me is all this high-tech security. Only a man swimming in money would go to these extremes. It was like he thought doomsday was coming."

Both Jet and Lena laughed. "And he was right," Lena said. "He just didn't expect it to come so soon for him."

"I still don't understand," Drey said. "If you found the safe—"

"Opening it turned out to be a small problem," Lena said. "That's where you come in."

"I don't know the combination." She hadn't even known there *was* a safe hidden somewhere in the house. But she should have. Of course Ethan would have one. Was that where he planned to put the money he had sent to her?

"What's in the safe that you're so desperate for?" she asked not really expecting him to tell her. Something Jet wanted or needed so badly that he'd kept her drugged up while he searched for it, she realized.

"Everything I need to keep from going to prison and more," he said with a smile as he pressed a spot on the wall and the panel began to slowly slide back to reveal a huge safe.

She stared at it, wondering how they thought she was going to be able to help them open it.

Jet reached into his pocket and took out a small plastic bag.

She recoiled when she saw what was inside.

"Surprise," he said as he carefully withdrew the thumb with obvious distaste.

"Oh my God." Drey took a step back only to run into Lena and the barrel of the gun she had on her. "It *is* Ethan's." That was how he'd opened her husband's phone.

Jet was studying the thumb and looking unhappy. "I'm not sure how much longer this is going to be any good. It's now or never."

Lena pushed her toward the safe.

"First yours," Jet said as he grabbed Drey's hand and dragged her closer to the safe. Her hands were trembling as he wrenched her thumb to turn it and force her thumb pad against the small glowing disk.

A green light came on and pulsed before turning red again.

Jet grinned and shoved her back at Lena. "Just as I thought. My brother, the crafty bastard." He pressed Ethan's thumb to the glowing disk on the front of the safe and seemed to hold his breath. She could see Jet's expectant face. He was almost salivating.

Nothing happened. He pressed the thumb again and swore. "I should have left it in the freezer." He gave Drey a withering look as if it was all her fault. She gagged and tried not to throw up. Ethan's thumb.

"You killed your own brother?" she cried. She didn't want to think about how Jet had gotten it, but she suspected it meant Ethan was dead. Had been dead this whole time? She gagged again.

"I just took his thumb," Jet said. "If he had simply opened the safe, he would still have it." Her stomach roiled. "Don't you dare throw up," he warned.

"I told you we should have made the glue copy," Lena was saying. "They walk you right through it on the internet. But you were so sure it took the real thing. Now what are we going to do?"

Drey couldn't believe this. Ethan's safe took both of their prints? As a precaution because he knew his brother?

"We have no choice," Jet said with a curse. He

threw the thumb across the room. It slid on the white marble, coming to rest next to one of the conference chair legs.

"There's only one thing to do." Jet looked at Lena. "We'll have to use the other one of Ethan's thumbs, which means it's time to pay my brother a visit."

CHAPTER TWENTY-SEVEN

LILLIE ANSWERED ON the first ring. "So? Did she change her mind?"

Hawk's stomach dropped as his heart began to pound. "What?"

"Drey? She decided to stay with you, right? I knew you both would come to your senses and realize you belong together." She sounded delighted at that prospect. "Maybe she can get the marriage annulled or something, I don't know, and then—"

"Lillie." His blood ran cold. "What are you saying? Drey isn't there?" He knew the kind of people they were dealing with. Look what Jet and Lena had already done to Drey. If they had her—

"Drey? No. I thought she was with you." Fear immediately made his sister's voice break. "Hawk, she texted and said she was sorry but she had other plans."

Hawk let out a curse. "That's all she said in her text?"

"Yes, I just thought she was with you. Tell me she hasn't gone back to that house."

"I have to go." He disconnected, his mind spinning. She wouldn't have gone back to the house. Not unless she was forced to.

DREY DIDN'T WANT to believe Jet's words meant what she knew they had to. *Get the other one? The other thumb?* She shuddered at the thought. But at the same time, she felt a sliver of hope. That meant they were going to wherever Ethan was. Ethan really was in this house. Hawk had said it could be what was called a billionaire bunker. She had no idea what that meant, but even if it was a fancy bomb shelter, she didn't believe Ethan was hiding there. But she feared, she was about to find out.

Was it possible he really had been watching her all this time on his latest-technology surveillance equipment? No, she thought with a shudder as she glanced at the thumb lying on the floor. What kind of shape was Ethan in if he was already missing one thumb?

"Stay here," Jet ordered. She heard him take the stairs down to the kitchen. She kept thinking about Ethan, somewhere in this house, missing one thumb. Alive? Was it possible? But wouldn't he have left to seek medical attention? If he could have.

She looked at Lena and realized Ethan must be being held as a prisoner. It was the only thing that made any sense. But how? He'd designed the house himself. He would know how to get out unless he was trapped. Or dead. Or in such bad shape… She refused to let her mind go there.

Jet returned with a large butcher knife, the lethal-looking blade catching the light. She recoiled from it. If he would cut off his own brother's thumb to get into his safe, she didn't dare think about what he would do to her if she didn't cooperate.

"Let's go," he said and shoved her toward the elevator again. "Keep the gun on her. If she tries anything, shoot her. We can always cut off her thumb."

Drey felt like she'd been drugged again as they left in the elevator. This was all too surreal. This time, she wished it was a drug-induced dream and not a living nightmare.

As much as she tried not to, she kept thinking about the first night she saw this house and the premonition she had. *You will die in this house.* If only she had run then. If only she hadn't married Ethan. If only she could change the past. By now she and Hawk would be happily married with children—

The thought broke her heart. She felt a sob rise up from her chest and swallowed it back. Crying wasn't going to save her. Nothing probably could. But if she fell apart, she would have no chance.

From the time she'd entered the SUV, Lena'd had the gun on her. Now Jet had a knife. She had no idea how she could possibly get out of this alive, but she was going to try. She thought of Hawk. Her throat constricted. She couldn't think of what might have been this second time around. She had to think only about survival. It was her only hope.

No opportunity to escape had presented itself thus far without endangering Flint and Hawk. Now she was trapped in the elevator with Jet and Lena on their way to see Ethan. That he really was in the house seemed impossible and yet she hadn't known about the surveillance room or the hidden safe or that he'd had a bomb shelter built. But Jet seemed to know, she thought, as the elevator stopped on the master suite floor.

HAWK DROVE LIKE the crazed man he was. He should have gone with Drey. Or at least found out right away if she'd arrived at his sister's house. But he hadn't been worried as long as she didn't go back to Ethan Baxter's house.

Both he and Drey thought that what Jet and Lena wanted was hidden in that house. Why else had they drugged her but to keep her out of their way while they searched for it? So why would they want to take her back there? If they had her?

He knew he was jumping to all kinds of conclusions, but they'd both heard Jet and Lena plotting. He'd been so sure with Drey away from the house that she'd be safe.

The one thought kept coming back: she wouldn't go there alone. Which meant someone had her. Ethan? And if he was right and she was at the house… whoever took her needed her there for some reason.

Every reason he could think of only terrified him more. He dug out his phone, realizing he should have called his brother from the house. But all he could think about was getting there. Getting to Drey.

"Drey never made it to Lillie's," he said into the phone the moment Flint answered. "I'm headed for the house." He didn't think he needed to clarify more. They both knew.

"Have you tried to reach her?" Flint asked.

"She's not picking up."

"You don't think she went by there to pick up a few things, do you?"

"Not a chance. She wouldn't have gone there on her own."

"Wait for me, then," Flint said.

"I can't do that. I'll leave the gate open for you." He disconnected, fearing that too much time had already gone by.

AS THE ELEVATOR door slid open, Drey said, "I know you were in this house on my wedding night."

He glanced over at her. "How do you know that? I erased it on the security system."

"You left one of your toothpicks on the floor in the sunroom downstairs," she said and saw that he didn't like being shown up. He thought he was much smarter than everyone else, especially his brother.

"You and your stupid toothpicks," Lena said under her breath.

Jet motioned for them to go first. Lena jabbed her with the barrel of the gun and she stumbled out into her bedroom. What were they doing here? Ethan wasn't hidden in the bedroom. It felt as if she really was back on those pills, confused, disoriented, sick to her stomach.

Jet stepped out of the elevator, brandishing the knife. "I was here that night just as Ethan had planned. What he didn't know was that I was onto him. I'd gotten a heads-up from a friend of mine who works at the company. Ethan planned to let me take the fall with the FBI. But I played along as if I was still in the dark. Ethan thought he was so smart."

"You weren't the only one he was going to let take a fall for the mess he'd made of the company. He was going to let me go down, too," Lena reminded him.

Jet waved that off as of little consequence, making his girlfriend's expression turn ugly. Drey had wondered what Lena saw in a man like Jet. Right now, she didn't seem to see anything worth hanging on to, which made Drey only more nervous. All she needed was for these two to get into a huge fight.

Or maybe that was exactly what she did need, she thought. Anything that would give her a chance to escape.

"So you talked that night," she reminded Jet as she frantically tried to put all the pieces together.

He nodded, his gaze distant for a moment as if he was reliving it. "I could see how proud he was of his place. Ethan's Ego. It didn't take much encouragement for him to show me around. I wasn't acting very impressed so I knew he'd have to break out the good stuff."

Jet stepped to the wall just outside the double doors to the stairs outside the master suite. "This is the good stuff." He stopped at the back wall and touched a spot. The wood panel began to whir back into the wall behind Ethan's bathroom.

Behind it was another wall. This was one had a small keypad screen in the middle of it. Jet reached back, grabbed Drey's hand and pulled her up next to him. Taking her hand, he pressed her right thumb against the keypad. The device beeped twice and this wooden panel also slid silently away. She found herself staring at a huge steel door.

This must be the way to the bomb shelter Hawk had found out about. Was this where Ethan had been all this time?

"Bulletproof, soundproof, just not Jet-proof," Jet said with a laugh. Again he pressed her thumb to the pad in the middle of the door. Something clicked, and Jet grabbed the handle and opened the door. Lights came on in the ceiling, illuminating what appeared to be a tunnel.

Drey recoiled. She didn't want to go in there. She couldn't imagine that Ethan was in there. She looked into the dim darkness of a passageway that went back into the depths of the mountain behind the house, her throat constricting.

If Ethan was in here… If he'd been here the whole time…

"Ethan!" she screamed. "Ethan!"

"Save your breath. Even if he could hear you, he wouldn't come save you." Jet gave her a pitying look. "You still don't get it. My brother got me to Montana to fake his death. The stunt down by the dock? That was supposed to be him. Body disappears but enough blood to make the local cops believe it happened. Ethan disappears."

"I don't understand," Drey said, hating that her voice broke.

Jet shrugged. "You would stay here and deal with the FBI, I guess. I would take my money and get on the first plane out of the country." So Ethan really had been planning to leave her behind to face the FBI?

"But you didn't do it," she said.

"No, like I said, he tried to double-cross me," Jet said with a curse. "Ethan was going to throw me to the wolves. When I called him on it, he admitted it. He offered me money to take the fall for everything. He promised to get me a good lawyer and enough money to live comfortably when I got out of prison. Still think Ethan is your Prince Charming?"

So he was guilty. That's why the FBI had been investigating him and his company.

"I realized he must have evidence he planned to leave behind that would make it look like I was the one involved in the fraud," Jet was saying. "When I turned down his offer…" He let out a bitter laugh. "The bastard said if I didn't do everything the way he had it planned, he'd take me down. What a fool. I decided why fake his death when I could kill him and get away with it—with your help."

"So the dock stunt was just to make it look as if I was losing my mind. You wanted me to think I was crazy so I would take the pills." She saw the two exchange a look.

"It's simple, sweetie," Lena said. "You being crazy would explain what happened to poor Ethan." She smiled.

"While you and Jet flew off to some island, never to be seen again," Drey said.

"Pretty much." Lena chuckled. "You were perfect since I knew how you were on those antianxiety medications. By then we would be long gone," Lena said. "The feds would be happy because they had their man. You would be convicted of his murder—if you couldn't get off on an insanity plea."

Jet laughed. "My brother and this damned house… He made it so easy." He pushed her down the passage-way ahead of him as if he'd forgotten about Lena. "I used to listen to him tell me about this house until I wanted to scream. How ultramodern and high-tech it would be. Nothing like it. The best security money could buy." His laugh echoed down the dark tunnel.

Ahead she saw another door.

CHAPTER TWENTY-EIGHT

AT THE GATE, Hawk sped up his pickup and braced himself.

The gate was stronger than it looked. The force of the collision set off his airbag, but it quickly deflated once the gate fell away and he was on the road up the mountain.

As he took the first curve and the house came into view, he saw that all the lights were on. Was it possible Ethan had come back, called her and Drey had agreed to meet him at the house?

No, wouldn't she have called Flint—if not him—to let him know? Also, she had to know him well enough to know that he would check up on her tonight at Lillie's. Also Drey wouldn't have texted her friend. She would have called her to tell her that she'd changed her mind.

All his instincts told him that Drey was in trouble. She wasn't fool enough to go to the house alone even to meet her husband. At least he wanted to believe that.

He turned out his headlights, but thought busting through the gate might have already warned those in the house that the property had been breached.

Hawk roared up out front. He didn't see another vehicle aside from Ethan's sedan, but he knew someone was in that house. At home he'd grabbed a handgun and a shotgun. Now he got out, tucked the handgun into the back of his jeans and, taking the shotgun, turned toward the house.

The night was pitch-black; low clouds had moved in, hiding even the starlight let alone any moon. He moved toward the front door. It seemed too quiet. He couldn't see into the house because of the dark glass, but he knew anyone inside could see him.

He tried the door. Locked. Turning the shotgun on the lock, he started to fire, but changed his mind. He had no doubt that whoever was in the house had to know he was here. Which meant they would expect him to come busting in the front door.

He swung the shotgun strap over his shoulder and moved along the front of the house to the side. He'd climbed the balconies once before. He would be able to see inside through the balconies as he climbed. He had no idea why someone had gotten Drey back here or what floor she might be on.

All he knew was that he had to find her and fast.

Moving along the dark side of the house, he reached the first balcony. Once he climbed up onto it, he stood on the railing and reached for the next one. As he passed each floor, he peered in. Where was Drey? He could feel his heart pounding out each second—and time running out.

"ETHAN THOUGHT OF EVERYTHING," Jet was saying as they neared the door. "A bomb shelter/panic room with climate control." He pulled Drey up beside him and pressed her thumb to the screen, and the door began to move.

Drey was suddenly terrified to see what was waiting for them on the other side. As the door began to open, a gust of icy cold air rushed out. That and a smell made her gag. Nothing could prepare her for what she saw.

The bunker was decorated much like the house with all the usual amenities. Except for outside windows, it appeared to be a completely separate house with all the luxury Ethan could afford. A billionaire bunker.

She instantly saw how easy it would have been for Ethan to hide out here after faking his death until it was safe for him to leave.

Unfortunately, she saw at once that he wouldn't be leaving. Ethan sat in a recliner, his arms resting on each side. He looked so normal—except for his missing thumb and the dark stain on the chair under it—that for just a moment she thought he was alive.

But as Lena jabbed her in the back with the gun and she was prodded closer, she saw that his face was covered with a thin coat of ice—and so were his blank, dead blue eyes. She let out a cry as she was shoved closer to him and saw the bullet hole at heart level along with more dried blood.

As Jet stepped to Ethan and began to saw away at his brother's other thumb, she turned away and threw up on the marble floor.

CHAPTER TWENTY-NINE

HAWK SAW LIGHTS on the road below and knew it was probably Flint headed this way. He stopped on one of the balconies and pulled out his phone. Hitting the sheriff's number, he waited as it rang once, then twice.

"Hawk, where are you?"

"The front door was locked. The whole place is shut up tighter than a drum. I'm climbing the balconies. I need you to give me a few minutes until I find out whether or not Drey is in this house and what is going on. Can you do that?"

"I'm just turning off onto the road up to the house. Nice what you did to the gate. You realize if you're wrong—"

"I'll buy Ethan a new gate. An even better one." But he knew he wasn't wrong. Not about any of it. Especially about Drey being in trouble. He felt it gut deep. "Give me fifteen minutes. If you don't hear from me by then—"

"Ten minutes and I don't even like that. Let me know the minute you see Drey."

"I will." He pocketed his phone and began to climb again.

But at each level he saw no one. No sign that anyone had been there. Was it possible she wasn't here? So why were the lights on? He knew Ethan could have set them so they came on at a certain time each night. He realized he should have checked the underground garage. If there wasn't an extra car there...

He considered breaking in like he had the night he'd heard Drey scream, but if he was wrong and she wasn't here...

Dropping down to the kitchen-level balcony, he realized he was losing what could be critical time if Drey was in there somewhere.

Hell with it, he thought and pulled the strap off his shoulder, he turned the shotgun butt end first and broke the window. Stepping through, he waited for someone to come running. For an alarm to go off.

Nothing happened. He ran down the stairs to the basement garage, telling himself that the FBI weren't going to be happy about this. If Ethan had been here, maybe he'd gotten Drey and taken off for Mexico or some other part of the world.

DREY FELT DAZED as she was pushed back down the tunnel and into the main house. She couldn't get the image of Ethan off her mind. Had he been dead when Jet had turned up the climate control to near freezing? Was he killed on their wedding night?

The horror of realizing he'd been so close all this time... She shuddered as they reached the floor where the safe had been hidden in the wall.

"Stay here," Jet ordered as he headed for one of the guest-room bathrooms. "Shoot her if she even looks like she wants to run," he said to Lena. He left the door open and a moment later Drey heard the sound of water running.

"Running hot water on it isn't going to work," Lena called to him. "I told you not to kill him. If you'd made a copy of his print when I told you to—"

Jet cursed and yelled back for her to shut up. "You better hope this works. Otherwise we are both going down for this."

He came out of the bathroom, holding Ethan's thumb in a towel. Stepping to the safe, he pressed the thumb against the screen. Drey could feel the two of them holding their breaths.

The light flashed and Jet let out an exuberant yell. "Get her over here."

Lena shoved her to him. Again he grabbed her hand and, twisting her thumb painfully, pressed it to the screen.

Something inside the safe clicked. Jet shot Lena a look, then reached for the handle, shoving Drey aside.

The handle dropped down and the door opened. Jet let out another jubilant yell and Lena seemed to relax. Still, though, she kept the handgun steady, making it clear she hadn't forgotten about Drey.

"Is it in there? You know he could have been lying to you," Lena said.

Jet shot her an impatient look. "I knew my brother probably better than you did. I don't need you telling me what he was like, all right?"

Jet pulled a series of files from the safe, opened them and thumbed through them before turning to her and smiling. "It's all here. Hand me your bag," he ordered.

Lena pulled it off her shoulder and handed it to him. Jet began to fill it first with the files, then with the stacks of money piled to one side of the safe.

Drey watched, telling herself that they'd gotten what they wanted—which meant they didn't need her anymore. Not that she thought they could let her go. She knew too much, and there was Ethan... Just the thought of him made her want to throw up again.

Once Jet was sure that he'd taken everything from the safe, he closed the door, put the panel back in place and turned to Lena.

"You know what has to be done now," he said.

Drey felt her scalp shrink with fear. "You have what you want. Just take it and leave."

"If only it was that simple," Jet said with a shake of his head. He dug in Lena's bag for a moment and pulled out a bottle and a syringe.

Drey took a step back, the word *No!* escaping her lips before she stumbled into the wall.

"Your choice. Lena blows your head off to make it appear to be a suicide or you drift off peacefully," he said. "You got it much easier than Ethan. His first thumb came off when he was alive."

Drey knew she had little choice. But she wasn't one to give up easily. She lunged for Lena and managed to knock the gun from her hand. It skittered across the marble floor. Lena swore and backhanded her as Jet grabbed her arm and dragged her into a headlock.

"Let's take her upstairs to the master suite," Lena said. "I have an idea. We can still pull this off."

"I don't know why we can't kill her right here with the drugs."

"You want to get out of this clean? Then for once, listen to me. We don't want to kill her. Not like this."

Drey tried to fight Jet, but it was useless, as he dragged her up the steps to the master suite. Throwing her down onto the bed as Lena told him to, he held her while Lena got the shot ready. Drey struggled, but she was outnumbered and defenseless. She felt the needle bite into her arm.

Jet continued to hold her down until she quit struggling as the drug raced through her veins.

"Go fill the bathtub while I get her undressed," Lena ordered. He started to argue that they were wasting valuable time. "Just trust me for once."

Drey felt fingers slowly begin to unbutton her blouse but she couldn't raise her arms to stop them. The drug was fast acting. She suspected Lena had given her enough to kill her.

Cool air brushed over her naked skin as Lena removed her clothing. She could hear the sound of running water.

"Now, help me get her into the tub."

Jet picked her up, made some crack about how Ethan was a fool not to take more advantage of Drey's body, before carrying her into the bathroom. The room had begun to steam over as she was lifted into a tub of warm water.

"You really are a jackass," Lena said from the doorway.

"You sure she can't get out of there?" Jet asked.

"Let's just give it a minute." Lena started to leave the room.

"I need a drink," Jet said. "I'll come with you. It's not like she's going anywhere."

Drey struggled to keep her eyes open. She felt so woozy. The huge tub was full, but it sounded as if the water was still running. She tried to grab the sides of the tub to pull herself up, but her arms refused to work. Lethargy had left her too weak to resist the pull of the drug or the water that was pulling her downward.

The sound of the gunshots didn't even startle her.

Water lapped up over her face. She tried to hold her head up, but it was as if all her muscles were attached to a wire that had been cut. Her head lolled to the side. Water covered her mouth and nose.

Slowly she began to slide deeper into the tub, her head going under as the drug lulled her into a deep endless sleep.

CHAPTER THIRTY

HAWK HAD REACHED the underground parking garage. There, sitting in the semidarkness, was the SUV Drey had been driving. His blood turned to slush. She *was* here—just as he'd suspected. So why hadn't he seen her?

The bunker! He had no idea why whoever had taken her would bring her here—let alone take her to the bomb shelter. It made no sense. But then nothing about her marriage had.

He turned and quickly started up the stairs. Taking the steps three at a time, he raced up through the house looking for the entry to this bunker Ethan had built for himself. Hawk was almost to the kitchen level again when he heard the gunshots. His stomach dropped. He pulled his handgun.

"Drey!" No answer. "Drey!"

When he reached the kitchen, he saw the blood on the white marble floor. It had pooled next to the white shag rug under the dining table and turned a corner of the rug crimson. No body, though.

He rushed up the stairs, fear a ball of fire in his chest. "Drey?" He kept calling her name, but getting no answer. Terror gripped him by the throat. She had to be alive.

As he pushed through the double doors of the master suite, he'd expected to find Drey lying in a pool of her own blood.

But to his surprise and relief, he didn't see her. For a moment, he didn't hear the sound of running water over the thundering beat of his heart.

He pulled off the shotgun, tossed it on the bed and rushed toward the sound of water. The minute he stepped into the bathroom, all he could see at first was steam. Then he saw the water cascading across the floor. The bathtub. It had to be overflowing. He rushed to it. Water splashed down the side and ran across the floor.

Drey lay just under the surface of the water.

"Drey!" He scooped her out and rushed her to the bed. Putting her down, he began CPR. "Drey, come on, baby. Please." He kept at it, wanting desperately to stop and call 911, but he feared if he stopped... He told himself that Flint would be here soon.

Suddenly she coughed. She made a choking sound and tried to sit up, but her body didn't react. He spotted the syringe and bottle beside the bed and swore. Fumbling out his phone, he kept saying, "You're all right, Drey. You're going to be all right." All he could do was pray that she hadn't been given enough of the drug to kill her before the EMTs could get there.

The phone began to ring and was answered quickly. "I need an ambulance. Overdose and near drowning.

Please hurry. Ethan Baxter's house outside of town. Hurry! The gate's open."

He dropped the phone as he saw that Drey was trying to say something. He leaned closer. Her voice came out a low rasp. He wrapped the duvet around her.

"Help is on the way. Don't try to talk. You're going to be all right."

She shook her head, what little she appeared to be able to move it. She tried again to speak. He leaned closer. Her trembling lips brushed his ear. "She's… still…here."

He felt the hair rise on the back of his neck as he pulled back to look at her. Her eyes closed, then opened to glance toward the door. He saw her pupils widen in alarm only a second before he swung around to find Lena standing over him with a gun pointed at the two of them.

CHAPTER THIRTY-ONE

As FLINT PULLED up to the house, he saw Hawk's pickup out front next to Ethan's sedan. There was no sign of anyone. Jumping out, he drew his weapon and started for the house. The front door was unlocked. That surprised him. Then he figured that was his brother's doing, remembering that Hawk had said he'd climbed the balconies to get to Drey.

Just then, he heard something clank and realized it was the underground garage door rising. Working his way around the side of the house in the darkness, he waited until the door was high enough and, gun drawn, ducked under it.

The garage was only dimly lit. He heard an odd shuffling noise on the concrete floor, then what sounded like someone trying to open one of the vehicles' doors. He moved quickly toward the sound, keeping to the shadows until he saw the figure struggling to climb into the SUV Drey had been driving.

As quietly as possible he moved forward. A trail of blood led from the stairs into the garage and across the concrete floor to where the figure was still struggling to pull himself behind the wheel. Jet.

"Freeze!" Flint called when he was within feet of the man. "Sheriff's department. Freeze!"

Jet didn't freeze. He made a last-ditch effort to get into the vehicle. But clearly he was hurt too badly to pull himself up into the SUV. He slumped back against the open door and looked at the sheriff. Then his eyes seemed to dim and he slumped the rest of the way to the ground.

HAWK ROSE SLOWLY to his full height. Immediately Lena looked nervous.

"I've already killed one man," she said with bravado. "I can kill you just as easily. You're going to help me get out of here." She looked over at Drey lying on the bed. "We'll take her as our hostage."

Hawk shook his head. "She can't move, thanks to you. If you're taking anyone as your hostage, it's going to be me." He could see that he made her anxious. Good, he thought. Flint would be here any minute, in fact he might already be in the house. "Let's go, because any minute this place is going to be swarming with lawmen."

She swallowed, looked toward Drey, then motioned with the gun. "Your pickup is out front. Too bad you didn't leave the keys in it."

Too bad, he thought. He looked at Drey, then leaned down and whispered, "I'll be right back." He kissed her cheek. She gave him a lopsided smile, but there was worry in her eyes. He could see that some of the drug was starting to wear off because she tried to grab his hand.

Lena stood back to let him pass, then followed him down the stairs. He moved quickly, making her have to run to keep up. She needed him to get out of here and they both knew it, so he doubted she would shoot him in the back.

He stopped at the front door, realizing she could, however, go back upstairs and finish Drey off. She looked a little out of breath and definitely worried.

Once outside she motioned for him to get into the passenger side and slide over so she could keep the gun trained on him. He did as she ordered, pulled out his keys and started the pickup, swinging it around and heading down the hill. He had to get this over with and get help for Drey.

Out of the corner of his eye, he saw a figure come running out of the underground garage. Flint. Hawk flew past him. He could hear sirens. The EMTs would be arriving. Flint would find Drey. He'd get her help. Right now that was all that mattered.

"Keep going!" Lena ordered as they came around a curve in the road and the lights of several patrol SUVs and an ambulance flashed below them on the mountain.

Hawk gave the pickup more gas, swerving around the first patrol SUV. The next one he had to leave the road to get around. Dirt and clumps of grass flew up over the windshield. He swerved back onto the road.

The ambulance had pulled over to let him past.

"You can slow down now," Lena said. She had the gun in her left hand and was hanging on to the door handle with her right. He saw that she hadn't buckled her seat belt and smiled to himself as he gave the pickup even more speed. He never got into a vehicle without buckling up.

They were almost to the county road. On the other side of it was an old rock wall from one of the original settlements.

"Slow down, you're not going to be able to make the turn," Lena cried. Her eyes were wide as he hit the county road, the front of the pickup smacking down, the bumper grating on the asphalt.

Lena screamed, dropping the gun as she tried to brace herself on the dash.

The pickup plowed into the rock wall. The impact was even worse than Hawk had expected. His airbag had already deployed earlier. He hit the steering wheel hard. His head connected with something even harder. The last thing he saw was Lena Franklin taking out the windshield as she flew through it and disappeared over the rock fence.

CHAPTER THIRTY-TWO

HAWK DRIFTED IN and out of consciousness. He couldn't tell what was real and what was a dream. He thought he might be dead, but if he was, then Drey was here with him. No, that couldn't be. Flint would have gotten to her. The EMTs…

He blinked at the bright light and felt himself move toward it, giving his head a shake to help clear his mind. As he surfaced, he knew he couldn't be dead; his head hurt too badly for that. Squinting, he looked around, trying to understand where he was. A nondescript room, sunlight coming in the window. A hospital room.

Closing his eyes, he turned his face away from the bright light of the window. When he opened them again, he saw Drey sitting in the chair next to his bed. Her caramel-brown eyes widened. A smile broke out on her face as she shot to her feet.

"You're awake!" Tears instantly filled those eyes.

He smiled and reached up to brush a lock of her beautiful auburn hair back from her face. His knuckles brushed across the silk of her skin.

"Oh, Hawk." She was crying now as she caught his hand and drew it to her lips. She kissed it softly, squeezing his hand as a nurse came into the room, followed by a doctor.

He felt her let go, closed his eyes and drifted for a while—a smile on his face.

BILLIE DEE WAS still pinching herself the day Gigi headed back to Texas. She was in the kitchen at the saloon making chicken and dumplings, when Ashley Jo came in after seeing her friend off.

Gigi had stuck around longer than she planned—no doubt AJ's doing. AJ was determined that her friend see some of Montana before she went home.

"Oh, Ashley Jo." Billie Dee turned from her cooking to hug the young woman.

"My friends call me AJ," she reminded her. "You're not mad at me for deceiving you?"

"Good heavens, no. How can I ever thank you?" Billie Dee felt as if her heart would burst with all the love and gratitude she had for AJ. "If you hadn't been determined to find me for your friend…"

"Once I met you, I just knew that Gigi had to, as well." She drew back from the hug to check out what the cook had going on the stove, then pour them both a cup of coffee. "She's pigheaded, determined, strong, smart and talented, but also sweet and caring. Kind of like you. I really hope the two of you can have some kind of relationship."

"So the only reason you came up here was to find me?" Billie Dee said as she took a cup and sat down at the kitchen table.

AJ pulled out a chair, cradling her coffee cup in

both hands. "Find you, see if you were okay and then decide if I should tell Gigi."

"I'm honored that I passed the test."

"Don't be silly. Once I fell in love with your cooking and then you, I had to tell her," AJ said. "We'll just give her some time. I'm sure she'll come around."

Billie Dee reached over and took the young woman's hand. "You two could be sisters, you look that much alike. The first time I saw you, the day you came in for the interview, I almost had a heart attack. You looked so much like I did at your age. I thought for sure you were my daughter."

"I wish." AJ grinned as she set down her cup. "Then you saw Gigi. I thought for sure I'd killed you when you fainted. You knew right away, didn't you?"

She nodded. "You're my honorary daughter as of this moment. But your mother is still alive, isn't she?"

"Alive and well and saving lives as a top-ranked surgeon in Houston. My father has his own corporation. He's still hoping that I will use my law degree and join him."

"But?"

AJ laughed. "But I find I want something…different."

"I've seen you making eyes at Cyrus Cahill."

The young woman groaned. "Lillie said the same thing to me. Honestly, I can't have a crush without everyone knowing it?"

"So it would seem."

AJ smiled over at her. "He took me horseback riding the other day. I think I'm in love with Montana, horses and…" She laughed. "Anyway, now that you've found your daughter, there is nothing to keep you from getting married. This is what you've been waiting for, isn't it, Billie Dee?"

AFTER EVERYTHING THE family had been through, it was decided that they should get together for a picnic—after all, it was summer in Montana.

They all gathered at the Cahill Ranch. The men had a pig turning on the outdoor pit. The women had made an array of salads and desserts for the celebration feast.

As Drey looked around at the family she'd always loved, they all had something to celebrate. But especially her and Hawk. Some days she thought it had all been a dream—and a nightmare. But then she would awaken and Hawk would be there and she would close her eyes and thank God. They'd both almost lost their lives.

That was something she tried not to think about. On a day like today with the sun shining, a cool pine-scented breeze cooling the afternoon air, and the love of this family, she couldn't think anything but happy thoughts.

Hawk caught her eye and she smiled at him across the ranch yard. Every time she looked at him, her heart beat a little faster. He was so handsome, so strong, so Montana tough. She loved that cowboy with all her heart.

That they shared another secret didn't bother her in the least. The family would find out soon enough.

"LILLIE IS IN hog heaven," Cyrus said as he joined his brother. "Two weddings to help plan."

Hawk said nothing. He hated to disappoint his little sister but there was no way he and Drey were waiting to get married. He told himself that Lillie would get over it. She could plan to her heart's content Billie Dee and Henry's wedding, he thought, smiling to himself as looked over at the woman he'd loved all of his adult life.

Lillie used to tell him that Drey was the only woman for him. He'd thought after they'd broken up that maybe he was born to be a bachelor.

"You do realize you're the last of the Cahills to make that trip down the aisle," Hawk said to Cyrus. "Lillie is going to be planning your wedding next."

Cyrus shook his head. "I don't think so."

But Hawk noticed how his gaze went to Ashley Jo, or AJ as they were all calling her now. The story had come out about Billie Dee and Gigi and how AJ had brought mother and daughter together. There had been some tears of joy shed over that story.

Now everyone was excited about Billie Dee's upcoming wedding. The whole family would be standing up with her—including her daughter, who would be flying in for the ceremony. Lillie and AJ were planning the whole shindig.

Hawk had to laugh. If his brother wasn't smitten, well, he would eat his hat.

He looked around the ranch yard at his growing family. Tucker and Kate were curled in a corner laughing about something. Darby and Mariah were cooing at their son sitting in a carrier on the picnic table with Lillie and Trask doing the same thing. Lillie was saying the two boys would be like brothers growing up. From the gleam in Lillie's and Mariah's eyes, he suspected it wouldn't be long before they had another announcement.

But it was Flint and Maggie that held his gaze. Flint had his hand over the baby growing inside her. He'd never seen this Flint before. A blissful family man.

His gaze shifted to Drey, who had been talking to AJ. Now she met his gaze. He felt that spark across the entire yard. She grinned and raised her water bottle to him. He raised his beer and couldn't help the fool grin that he knew spread across his face. Men in love, he thought. Could they be any goofier?

Hawk was glad that no one brought up what they'd recently been through. He was almost fully recovered and so was Drey. Ethan's body had been removed from the house, the government taking possession of all his assets. Jet's body was also removed, the information he was trying to escape with to be used as well as what they had against Ethan in the investigation. Lena had been up to her neck in the crime. But she, too, was gone.

Fortunately, it hadn't taken long to clear Drey of any involvement. She had been able to get her old job back as the local librarian, a job Hawk knew she loved. She wanted to work—just until they had their first baby. He couldn't wait and was thankful that the doctor had given her assurances after her miscarriage all those years ago that she should have no problem getting pregnant again.

Drey had said she didn't want to wait so they would be working on that real soon, he thought, grinning again.

"I'm sorry Dad couldn't be here," Cyrus said. "I'm tempted to go up into the mountains to check on him."

"It's summer. You'd have a hell of a time getting him out of the mountains," Hawk said. He didn't say what he'd been thinking about Ely Cahill. That he probably didn't have that many summers left. "I'd leave him be. He's happy wherever he is. Anyway, you need to go to Denver and pick up that bull."

Cyrus grumbled. "You really aren't going to go?"

Hawk shook his head, still watching Drey. "I have other plans."

EPILOGUE

HAWK STUDIED DREY in the light from the campfire. Her cheeks were flushed from the crackling fire's warmth. Sparks rose and drifted out over the lake like fireflies before winking out. Overhead, stars twinkled in a deep blue velvet Montana sky. The warm breeze carried the summer scents. Only a sliver of moon hung on the horizon above the dark pine-covered mountain.

Drey was looking into the flames. He wondered what she was thinking. He hoped she wasn't reliving the horror. Coming that close to dying...

Her gaze rose to him as if she'd sensed him watching her. She smiled across the campfire at him.

"I'd offer a penny for your thoughts..."

"I was thinking how much I love this." She looked out at the lake, the surface silvery under the starlight. "How much I love being with you here," she said, her gaze coming back to him.

He moved around the fire to sit down next to her on the blanket. "Warm enough?"

She nodded as he put his arm around her and she leaned into his chest. He felt as if he had been blessed and didn't deserve it. For so long he thought they would never find their way back to each other.

It had taken almost losing her to make him come to his senses. He regretted each lost year, month, minute, second and promised himself he'd never make that mistake again.

It was why he'd asked her to marry him in front of his entire family at the family summer picnic. She'd smiled and said yes, throwing her arms around him. They'd been oblivious to the family's cheers and applause. It had been only the two of them lost in the moment. That night, they'd run away and gotten married.

He knew his sister, Lillie, would eventually forgive him. She loved nothing better than a huge family wedding. Let Cyrus give her one, he'd told her. She was busy with Billie Dee's wedding, so that had taken some of the sting out of it for her.

Also, when he'd told his sister that he couldn't wait another day to be married to Drey, Lillie had cried. The woman was a true romantic. "I knew she was the only one for you. Didn't I tell you that?"

"Numerous times," he'd said with a groan.

The horses whinnied from the darkness as he got up to throw another log on the fire.

"You know what I want?" Drey asked.

"Name it." Hawk knew he would move heaven and earth if she asked him.

She stood and started taking off her clothes.

"I'm not sure where exactly this is headed, but I'm liking it," he said as he began to take off his clothing, as well.

She laughed and dropped the last of her clothes on

a log next to the fire, then ran to the edge of the water and jumped in.

Montana lakes never got what anyone in the South would call warm. But it was summer, the warm air like a caress, and his beautiful wife was naked and calling to him from the starlit water.

He finished undressing and raced out to dive in and swim out to her. Her body felt silken as he pulled her to him. Water beaded on her lashes. He'd never seen anyone more beautiful. He kissed her until they both went under.

Surfacing, she said, "First one to the tent…" She swam toward the shore as if trying out for the Olympics.

He watched for a few moments, in wonder at the woman he'd married, then he swam after her, anxious to find out what the loser of the race would get. Smiling, he couldn't wait. Tonight they would make love beside the lake just as he'd dreamed for so long. He was so filled with joy that he felt as if he would burst.

Drey was waiting for him in the tent. She tossed him a towel. "You know I used to dream about this."

"Me trying to get you into my tent?"

Laughing, she said, "You and me up here like this. Married, planning our future." She lay down on top of the sleeping bag. "For so long I never thought it could happen."

"I know," he said as he dried himself off with the towel. "I'm sorry it took me so long, Mrs. Cahill."

Firelight played on the side of the tent, making warm gold patterns across her naked body. "Mrs. Cahill. I do love the sound of that."

He dropped the towel and joined her on the sleeping bag.

"Let's make a baby tonight," she whispered.

He looked into her beautiful eyes. "Oh hell, let's make two."

* * * * *

*Read on for a glimpse of what is in store for
Cyrus Cahill in* Wrangler's Rescue,
the exciting conclusion in New York Times
bestselling author BJ Daniels's
The Montana Cahills series.
Available wherever HQN Books *are sold.*

ASHLEY JO "AJ" SOMERFIELD couldn't help herself. She kept looking out the window of the Stagecoach Saloon hoping to see a familiar ranch pickup. Cyrus Cahill had promised to stop by as soon as he returned to Gilt Edge. He'd been gone for over a week down to Denver to see about buying a bull for the ranch.

"I'll be back on Saturday," he'd said when he'd left. "Isn't that the day Billie Dee makes chicken and dumplings?"

He knew darned well it was. "*Texas* chicken and dumplings," AJ had corrected him since everything Billie Dee cooked had a little of her Southern spice in it. "I know you can't resist her cookin' so I guess I'll see you then."

He'd laughed. Oh, how she loved that laugh. "Maybe you will if you just happen to be tending bar on Saturday."

"I will be." That was something else he knew darned well. "I'll tell Billie Dee to make the chicken and dumplings extra special just for you."

He'd let out a whistle. "Then I guess I'll see you then."

She smiled to herself at the memory. It had taken Cyrus a while. One of those "aw shucks, ma'am" kind of cowboys, he was so darned shy she thought she was going to have to throw herself on the floor at his boots for him to notice her. But once he had, they'd started talking, joking around, getting to know each other.

They'd gone for a horseback ride before he'd left. It had been Cyrus's idea. They'd ridden up into one of the four mountain ranges that surrounded the town of Gilt Edge—and the Cahill Ranch.

It was when they'd stopped to admire the view from the mountaintop that overlooked the small Western town that AJ had hoped Cyrus would kiss her. He sure looked as if he'd wanted to as they'd walked their horses to the edge of the overlook.

The sun warming them while the breeze whispered through the boughs of the nearby pine trees, it was one of those priceless Montana fall days before the weather turned. That was why Cyrus had said they should take advantage of the beautiful day before he left for Denver.

Standing on the edge of the mountain, he'd reached over and taken her hand in his. "Beautiful," he'd said. For a moment she thought he was talking about the view, but when she met his gaze she'd seen that he meant her.

Her heart had begun to pound. This was it. This was what she'd been hoping for. He drew her closer. Pushing back his Stetson, he bent toward her. His mouth was just a breath away from hers—when his mare nudged him with her nose.

She could laugh about it now. But if she hadn't grabbed Cyrus, he would have fallen down the mountainside.

"She's just jealous," Cyrus had said of his horse as he'd rubbed the beast's neck after getting his footing under him again.

But the moment had been lost. They'd saddled up and ridden back to the Cahill Ranch.

AJ still wanted that kiss more than anything. Maybe today when Cyrus returned home. After all, it had been his idea to stop by the saloon his brother and sister owned when he got back. She thought it wasn't just Billie Dee's chicken and dumplings he was after and bit her lower lip in anticipation.

SHERIFF FLINT CAHILL had been thinking about how quiet Gilt Edge had been lately, when a call was put through to his office. Before he could pick it up, the dispatcher appeared in his doorway looking worried.

Betty said nothing as he lifted the receiver, but he was already praying the call wasn't about the baby. He'd recently become the proud father of a baby girl who was the spitting image of her mother. But little Elizabeth, named after his sister, Lillie, had been small and he worried.

"Sheriff Cahill," he said into the phone and held his breath.

But it wasn't his wife Maggie's voice on the other end of the line with bad news.

"Sheriff Flint Cahill?" a man asked in a West Indian accent.

He glanced up to see that Betty was no longer standing in his doorway. He began to breathe a little easier. "Yes? How may I help you?"

"I'm sorry to be the bearer of bad news. Your brother Cyrus Cahill?"

"Yes." He sat up a little straighter, holding the phone tighter.

"He has disappeared and is believed to have gone overboard."

"Gone overboard?" Flint repeated, thinking he must have heard wrong.

"Yes, he has fallen off the cruise ship he was on."

Flint shook his head. "I'm sorry, who did you say you were?"

"The police commissioner here on the island of St. Augustus in the Caribbean."

He felt a surge of relief. Was this some kind of scam call? "I'm afraid there's been a mistake. My brother is nowhere near the Caribbean. Why don't you give me your number and I'll call you right back?"

That usually took care of the scam calls.

"Of course." The man gave him a number, taking Flint by surprise. If this was some trick to get money out of him... He checked with the operator before dialing the number and was told it definitely was a number on the island of St. Augustus in the Caribbean.

Flint couldn't imagine what was going on. Was it possible Cyrus's identity had been stolen?

The police commissioner answered on the third ring. "I know this must come as shocking news."

"Shocking, yes, since my brother is on his way home from Denver, Colorado." Cyrus had gone down to look at a bull he was considering buying for the family ranch. "The last place he would be is on a cruise in the Caribbean. But if someone is using his name…"

"Perhaps this will clear everything up," the man said. "I can email you a photograph taken on the ship after the couple was married by the captain."

He almost laughed. There was definitely a mistake. Cyrus married—let alone on a cruise ship in the Caribbean? Flint gave him his email address and waited.

Moments later an email popped up on his computer. He clicked on the mail from St. Augustus Police, assuring himself that this mistake would be rectified quickly once he… Flint felt all of the breath rush from his lungs.

In the photograph Cyrus was wearing a dress suit. He had his arm around an attractive blonde in an emerald green gown. Both were smiling at the camera. In the background was a turquoise blue sea. Closer was the name of the ship: *The Majestic Goddess of the Caribbean*.

Rachel McCall never thought she'd return to her hometown of McCall Canyon, Texas. But when long-buried family secrets come to light, she has no choice. And the only person she can turn to for help is the one man she'd hoped to avoid: Texas Ranger Griff Morris. Because it won't take long before he learns she's carrying his baby...

Read on for a sneak peek at USA TODAY *bestselling author Delores Fossen's* Finger on the Trigger.

Chapter One

Something wasn't right.

Rachel McCall was sure of it. Her heartbeat kicked up a notch, and she glanced around Main Street to see what had put the sudden knot in her stomach.

Nothing.

Well, nothing that she could see, anyway. But that didn't help with the knot.

She walked even faster, trying to tamp down her fears. It had been only a month since someone had tried to kill her father and had kidnapped her mother. That wasn't nearly enough time for her to force the images out of her head. The sound of the shot. All that blood. The fear that she might lose both her parents.

There were images and memories of the other things that'd happened over the course of those two days, too.

Remembering that wouldn't help her now, though. She had to get to her car, and then she could drive back to the inn on the edge of town and figure out why this "not right" feeling wouldn't budge.

She continued to walk from the small pharmacy up

the street to where she'd parked her car. There had still been plenty of daylight when she'd gone into the pharmacy twenty minutes earlier to wait for her meds to be ready, but now that the storm was breathing down on her, it was dark, and the sidewalks were empty. There were so many alleys and shadows. Enough to cause her nerves to tingle just beneath her skin.

Rachel silently cursed herself for not parking directly in front of the pharmacy, but instead she'd chosen a spot closer to the small grocery store where she'd first picked up some supplies before going for the meds. That grocer was closed now—as was seemingly everything else in the small town of Silver Creek.

She'd chosen this town because in many ways it'd reminded her of home. Of McCall Canyon. But bad things had happened there, and they could also happen here.

The moment her car was in sight, she pressed the button on her key fob. The red brake lights flashed, indicating the door was unlocked, just as a vein of lightning lit up the night sky. A few seconds later, the thunder came, a thick rumbling groan. And it was maybe because of the thunder that she didn't hear the footsteps.

Not until it was too late.

Someone stepped out from one of those dark alleys. She saw only a blur of motion from the corner of her eye before that someone wearing a white cowboy hat pulled her between the two buildings.

The scream bubbled up in her throat, but she didn't manage to make a sound before he slid his hand over her mouth.

It was a man.

Rachel had no trouble figuring that out the moment her back landed against his chest. But she didn't stay there. The surge of adrenaline came. And the fear. She rammed her elbow into the man's stomach, breaking free, and turned to run. She didn't make it far, however, because he cursed and hauled her back to him.

"Shh. Someone was watching you," he said.

She continued to struggle to get away, until the sound of his voice finally registered in her head. It was one she definitely recognized.

Griff.

Or rather Texas Ranger Griffin Morris.

How the heck had he found her? And better yet, how fast could she get rid of him?

Rachel pushed his hand away from her mouth and whirled around to face him. She hoped the darkness didn't hide her anger. Even if it didn't, Griff didn't seem to notice, because his attention was focused across the street.

"Shh," he repeated, when she started to say something.

Rachel nearly disobeyed him on principle just because she didn't want Griff telling her what to do. But she wasn't stupid. His own expression told her loads. Something was wrong. The knot in her stomach hadn't been a false alarm.

She followed Griff's gaze and tried to pick through the darkness to see if she could figure out what had caused him to grab her like that. There was a row of buildings, mom-and-pop type stores, all one and two stories high. Like the side of the street that Griff and she were on, that one had alleys, too. If someone was hiding there, she couldn't see him.

"Who's watching me?" she whispered. That was just the first of many questions she had for Griff.

He didn't jump to answer, but merely lifted his shoulder. Since he still had his left arm hooked around her waist, she felt his muscles tense. Felt the handgun that he'd drawn, too. Apparently Rachel wasn't the only one who'd thought something was wrong.

"Is this about my father?" she pressed.

That only earned her another shoulder lift. For a couple seconds, anyway. "Your dad's alive, by the way. Just in case you want to know."

She hadn't needed Griff to tell her that. Rachel had kept up with the news about his shooting. Her father had survived the surgery and had been released from the hospital. She hadn't wanted him dead. But Rachel no longer wanted him in her life.

That applied to Griff, too.

"I got here about five minutes ago," Griff went on. He tipped his head toward the end of the street. "I parked up there and came to your car to wait for you. That's when I saw the guy across the street. He's about six feet tall, medium build and dressed all in black. I didn't get a look at his face because he stepped back when he saw me."

Even though Griff and she were at odds—big odds—she believed everything he'd just said. Griff wasn't the sort to make up something like that just to get her in his arms again. Though it had worked. Here she was, right against him. Rachel was about to do something about that, but Griff spoke before she could put a couple inches of space between them.

"Keep watch of the alley behind us," he said. "I don't want him backtracking and sneaking up on us."

That tightened the knot even more, and Rachel wished she'd brought her gun with her. Too bad she'd left it at the inn.

"There might be nothing to this," she whispered. However, she did turn so she could keep an eye on the back alley. "Unless..." She almost hated to finish that. "Has there been another attack? Did someone try to kill my father again?"

Griff didn't answer right away, but he did spare her a glance. He looked down at her just as she looked up at him. Their gazes connected. It was too dark to see the color of his eyes, but she knew they were gunmetal gray.

Rachel also knew the heat was still there.

Good grief. After everything that had happened, it should be gone. Should be as cold as ice. But here it was, just as it always had been. Well, it could take a hike. Her body might still be attracted to Griff, but she'd learned her lesson, and she wouldn't give him another chance to crush her.

"There have been new threats," he finally said. A muscle flickered in his jaw. "Both emails and phone calls. Have you gotten any?"

She shook her head. "No, but then I closed my email account and have been using a burner cell."

Of course Griff knew that, because he was the rea-

son she'd gone to such lengths. Rachel had been trying to get away from him.

"How'd you find me?" she snapped. "*Why* did you
find me? Because I made it clear that I didn't want
to see you."

There was too much emotion in her voice. Not
good. Because it meant she was no longer whispering. Rachel tried to rein in her feelings so she could
keep watch and put an end to this visit.

"Your meds," Griff said.

Because she was still doing some emotion reining,
she didn't immediately make the connection. Then
Rachel remembered she'd needed the pharmacist to
call her former doctor in McCall Canyon to verify the
prescription for her epilepsy medicine. Without them,
she would have had a seizure, something that hadn't
happened in two years.

Rachel cursed herself for that lapse. She should
have figured out a way to get the meds without anyone having to contact Dr. Baldwin. Of course, Dr.
Baldwin shouldn't have ratted her out to Griff either,
and as soon as she could, she'd have a chat with the
man about that.

"I'd been so careful," she mumbled. She hadn't
meant to say that aloud, and it got Griff's attention
because he glanced at her again.

"No. You haven't been. You shouldn't have parked
here. If I could find you, then so could the person who
made those new threats."

She couldn't argue with that, but what Rachel
could dispute was that the person who'd made those

new threats might not even be after her. Yes, a month ago someone had put a bullet in her father's chest while he'd been in the parking lot of the sheriff's office where both her brothers worked. But that person, Whitney Goble, who'd been responsible for the shooting, had tried to kill Rachel's father so Whitney could set up someone else that she wanted to punish. Now Whitney was dead.

Not that it helped lessen the memories just because Whitney was no longer alive.

No. Because of everything else that'd happened in the twenty-four hours following the shooting. That was when they'd learned that her father also had secrets.

Well, one secret, anyway.

That, too, twisted away at her. Just as much as reading the threat he'd gotten and seeing him gunned down in the parking lot. But the truth was her father had been living two lives and had a mistress and a son living several counties over. Her brothers, Egan and Court, hadn't known. Neither had her mother, Helen.

But Griff had.

Of course, Griff hadn't breathed a word about it. Not after the shooting. Not even when later that night she'd gone to his bed to help ease the worry she was feeling for her father. That's why the cut had felt so deep. Griff had known, and he hadn't told her.

All of those emotions came flooding back. "I don't want you here," she said.

If her words stung, he showed no signs of it. "Yeah, I got that, but I made a promise to your mother that I'd keep you safe."

It didn't surprise her that her mother had made that request. Or that Griff had carried it out. But there was possibly another side to this. "Are you using this as a way to mend fences with me? Because if so, it won't work."

He didn't even acknowledge that, but Griff did push her behind him. He brought up his gun as if getting ready to fire. That put her heart right in her throat, and Rachel came up on her toes so she could see over Griff's shoulder. She shook her head and was about to tell him she didn't see anything.

But she did.

Rachel saw someone move in the alley to the right of the small hardware store. Since it was only 8:00 p.m., she reminded herself that it could be someone putting out the trash. However, that knot in her stomach returned. It was a feeling that her brothers had always told her never to ignore.

Was this the person who'd made those new threats against her family?

Maybe. Whoever it was definitely seemed to be lurking. And looking in their direction. Rachel doubted the person could see them because Griff and she were deep enough in the shadows on this side of the street. Or at least they would be unless there was more lightning. Which was a strong possibility. She could hear more thunder rumbling in the distance.

"Why would someone want to hurt me?" she whispered.

"To get back at your father. At Warren," Griff answered without hesitation. "Everyone in the McCall family could be at risk. Don't worry," he quickly added. "We have a guard on your mother's room at the hospital."

Good. Because her mother was mentally fragile right now. Suffering from a breakdown. Helen didn't need to be fighting off idiots obsessed with getting back at Warren.

Rachel felt the first drops of rain hit her face. They no doubt hit Griff, too, but they didn't cause him to lose focus. He kept watching the man across the street. But the guy wasn't moving. She did see something, however. The flash of light, maybe from a match or lighter. A moment later, a small red circle of fire winked in and out.

That caused her to breathe a little easier. "He's just smoking."

But Griff didn't budge. "He's carrying a gun."

Rachel certainly hadn't seen anything to indicate that, but she took a closer look. She had to wait several snail-crawling moments, but she finally saw the glint of metal. Maybe a gun in his right hand.

More raindrops came. So did the vein of lightning that lit up the sky, and Griff automatically moved her deeper into the alley. He also took out his phone.

"I'm calling the locals for backup," he said, without taking his attention off the man. "Yeah, it's me again," he added, speaking to whoever answered.

That probably meant Griff had already been in touch with local law enforcement. In fact, he'd probably called them as soon as he'd figured out she was in Silver Creek.

"Do a quiet approach," Griff instructed. "If you can, try to get someone behind this guy so we can take him into custody." He ended the call and put his phone away.

She doubted it would take long for someone to arrive, but it would feel like an eternity. And might be completely unnecessary.

"If he means to do me harm, why hasn't he fired at me?" Rachel asked.

Again, Griff took his time answering, but judging from the sound of agreement he made, it was probably something he'd already considered. "Maybe he's waiting for a clean shot."

That gave her another jolt of memories. Of her father's shooting. They hadn't seen the gunman that day because he or she had fired from a heavily treed area behind the police station. But it had indeed been a "clean shot" that went straight into her father's chest. It was a miracle he'd survived.

"We can cut through the back of the alley and then get to my truck that's parked up the street," Griff whispered. "That way you're not out in the open."

"My car is right there," she pointed out. "Only about ten feet away. And the doors are already unlocked."

"If this man wants you dead, he could shoot you before you get inside."

That caused her breath to stop for a moment. Griff normally sugarcoated things for her, but apparently those days were over. Maybe he truly understood that their friendship—and anything else they felt for each other—was over, too.

"There's a deputy," Griff said.

Rachel immediately looked out and spotted a man on foot coming up Main Street. He had his gun drawn and was ducking in and out of doorways of the various shops. He was still three buildings away when the guy who'd been watching them turned and started running out the back of the alley. He quickly disappeared from sight.

"He's getting away," she blurted out.

"The sheriff might have had time to get someone back there." Griff didn't sound very hopeful about that, though. "Come on."

He took hold of her arm to start them moving, and she saw his truck. It was indeed at the back of the alley. But they had barely made it a step before a deafening noise blasted through the air. Not lightning or thunder from the storm. The impact slammed Griff and her into the side of the building.

And that was when Rachel saw that her car had exploded into a giant ball of fire.

Can Griff protect her and the baby he doesn't know she's carrying before a killer takes his shot? Find out when Finger on the Trigger *by* USA TODAY *bestselling author Delores Fossen goes on sale September 2018.*

First night back at the All Things Wild Safari and Resort in Kenya, Africa, and Harmon "Harm" Payne had trouble sleeping. Their commander had granted the team a bonus week of vacation. After a particularly difficult mission in South Sudan, cleaning up the damage done by a ruthless warlord bent on wreaking havoc with the locals and stealing their children for his army, the SEAL team deserved this time to unwind.

Though his week of rest and relaxation had begun, he couldn't rest or relax. He paced the sleek wooden floors of his cabin, hoping to get sleepy, but so far, nothing was working.

As a US Navy SEAL, he was used to snatching some shut-eye whenever he had fifteen minutes to spare. Why couldn't he do it now?

He stood by the window, staring out into the darkness of night, studying the myriad of stars twinkling in the heavens. The setting was perfect, the mission had been a success, but he couldn't calm his racing pulse. Harm felt on edge, as if he teetered on the precipice of something.

He lay on the bed, forced his eyes to close and counted bullets, hoping the monotony of the numbers would lull him to sleep. Around fifty, he must have slipped into a troubled sleep. The numbers became the beat of a drum; the sleek bullets became gyrating bodies, shiny with sweat and paint, dancing in the flames of a bonfire. The rhythm grew stronger, the dancing more erratic, and a voice called out words in a language he could not understand. A flowing red scarf drifted through the dancers and into the fire, becoming part of the dancing flames.

What did it mean? Why was he there?

A movement in the shadows surrounding the fire caught his attention. The face of a coyote, wolf or jackal appeared, its golden eyes reflecting the glow of the burning embers.

For a moment, Harm's attention remained riveted on the jackal, his heart beating fast and furious, slamming against his ribs, as if eager to escape the jackal and the confines of his ribs.

Harm swayed with the drumbeat, his body drawn like a moth to the flames, his gaze captivated by the jackal's eyes, mesmerized in the effect of the dancing flames. His feet moved as if of their own volition, taking him within reach of the blaze. He would have fallen in had an owl not swooped low, screeching loudly at just that moment.

The sound jerked him back from the fire. The jackal disappeared and Harm sat up in the bed, his heart racing at the close call in the dream. He rubbed his eyes, swung his feet over the side and stood, letting the night air cool his sweating body.

Obviously, sleep wasn't coming anytime soon.

Don't miss
Four Relentless Days *by Elle James,*
available August 2018 wherever
Harlequin® Intrigue *books and ebooks are sold.*

www.Harlequin.com

Get 4 FREE REWARDS!

We'll send you 2 FREE Books <u>plus</u> 2 FREE Mystery Gifts.

FREE
Value Over
$20

Both the **Romance** and **Suspense** collections feature compelling novels written by many of today's best-selling authors.